Pride Publishing books by Bailey Bradford:

Breaking the Devil
Dark Nights and Headlights
Texas and Tarantulas
Belt Buckles and Cowboy Boots
Something Shattered

Southwestern Shifters
Rescued
Relentless
Reckless
Rendered
Resilience
Reverence
Revolution
Revenge
Reluctance
Renounced
Retrograde

Southern Spirits
A Subtle Breeze
When the Dead Speak
All of the Voices
Wait util Dawn
Aftermath
What Remains
Ascension
Whirlwind

Love in Xxchange
Rory's Last Chance
Miles to Go
Bend
What Matters Most
Ex's and O's
A Bit of Me
A Bit of You
In My Arms Tonight
Where There's a Will
My Heart to Keep

Leopard's Spots
Levi
Oscar
Timothy
Isaiah
Gilbert
Esau
Sullivan
Wesley
Nischal
Justice
Sabin
Cliff

Mossy Glenn Ranch
Chaps and Hope
Ropes and Dreams
Saddles and Memories
Fences and Freedom
Riding and Regrets
Broncs and Bullies
Hay and Heartbreak
Vaqueros and Vigilance

Yes, Forever
Yes, Forever: Part One
Yes, Forever: Part Two
Yes, Forever: Part Three
Yes, Forever: Part Four
Yes, Forever: Part Five

Spotless
Hide
Hunt
Home
Heart

Coyote's Call
Off Course
In from the Cold

SOMETHING
SHATTERED

BAILEY BRADFORD

SOMETHING SHATTERED

Dedication

You're stronger than you know.

Chapter One

Jesse Martin sat on the porch steps of his rented trailer, looking at the sparse patches of grass in his tiny yard. The New Mexico sun was bright in the clear blue sky, the heat beyond oppressive and bordering on hellish.

The beer bottle in his hand was sweating almost as much as he was, and he wondered if the yellowish-brown color of the grass meant it was dead or just severely dehydrated. Maybe if he watered the grass, it would eventually become a lush green carpet like his neighbor's. That was one pretty lawn across the street.

Right. Like he would remember to water the pathetic splotch that was his yard—and he sure didn't want to know what that would do to his water bill. If the landlady didn't like the crappy lawn, then *she* could foot the bill and take care of the stuff. At least this way he didn't have to mow.

Still, he couldn't help but be a little envious of that thick, green grass across the street. The neighbor must be some kind of plant-life miracle worker. Even the man's back yard was flourishing. It was possible that he had an in-ground sprinkler system or something, which was well beyond Jesse's means.

Jesse took a drink of his warm beer. *Still nasty*. If he were smart, he'd sit out here with a little ice chest, though even then he'd have to really chug the beer to get it down before the temperature did a number on it.

Glancing at his watch, he saw it was five till three. He turned his attention to the house across the street. From behind darkly tinted sunglasses, he watched, waiting for the door to that home to open. A ripple of anticipation went through him.

Sure enough, as had happened Monday through Saturday every afternoon for the past month, the door slowly opened.

Jesse's anticipation doubled. He tensed, waiting for what would happen next. When he saw it, he slumped with relief. Nothing had changed today.

One thin arm slipped out of the opened door, inch by inch.

Then, Jesse's heart did its usual odd skippy-thing that happened every time he watched.

A man appeared, cautiously moving through the doorway. Beat-up tennis shoes, baggy denim jeans, a ratty T-shirt about two sizes too big for his frame, a cast on his lower right arm that had gotten dingier since Jesse had first seen it. Everything the neighbor had on was pretty much the same outfit Jesse had seen before. Whether this was due to the guy having a bunch of the same shirts, bad hygiene, or a limited wardrobe, Jesse hadn't a clue. It wasn't like he could just ask either — they weren't exactly on speaking terms.

After only a few seconds' hesitation, the man moved through the doorway and stepped onto the little cement porch. Jesse checked him out as inconspicuously as possible. Not quite short, and thin to the point of gauntness, the man was a mystery to everyone in the small town of El Jardin. Tongues were wagging, and gossip spreading. Some of the stories people told were unbelievable and, to Jesse, solid proof that the creators of those tales had too much time on their hands.

Besides, he remembered very clearly what it was like to be the new kid in town, even though ten years had passed. Jesse still wasn't completely accepted by all the natives. More than a few of them talked about him, but he ignored them. For some reason, that was harder to do when the gossiping was about his new neighbor. Even his coworker, Officer Pat Monroe, made remarks here and there. But that didn't surprise Jesse. Monroe was an asshole who never missed an opportunity to make snide remarks. Some days it seemed Monroe spent more time talking trash than performing his duties as a police officer.

Jesse tried not to give such talk any credence, with the exception of ensuring there wasn't some pervert living across the street. No, he'd rather get the truth from the source, but that was kind of hard to do when the source wasn't talking.

Granted, Jesse hadn't tried too hard, just knocked on the door the day after the guy had moved in. When his knock had gone unanswered, he'd figured his new neighbor was either asleep or maybe at a doctor's appointment, considering all the injuries he'd had. Jesse had walked back to his trailer and gotten ready for work. Right before getting in his car to leave, he'd glanced across and noticed that a printed sign now graced the door. Curious, Jesse had walked to the sidewalk, squinting in an attempt to read it.

DO NOT DISTURB THE TENANT.

Well. That had seemed pretty clear. Jesse hadn't been offended by the snotty sign at the time. Easy enough to understand, since the man was so banged up. Except, over a month later, the sign was still up. Pretty clear, but not so understandable. *Now* the sign just seemed rude.

Jesse took another drink of his beer, grimacing as the heated liquid hit his tongue. The neighbor was at the mailbox now. Well, not exactly *at* the mailbox — that would mean he had to step off the sidewalk and into the street. Instead, as was the norm on these little treks, he kept his feet firmly planted on the edge of the walkway while he leaned forward and stretched out his left hand to retrieve the mail. *Probably not uncomfortable,* Jesse mused, *but still, why not just take the few extra steps to actually* walk *to the mailbox?*

The man slapped the box lid shut and pivoted carefully. Jesse quit trying to pretend he wasn't watching and tipped his glasses down. Without the dark tint impeding his vision, he was treated to a brilliant display of gorgeous, curly auburn hair. The sun brought out streaks of red as well as glints of gold and orange in the silky-looking mess. Jesse's fingers tightened on the beer bottle — the urge to touch the colorful curls was nearly a physical thing.

He sat on the steps for several minutes after the neighbor had disappeared back inside, wondering how pathetic he'd become when this was the highlight of his day.

Caleb took a deep breath and steeled himself. He could do this, *he could.* It was a pretty sorry thing when a grown man had to work to find the courage to walk fifteen feet to his own mailbox. Some days it took longer than others to even open the door.

Maybe that cop will be sitting on his steps. He'd seen the man numerous times — there were times it made his trip outside easier, knowing there was a police officer just a few feet away. Sometimes it made him nervous, though, because Caleb was pretty sure the guy was watching him. Maybe it was all innocuous, or maybe the cop was watching him for other reasons. Did he think Caleb was a criminal, some kind of threat to the people in this town?

Caleb actually snorted at the idea as he made himself unlock the deadbolts then slip on the glasses. His fingers shook as he reached for the doorknob, but he managed to turn it with a slight twist of the wrist. Caleb gingerly opened the door, fighting to keep his muscles from trembling. A deep breath, then another, and he was able to take the step that brought him outside and onto his porch.

I can do this. Keeping his head down, Caleb willed his feet to move. Slowly, he shuffled down the sidewalk. The sun's heat seemed to seep inside him, warming the dark, frightened places in his mind. Caleb tipped his head up just enough to see the man sitting on his porch. He looked big and fit, a tight T-shirt clinging to sculpted muscles. *Safe. I'm safe as long as he's out here too.*

Caleb stopped at the edge of the sidewalk, fighting against the flush that crawled up his cheeks. *Why can't I take even one step off it?* The very idea made his heart race erratically, pound so hard he wondered if he might have a heart attack. *Just check the damn mail!* Caleb reached for the mailbox lid, not thinking until that moment just how bizarre his ritual must seem to an observer.

No wonder he watches me. I'm a damned freak. He dared a glance at the man. Now he was certain the guy was watching. Caleb fumbled as he grasped at the mail, his fingers not cooperating, hands shaking a little. Bending forward more, he managed to grab the envelopes and pull them from the box. Caleb slapped the lid shut and turned back to his house. He would not peek over his shoulder, he *wouldn't*. And he wouldn't run either.

It took all his concentration to keep his steps slow and steady, embarrassment and shame pushing at him as he felt the man's gaze prickling his spine. By the time he was back inside, the deadbolts firmly in place, Caleb's nerves were shot. He wondered how much longer he could go on the way he'd been doing the past month or so. *Will I always be this fucked up?* He didn't really want an answer to that because he knew it'd just depress him.

Caleb called his puppy to him. "Loopy! Come snuggle."

The adorable toy poodle came bounding into the room, and leaped up onto the couch where Caleb had sprawled. "Good baby." There was nothing like puppy kisses and cuddles to take his mind off unpleasant things.

* * * *

Inside the stuffy trailer, Jesse shrugged out of his clothes and pulled a uniform from the closet. As he dressed for work, he couldn't stop thinking about his neighbor. The man's odd behavior and general unfriendliness were reasons enough, in his opinion, to keep an eye on the guy. Add to that his mysterious arrival in the wee hours of the morning weeks ago, and Jesse couldn't help but be curious.

It was possible that a lot of people moved into a new place at three in the morning, but it seemed strange to him. He supposed it also played into the mystery about the neighbor, ensuring Jesse would continue watching him, working it all over in his mind.

He'd never seen the man at the store or anywhere out in public. Chances were, in such a small town, they would have run into each other at the local grocery store at the very least. The guy had to be getting food somewhere, unless he was stocked up in preparation for doomsday. He wouldn't be the only one in El Jardin to do so.

Jesse did glean some things about his neighbor, like that he must be a sucker for animals, because there was a yappy dog in the big back yard sometimes. There was also a gray tabby cat that was, as far as Jesse could tell, more than a little on the feral side. The few times he'd tried to approach the cat had resulted in the tabby bolting for cover. Still, he'd seen the animal crouched on the porch, nibbling away at a pile of cat food. The free meals didn't put a dent in the tabby's hunting stints. Jesse was pretty sure the cat was responsible for the deaths of a quarter of the local bird population, despite the meals his neighbor provided.

Is the guy just crazy, though? Or is he suffering from the aftereffects of whatever violent event happened to him before he moved here?

More fuel had been added to the fire last week when Jesse had overheard Lisa down at the tax office talking about how the house had been purchased in a woman's name. Shannon, Lisa's coworker, had pointed out that her sister worked for the utility company, and those too had been put in a woman's name. It had been on the tip of Jesse's tongue to inform them they were sharing information that, by law, they shouldn't have, but he *had* listened. Besides, a scolding from him wouldn't have stopped them anyway, and it'd just have made Jesse look like a prick.

All these things pushed Jesse to find some answers. The truth was, on the off chance someone had personally assaulted his neighbor… Well, it would be better for the neighbor if Jesse knew that, even if the person responsible were in jail. If it was some sort of accident, maybe he could drop a hint about that here and there around town, try to turn the tide of small-town disapproval. Nothing major, just some basis for telling the wagging tongues to back off.

Was he going a little too far with his determination to find out more about the man? If he was, he wasn't alone. There were enough people in the dinky town just waiting and watching, wondering what the *odd* new guy in El Jardin was doing. At least Jesse only wanted to know because his cop senses were tingling. He had no intention of spreading gossip. And it had absolutely nothing to do with the fact that he found himself oddly attracted to the man.

Chapter Two

Another week passed before Jesse caught what he hoped was a break. The little reddish-orange canine ball of fur bounced around his ankles. A smile bloomed as he realized why the poodle looked familiar. *Bingo and a home run.* The hyper creature was the same one he had seen in his neighbor's back yard.

Now he had an excuse to go bang on the door, regardless of what the snotty sign said. So far, he had still been waiting patiently for the story to unfold. Maybe there, in the form of a six-pound bundle of shivering canine excitement, was the thread that would unravel the whole tale.

"Come here, boy." Jesse squatted and reached for the poodle, earning himself a face full of dog kisses. "Ick. I'm not kissing you back, dog." He wasn't really bothered by them. The pup was cute and sweet. He'd tolerate getting licked if it meant finally meeting the man who had refused to acknowledge his existence for over a month.

The guy couldn't be totally averse to visitors—Jesse just knew that he had to be lonely at times, so it was either personal or applied to all strangers. Jesse was definitely leaning toward the latter, since he opened the door to one person at least.

Or, to be exact, three people. A car had been there earlier, carrying an attractive woman and two little girls Jesse assumed were her kids. It was gone now. He'd seen it there before, though.

Once. He'd seen that car at his mysterious neighbor's house, and while the man hadn't walked outside to greet them, he had waited in the doorway and hugged his visitors before scurrying back inside. Jesse suspected they were family members. The woman was petite, her hair was reddish, and the little girls, with their auburn ringlets glistening in the sun, were like carbon copies of the man who had hugged them. They could have been the neighbor's kids.

They looked so much like him... Well, except for being female. Jesse's neighbor might be skinny, and he wasn't tall, at only about five-eight, but he didn't look feminine at all. It seemed to Jesse that his slight build was off in a way that seemed unnatural to the man's frame, as though as a result of whatever had happened to him, he'd lost a lot of weight.

Jesse had no doubt it had been a violent event, whether it was a wreck or something personal like attempted murder. The first week or so, the man had been covered in bruises and had moved as though every part of his body screamed in agony.

Now there was the added twist of family of some sort. Jesse didn't know if the woman was a family member or an ex. He didn't know if exes would be on such friendly terms as to hug and kiss cheeks or be as happy to see each other as those two had been. Wasn't sure they wouldn't be, either. He'd heard some exes got along great. It just wasn't anything he'd ever seen happen.

Another yap drew Jesse's attention back to the puppy still bouncing around. "Yeah, I see you, cutie. Come on, let's get you back to where you belong." He scooped the small dog up in one hand, then made his way across the street. Jesse thought he saw the blinds twitch in the living room window.

The idea that his neighbor might have been watching had Jesse's lips quirking up in amusement. He liked to think the man hadn't been able to ignore him after all. Hell, he could have his own timeline of Jesse sightings logged in some notebook for all Jesse knew.

On the porch, Jesse didn't stand on the last step up. He was already taller and bigger than his neighbor and didn't want to intimidate him. He'd just raised his fist to knock when the door swung open a few inches and a narrow strip of coppery hair appeared. The bundle of canine joy went into a fit of ecstasy, squirming and wriggling as it yipped. Jesse held on to the dog, waiting for the door to open the rest of the way.

The first thing that hit him was the jewel-bright green of the man's eyes. Damned if Jesse had ever seen eyes like that. The fact that he could see the color through his own dark-tinted lenses surprised Jesse and had him sliding the black frames on top of his head. He looked for a ring around the irises, some sign of contacts, but could find none. Jesse noticed little flecks of deeper green and brown close to the pupils, creating a riotous starburst pattern that was... *Breathtaking* was the only word he could think of. Thick, dark lashes provided a contrast for those wide, vibrantly colored eyes.

Jesse realized he was staring as he memorized every detail. But hell, it wasn't like the other man wasn't looking too. Goosebumps rose on his skin everywhere that nervous gaze landed. He had the forethought to know that if it dropped to his half-hard cock, he might end up with the door slammed in his face. Who could blame the guy? What kind of sick jerk was he to be turned on by a man who was so obviously messed up and scared?

Clearing his throat, Jesse slowly stuck out his free hand, worried any sudden moves would send the man off in a panic. The gesture brought that glittering gaze back up to his face as a long, bony hand landed in his bigger one.

"I'm Jesse Martin. I live across the street." Jesse gestured over his shoulder, since the neighbor had withdrawn from the handshake as quickly as possible. Then he waited. There was a certain sort of power in silence that most people couldn't tolerate. He was betting this man wouldn't be any different. Already, his eyes were darting around nervously.

Jesse almost felt bad knowing the neighbor was uncomfortable, but whatever caused such nervousness — *and, okay, fear* — needed to be confronted, to Jesse's way of thinking. The little dog squirmed and yipped again, breaking the silence and giving the auburn-haired man something to focus on.

"May I have Loopy back?" The question was rushed out, the words almost blending together.

Jesse nearly dropped…Loopy. *What the hell kind of name was that? What about Rex or King or…* Eyeing the fur ball, Jesse realized Loopy was probably a good fit. The dog did seem more than a bit ditzy.

"Sure, of course." Handing the dog over, Jesse subtly let his hand brush against the warm skin of the man's hand. The jolt of sensual awareness that shot through him had him almost dropping the dog. Judging by the startled gasp from his neighbor, Jesse wasn't the only one who felt it. Then again, maybe the guy simply didn't like being touched. And damn it all, Jesse was tired of not knowing the guy's name. It didn't look like he'd be offered it freely. There was no help for it. He had to ask.

"What's your name?" Rough and gravelly, Jesse's voice sounded unnatural to his ears.

The man's gaze shot up to his. There was an audible swallow, then another and another before Jesse got an answer.

"I'm Caleb, with a C. Tomas. I mean, Caleb Tomas."

Caleb. Different and interesting, like the man it belongs to. Now Jesse had a name for his gorgeous neighbor.

"Thank you for bringing Loopy back." Caleb stepped back, and before Jesse knew what was what, that damned front door started closing in his face.

Reflexes had him slapping a hand against the heavy panel, stopping it forcefully and giving Caleb a severe start. Caleb's eyes were huge and he'd jumped like he'd been jabbed with a sharp stick. *Shit! Wrong move, moron!* He hadn't meant to scare him.

"Sorry." Jesse didn't have to fake the apologetic note in his voice. "I didn't mean to, ah, freak you out or anything, honest."

Caleb's head bobbed up and down before he caught himself. Still, he wouldn't look at Jesse.

"Caleb."

The panic in those green depths didn't subside, but Caleb did succeed in looking in his eyes.

Christ, the power behind that look sent a coil of heat throughout Jesse's body, but more than that, it made Jesse want to hold Caleb close and keep him safe. *What the fuck?*

"Wh-what?" A sheen of sweat broke over Caleb's brow and trickled down his temples.

Jesse wanted to trace the path that sweat was taking, either with his tongue or his finger. His hand was moving before he realized it, and he probably wouldn't have stopped if Caleb hadn't made a strangled sound that hit him straight in the heart. So intense and surprising was the feeling, Jesse pulled back his hand and pressed it against his chest in an attempt to counteract the pain. He could do nothing to squash the overwhelming need to reassure his neighbor, though.

"I'm sorry, Caleb. I wasn't going to hurt you, just wanted to brush something off the side of your face. I won't make any sudden moves like that again." Fear, shame, self-loathing—Jesse saw those things and more flash across Caleb's face. All those bad feelings were because of Jesse being an idiot. "Hey, it's okay. It was my fault."

Caleb just shook his head, looking so broken Jesse was at a loss as to what to do.

"What can I do to help you?" Right now, Jesse would do anything to get that look off Caleb's face, out of his haunted eyes.

"Let me shut my door," Caleb whispered, staring at his feet.

Sick with guilt, Jesse could only comply. He pulled his hand back and watched the door shut, listening as several locks clicked into place before he turned and headed back to his trailer.

Caleb leaned against the door, holding Loopy to his chest until his demands to be put down reached the scratching-and-nipping phase. He lowered the dog to the floor, unsurprised when Loopy bolted across the room and jumped onto the couch, happily ensconcing himself in the multitude of colorful pillows. The cuteness factor usually made Caleb feel warm and fuzzy, but right now nothing could penetrate the depression sinking into his soul.

God, will I never be normal again? Tears burned his eyes and leaked out, making him so angry he wanted to scream and hit something. He *wasn't* like this! Damn it, he hadn't been this crying, scared man for the first thirty-one years of his life. How could he have changed so drastically?

Caleb walked to the couch, trembling and jerky and so tired of this person he had become. He lay down and snuggled as close to Loopy as the hyper animal would let him but still felt empty and utterly alone. Caleb wrapped his arms around a pillow, pressing it tightly against him in a bid to meet the welling need for comfort. It wasn't enough, never was, no matter how often he did it. This time it only made him feel worse, seemingly stoking the loneliness and fear growing inside him.

Curling into a fetal position to make himself as small as possible, Caleb closed his eyes and fought back the sudden panic. It was the last thing he was cognizant of doing before he welcomed the relief promised by the darkness engulfing him.

* * * *

Jesse sat on the wooden steps and checked his watch. He had spent the last twenty-four hours worrying about the way he'd botched things with Caleb. The fear and anguish in Caleb's eyes had been turned inward as though he was looking inside and was afraid of what he had become. That was just wrong. Jesse's actions had been inappropriate, especially for such a delicate situation. It was his actions that had wrought those dark emotions.

The knowledge he had put those feelings there, however inadvertently, had ridden him hard ever since. No one should have to live with so much pain. Somehow he would find a way to help Caleb. Someone needed to, and he was more than willing to step up and offer. After all, he was sworn to uphold the law and assist those in need.

Yeah, yeah, yeah, keep on telling yourself that's all it is. Doesn't have a thing to do with the fact that Caleb is the sexiest man you've ever seen. It has nothing to do with those gorgeous eyes or that tight little ass you pretend to ignore even when you drool over it. Nothing to do with that wide, sexy mouth or –

Jesse's internal rant was cut off by Caleb's front door sliding open. He waited for him to step outside and worried the longer that door stayed open and nobody appeared. *Should I go check that nothing's happened?* What if someone else was in the house and it wasn't Caleb who'd opened the door? Or if Caleb was hurt and needed help? It didn't matter that neither of the scenarios rushing through his head made sense. Jesse was on his feet and moving before he knew what he was doing.

The closer he got to Caleb's house, the more worried he became when Caleb still hadn't appeared. He was almost to the porch when he saw a leg lying on the floor. A bouncing ball of fur ran to the open doorway and yipped.

Pulling off his sunglasses for a better look, he realized Caleb was sitting splayed-legged in the carpeted entryway, with his back against the wall.

Not wanting to startle either Caleb or the puppy, Jesse strode closer, trying to keep from appearing aggressive. Caleb's shoulders were hunched, and hands covered part of his face. It was a heart-wrenching sight that tore something open inside Jesse. Once he was closer, he crouched and cautiously leaned his torso into the doorway.

"Caleb?" Jesse kept his voice soft and calm, much as he did when dealing with trauma victims. "Caleb, it's Jesse Martin, from across the street."

A slight tremor worked through Caleb's thin body, followed by a whimper that stomped Jesse's heart to pieces.

Jesus Christ, had he done this with his stupid need to pry? He must have. Jesse had to find a way to fix the damage. Loopy yapped, and Jesse reached for him but hesitated, unsure.

"Hey." Jesse's knees popped as he turned to face Caleb more fully. "Caleb, I'm going to sit here, okay? Just to take the pressure off my knees." When Caleb didn't offer any protest, Jesse put action to his words. He eased himself into a position that left his legs draped on the porch step. Loopy bounced between Caleb and Jesse before finally scrabbling off somewhere in the house.

Jesse watched for a sign Caleb was aware of him, some slight movement or an increase in the tension coiling the man's body into a rigid mass of anguished flesh, but saw no change whatsoever.

"Caleb, can you hear me?"

There was just the slightest nod of acknowledgment. Jesse's hands twitched with the need to touch and comfort. Holding himself back was sending little spasms of protest through his arms. He struggled for control, getting a tenuous grasp on it before continuing.

"Good. Okay, I'm going to scoot in," he warned and waited for a protest.

Caleb's body jerked in response to the words, but Jesse could not back away.

"It will be fine. You're safe, I swear it. Just let me sit beside you until you can tell me what's wrong." Jesse had been moving silently as he spoke and was now in the house, sitting almost hip to hip with Caleb.

The man looked so alone that Jesse risked everything he had accomplished to close that last scant inch. Just a light scoot and he was beside Caleb, no almost to it. They were actually brushing against each other when either breathed.

A gasp tore from Caleb's lips. His hand dropped with a *thud* onto the floor between his thighs. Seeing his tear-ravaged face, Jesse ached for him. Caleb was so obviously losing the battle against whatever demons tormented him.

"Caleb, I can't let you do this alone."

Caleb tipped his head up. There was no sparkle in those green eyes, no nervous darting from place to place like yesterday. Seeing the dull, hopeless look snapped the rest of Jesse's control.

"Please," Jesse murmured as he reached to pull Caleb in his arms. "Just let me help you. Please. You tell me to stop, to get away, and I swear, I'll do it. If not, I'm just going to hold you until you feel better. Okay?"

Caleb didn't speak or move away. Jesse twisted his torso and gathered the frail man close. He stroked Caleb's back, feeling the knobby ridges of his spine and ribs through his baggy clothing.

"It's okay, you're not alone. I'm here, and it's okay, Caleb." Jesse didn't know how many times he said those words, how long he petted and tried to soothe Caleb, but slowly he became aware of the slightest of movements not his own.

Tremulous touches, as Caleb brought his hands to Jesse's waist for only a moment before Caleb fisted them tightly enough into the cotton material that Jesse heard it tear.

Caleb rested his head against Jesse's chest. That minute show of trust—Jesse wanted to believe that was what it was— shook Jesse to his core. *He* was the person Caleb was clinging to, leaning on, letting in in some small way.

Caleb shuddered. Then he sniffled. He was breaking Jesse's heart.

A growing wetness on Jesse's chest told him Caleb was crying. Jesse rocked gently, swaying their bodies back and forth as he continued rubbing Caleb's back and crooning softly, humming more than actually speaking.

"I can't... I can't go outside. There's the hole in the back fence, and the mail came, and... I don't know what's wrong with me. *I don't know what's wrong with me.*"

The words from Caleb came so quietly Jesse thought he imagined them at first. The last repeated phrase sounded like a familiar refrain—something Caleb had asked himself numerous times. Another dozen things spun through Jesse's mind, but not a single one was about blaming Caleb for what he was going through—and several of them were about the fact that holding Caleb felt so damned right. He carefully considered what he wanted to say, then reconsidered it, but couldn't find anything better suited.

"I don't know what happened to you, Caleb, and I'm not asking you to tell me, not yet." Jesse tightened his arms around Caleb when he stiffened. "I don't think it's a matter of what's wrong with you so much as it's what happened to you before moving here. That's what's causing this." At least he hoped that was the case. For all he knew, the thin man had been institutionalized numerous times.

Caleb pulled back and Jesse had no choice except to loosen his hold and let him have a little space. He didn't let go of Caleb, though, and it didn't seem as if Caleb wanted him to.

Jesse wanted to look into Caleb's eyes and see if they were still dull and lifeless, or if they had warmed any, bringing those darker green and brown flecks to a sparkling shimmer. He debated whether he could touch Caleb's face. Yesterday it had nearly sent him into a panic.

Caleb leaned against him again.

That'll work.

"I wasn't always this way, not anything like this at all." Caleb's voice was barely more than a strangled whisper.

That was what Jesse had thought. He wasn't schooled in psychology by any means, but it seemed to him that Caleb might be agoraphobic. Then again, he could be totally off base with that.

"All right, then, you know this is a result of…something else. It didn't just start for no reason." Jesse paused, giving Caleb a chance to comment. After a half minute or so, he took the silence to mean that Caleb was waiting for him to continue. "When something traumatic happens to a person, the mind copes with that event or events in whatever manner possible to keep you going. It works to protect that person and keep them safe, even if it's not in a way the person likes."

"How do you know? What if there's something wrong with me?" Caleb asked.

Now those eyes looked a little less dull, a little less lifeless as Caleb sought Jesse's reassurance. The brown bits stood out in an entrancing display against the deep green. It struck Jesse again how pretty Caleb's eyes were.

He asked a question! Stop gawking at him and pull it together, moron. "You know I'm a police officer, right?"

Caleb nodded, his cheeks tinting. "I noticed before. I've seen you in your uniform."

Didn't that bear some thinking, that Caleb had possibly watched out of the window for a chance to see him? "I've seen a —" Jesse caught himself before he said 'a lot of victims of violent crimes'. He didn't want Caleb to pack up and move because of the crime rate here. "I've seen the way different people cope with things, and I'm telling you. That's what's going on here. You're not crazy. Your brain is just trying to find a way to cope. Now that you know what it's doing, you need to try to interject some changes."

"I don't know how, Jesse." That was the first time Caleb had said his name. It sounded all too right coming from his lips.

"Why don't we start by letting me help you to the mailbox?" Jesse saw the doubt clouding Caleb's eyes and barreled right over it. "If you wait, it'll just get worse. I'm here right now. I won't let anything happen to you."

Caleb still seemed hesitant, but he hadn't outright refused, so Jesse pushed more. "Think about how much you want to get past this. How much do you want to be the person you were before? I'll be right with you. I'll even keep my arm around you and hold you close to my side." *Like that's a hardship.* Jesse wasn't prepared for the heat that bloomed in Caleb's eyes — in fact, he was sure he imagined it — or the small smile that worked at his lips.

"I think... I think I might like that." Caleb's eyelids lowered, hiding some part of him.

As Jesse stared down at him, something, or the lack of something, caught his attention. "Hey, when did you get your cast off?" The clunky white hunk of plaster that had been on Caleb's right arm ever since he'd moved in was now gone.

"Um. Today. I took it off today."

Jesse's gaze shot up to Caleb's face. "*You* took it off?"

Caleb nodded and stared at Jesse as though daring him to say something.

Jesse didn't consider himself or Caleb stupid, so he wisely stayed quiet. Caleb was an adult. He wasn't crazy. He just had some issues, and as far as Jesse was concerned, everyone had some of those.

"Cool. So, you ready to do this?" Jesse stood and pulled Caleb up with him, keeping the small man wrapped in his arms.

Caleb gave him a start when he shook his head. "No, I'm not, but I— We're going to do it anyway." He drew in a deep, shaky breath before straightening his shoulders. "Okay, let's go."

Chapter Three

Caleb sat in the big leather recliner and stared at the muted television. He rarely watched TV, but he had it on constantly, muted. No doubt a psychiatrist would have a field day with that, along with the rest of his problems. Some mental health care might be beneficial, but the truth was, he couldn't handle leaving the house for appointments, and he couldn't handle having a stranger in his house either.

A vision of the very sexy Jesse Martin popped into Caleb's mind. Tall, dark and handsome, like some romantic fairy-tale hero. Those eyes, so warm and decadent—they reminded Caleb of melted milk chocolate rimmed in the richest dark coffee. The amber striations in those pretty irises brought to mind a sensual, smoldering heat.

The man was fucking hot and Caleb was almost certain sure Jesse was gay. A straight man wouldn't have been so willing to hold him, to touch and offer comfort so freely. Those touches had done more than just comfort and calm. They had ignited a spark of desire in Caleb that was still growing steadily.

Caleb wished the attraction was mutual, but Jesse hadn't said or done anything while Caleb was sitting in his lap. Had Jesse restrained himself from doing so out of concern for him? Or was Jesse afraid to get involved with his crazy neighbor? Caleb damned sure couldn't have been looking very attractive at that point.

But Jesse had been so nice. Surely if he hadn't wanted anything to do with Caleb, he wouldn't have spent time trying to calm him down and reassure him.

Caleb snorted at his stupidity. Jesse had found him a broken, sobbing mess. Was it any wonder he hadn't tried to come on to him? "Talk about a turn-off." Caleb scoffed at his idiotic thoughts. Tears and snot had to be on the top-five list of things that grossed out a potential date, right below clinginess, whininess and craziness.

Still, Jesse had shown considerable kindness. He hadn't pushed to come back inside once he'd helped Caleb to the mailbox. Instead, his friendly neighbor had walked around the house to the back yard and found the hole in the fence. Caleb had watched out of the back window while Jesse had dug around in the shed for some tools.

Caleb had stared at Jesse's firm ass as he'd bent to fix the fence. It'd been a gorgeous view.

Until Caleb had noticed the twitching of his dick. He hadn't gotten an erection, and had tried not to worry about that, since he'd been hurt. The fact that he was half-hard even now was a relief, to put it mildly.

And frustrating too, because other than jacking off, there wasn't much Caleb could do about his reaction to Jesse Martin. He hadn't even been able to open the back door while Jesse was working outside. It wasn't like Caleb had never opened that door. It was something he did multiple times every day to let Loopy in and out.

No, all the time Jesse had been in the back yard, Caleb had done nothing but watch from a window, occasionally blatantly, but mostly he just peeked. That became necessary when Caleb thought he might very well drool as he looked at Jesse's fine form. If Jesse had seen him, surely the man would have picked up on the lustful looks.

So Caleb had come off like a weirdo. God knew he felt like a pathetic fool when Jesse finished working and put up the tools before waving goodbye. "Like he knew I was watching."

Well, he had been. Caleb had also yearned to be able to move past his crazy shit. For over a month, he'd just let it consume him, but now, he thought he might want more freedom than he was currently able to allow himself. What he didn't know was how to fix himself, or if he could even *be* fixed. He thought about Jesse's warm brown eyes and the way it had felt to be held, and his cock began to firm up.

At least one part of him wasn't afraid of letting Jesse get close. Too bad that particular part didn't have control over whatever it was that kept him from functioning like a normal human being.

Frustrated, Caleb wandered into his office and turned on his laptop. While that started up, he went to the back door and unlocked the deadbolts. *Now* he didn't have any problem pulling the damn door open. Loopy bounced inside. Caleb couldn't fight back a grin as he shut the door and locked it while remaining upright, which was no mean feat considering how Loopy jumped all over him.

Why hadn't he been able to open the back door earlier? He *wanted* to talk to Jesse. As much as he loved his dog, Loopy wasn't able to hold a conversation, and he missed talking with someone who would listen and share his opinions. Why was he suddenly feeling so lonely instead of safe and sheltered as he usually did in his home? It irritated the crap out of him.

Caleb found himself muttering and cursing as he checked Loopy's food and water bowls. The need to interact with other people, specifically *one* other person, was preying on him, and while he could admit he wanted Jesse, he didn't have to like it. No matter what his randy dick tried to prove otherwise.

Caleb flopped into the chair at his desk and stared at the laptop screen. Giving in, he tapped a few keys and opened his account on the social-networking site. It wouldn't be the same as talking to the man he wanted to talk to, but at least he could almost guarantee that online there would be a few people to help keep him occupied so he didn't dwell on the empty feeling growing inside.

* * * *

Jesse wasn't concentrating like he needed to. He knew it and couldn't seem to do anything about it. He kept thinking about Caleb slumped against the wall, looking so broken and lost. That image would haunt his sleep for a long time. *Why* it affected him so much was a whole different concern. And distractions could be deadly for a police officer or anyone he was working with or trying to help. He knew that, yet he couldn't focus on his job like he needed to.

Adding to his confusion, while he'd been repairing the fence, Jesse had caught Caleb watching him several times. He'd thought, and even hoped, that Caleb would open the door at the very least. Maybe even speak to Jesse as he rewound the rusty piece of wire around the edges of the chain-link fence, but Caleb hadn't done anything like that.

The fact that Caleb was watching, along with that glimmer of interest in his eyes earlier, was part of why Jesse's mind was spinning with a whole new set of questions. Each of those came down to two important ones. Did Caleb want him, and if so, would it even be possible for the two of them to do...anything?

Jesse couldn't sort it out, didn't know if it was his desire making him want to believe there'd been anything other than other than caution and fear in Caleb's eyes. When he tried to imagine holding Caleb in a sexual manner, he all too easily pictured the anguished expression on Caleb's face that had been there when Jesse had found him looking so hopeless. That tended to wilt his hard-on immediately.

So Jesse figured he could either get his head out of his ass, or he could go back to the station and tell the chief he needed to go home. Of course, then Chief Chapel would demand to know why he wanted to take off early, and that was something Jesse didn't know how to explain to Chapel.

How could he explain it to someone else when he wasn't sure what was going on in his head himself?

Maybe if he did a quick drive by Caleb's house, he could relax a bit and quit worrying about the man. Though, seeing the house wouldn't really tell him anything. It could look safe and all on the outside, while Caleb could be huddled inside, going through God knows what.

Still, if there was a chance it would even partially ease his mind, he could give it a shot.

Jesse pulled into the parking lot of one of the three convenience stores in town and made a U-turn. Having decided to do a quick pass by Caleb's house, Jesse had already started feeling better.

A glance at his watch told him it was nearly one in the morning as he slowed the car and cruised down their block. Hopefully the fact that every light in Caleb's house was on meant everything was okay with him. Thinking about it, Jesse remembered the interior of the house had been dark when he'd found Caleb earlier.

It wasn't the reassurance Jesse would have liked, but it would do. Tomorrow, when Caleb came out to check his mail, Jesse would approach him, cautiously, and see if he could get him to take his cell number in case he needed help or anything, even just to talk or text. It would make him feel better knowing for certain that Caleb had someone to call on nearby, and he could admit he wanted that someone to be him. He just wished he knew why he felt that way.

* * * *

"There!" Caleb shut off his laptop and pushed his chair away from the desk. He'd spent hours interacting with fans and God only knew who else. His agent would do cartwheels at the amount of self-promotion Caleb had just done.

"Well, maybe not cartwheels." Caleb almost laughed. Macy Ferris wasn't the cartwheel type of person. She was a great agent, but Caleb could count on one hand the number of times in the past six years he'd seen her let loose a genuine smile. He should have probably shot off an email to let her know what a good boy he'd been, but since he'd really done it to counter his loneliness, he didn't feel like bragging.

The interactions had helped some. He didn't feel quite so empty inside. However, Caleb was still swamped with thoughts of Jesse. Admittedly, at first, that had led to a bit of Internet porn, something Caleb hadn't bothered with in quite a while. The combination of Jesse and porn had left him in his current state, which was achingly hard and hornier than he'd been in ages. He made his way into the living room and sprawled out in the recliner.

Caleb groaned at the uncomfortable pressure of his dick pressing against the buttons of his jeans. Uncomfortable, but having a hard-on again was so reassuring, such a normal thing for a guy his age, Caleb had no urgent need to beat off. Sure, after he'd had time to revel in the fact that he wasn't impotent, then he might have a go or two. It *had* been months, after all. And some lovely images lingered in his mind, although he did keep superimposing Jesse's face onto many of them. Who could blame him? The man was gorgeous and kind, and he had an ass to die for.

Caleb shifted in the chair, trying to keep the denim from pinching his aching dick. Every twitch threatened to make him come. And now he wasn't enjoying the fact that his cock throbbed with each heartbeat.

It was time to move to a more appropriate spot. His bed would probably be best, since he pretty much passed out after an intense orgasm. As aroused as he was, his impending climax would probably be the most intense one he'd ever experienced.

He wouldn't risk falling asleep covered in cum and waking up with a hyper pup trying to lick places he never wanted a dog to lick. "Gross." Caleb shuddered and forced himself to get up.

Chapter Four

Jesse swatted away the June bugs as he walked up to his front door. He hated the freaky flying bastards but didn't have the energy to do any serious damage to them or to shoo them away effectively. It had been a rough shift. There'd been three domestic violence calls, some idiots had attempted a beer run, and the worst of all, a wreck that had resulted in multiple fatalities. The latter had left him completely drained and more than a little depressed about the state of humanity.

The screen door wobbled and screeched as he pulled it open. He stepped forward and let it bounce against his shoulder as he unlocked the door. Jesse practically leaped into his living room, then shut the door quickly, hoping to prevent a full-scale June bug invasion. The dark paneling inside gave the room an almost sinister feel, but Jesse knew it was a carryover sensation from his shift. He turned the light on and winced as his eyes adjusted to the brightness. After a moment, Jesse found himself blinking at the bare walls, the cheap, dark paneling. He wondered briefly if Caleb's home looked more lived-in than his, then shrugged the thought aside. He hadn't paid attention to anything but Caleb once he'd seen him.

Jesse's eyes were gritty, and his stomach rumbled, but he wouldn't be able to eat a bite, not until the images of the fatality scene faded. The faint coppery scent of blood reached his nostrils and he glanced down, noticing a splotch on the left leg of his uniform pants. A teenage girl had been out joyriding with her friends. It had all gone to hell for them when the oncoming driver had tried to text and swig beer while steering with his knee. The resulting loss of lives ate at his soul.

Jesse was exhausted but he couldn't just strip and drop into bed, not with the lingering odor of death on him. He stumbled down the hall to his bedroom, unbuttoning his heavy belt as he went. Jesse put his weapon in a drawer of the nightstand, then placed a clip beside it and closed the drawer.

Then Jesse stripped and gathered the uniform. He carried it into the kitchen, where, he put it in a plastic bag. It wasn't what he normally did, but he didn't want to catch so much as a whiff of blood. Jesse tossed the bag on the floor beside the couch, then went into the bathroom to shower away the grime and memories.

The warm water coursed over his body. Jesse sighed as he rested the back of his head against the tiny shower stall. His chest hurt with a sudden aching loneliness. This was one of the times he wished he had someone to come home to. Not to share stories about the horrors of the day, but just to hold, be held, and draw comfort from.

Immediately he thought of Caleb, but this time the images his brain produced weren't of a scared, hurt man. Despite the fact that he was nearly dead on his feet, Jesse had no problem envisioning Caleb, his bright eyes wide with pleasure, his full lips parted, skittery breaths slipping between them with each hard thrust as Jesse buried his cock inside Caleb's hole over and over.

He fisted his own dick and Jesse imagined Caleb's snug, hot ass clamping around his shaft, squeezing and coaxing his climax out. Pleasure spiraled up from his groin. "Yeah. Fuck! Yes," he hissed, relieved to be somewhere other than a bad place in his head. Jesse gave himself over to the fantasy, imagining he could almost feel his balls slap against Caleb's ass with each thrust. Caleb would have a long, thick dick that'd fit perfectly in Jesse's hand. The head would be plump and red. He could just see it in his mind—a gorgeous shaft, perfect, with pre-cum glistening from the narrow slit.

Jesse groaned as he jacked off, squeezing tight and fucking his fist roughly, chasing the pain and pleasure that came from his grip. He used his other hand to play with his balls. Jesse rolled them in his palm as he jerked his dick even harder, urged on by his need to come.

A flick of his thumbnail in the slit of his dick and a tug at his balls weren't quite enough. Jesse let go of his balls and reached behind himself, almost frantic now for release. He buried a finger in his hole, shoving it in deep and hard. The jolt of having that digit in his ass sent Jesse over the edge in an explosion of heat and pleasure that tore a yell from his throat. Semen spurted from his dick in thick, white ropy sprays that were carried down the drain.

Jesse slumped against the shower wall, his knees weak and his breathing labored. His mind had gone blank with the heat and force of his climax. Now it'd gone right back to where it'd been the second before then, except in Jesse's fantasy, Caleb wore a blissed, well-fucked expression on his face as he snuggled against Jesse's side. His head rested on Jesse's chest, and one arm and leg were strewn over Jesse's stomach and thighs.

The image was possibly even more satisfying than the sexual fantasy. While that realization startled Jesse, maybe even scared him a little, it did nothing to dispel two simple facts he could no longer ignore. He wanted Caleb Tomas, wanted to help him, hold him, touch him, and he wanted him for more than just a simple fuck. A relationship, that was what he needed, wanted…which might be problematic in a town like El Jardin. Gay marriage was legal and all, but Jesse knew that didn't matter to some people. He was living in small-town New Mexico. There were those who thought their town should be the exception, and more than one of the local churches had posted some hateful shit on their signs when equality had won.

So, it could cause problems, almost certainly *would* for Jesse, if he were out. But it also might be worth the risk. In fact, he was inclined to think Caleb would be worth it. Jesse was beginning to believe that with everything he had. Caleb Tomas was worth taking a chance for.

Jesse washed quickly, his mind whirling with plans he discarded almost as soon as they formed. He could only be himself, offer only himself, but Caleb needed to know him first and learn to trust him. Jesse disregarded the nagging voice that said Caleb might not even be gay. He was certain Caleb played for his team. Jesse had never been one of those men attracted to straight guys. And there were those looks Caleb had given him from between the slats of the blinds.

Decision made, Jesse felt lighter than he had when he'd walked in the door. The image of holding Caleb in his arms was like a promise of the future dangling before him. It gave him hope, something he desperately needed, and it gave him a goal, a place to focus his attention.

Jesse climbed under the lightweight blanket with a smile on his face, eager to sleep so he could wake up and begin his campaign to win Caleb's trust.

* * * *

A flash of fur and yips greeted Jesse when he stepped outside. He grinned as he looked down at Loopy.

"You're trying to help me out, aren't you, boy?" Jesse sat on the steps and slapped his thigh. Loopy bounded up a step, then jumped into his lap. The dog was making an odd groaning sound, his entire back end shaking as his fluff-tipped tail zipped from side to side. Jesse couldn't hold back a laugh. How could he not be happy with such an enthusiastic greeting? And how had the little escape artist managed to slip from the back yard again?

Jesse scooped the dog up in both arms, because with all the jittery, ecstatic doggy joy, it took both arms to keep Loopy from doing a nosedive onto the hard ground. A glance across the street assured him Caleb was watching.

"Come on, Loopy. Let's get you back to your owner." Jesse wouldn't have believed it was possible, but Loopy wiggled even more, and Jesse felt more than a little concerned he might end up dropping the poodle and breaking him. Caleb would be crushed. Jesse readjusted his hold until he was confident Loopy was secure.

Jesse crossed the street. Loopy squirmed around. "Hey, now. Stop working against me here." Jesse hefted Loopy up higher in order to get a better grip, and once again found himself the recipient of a multitude of slobbery kisses. Jesse started to speak, then thought better of opening his mouth. Somehow he doubted Loopy was as discerning about where his tongue had been as Jesse.

And that's enough thinking about that. It would not be conducive to his plans for returning Loopy unharmed if he thought about where Loopy's tongue, which was now dragging across Jesse's nose, had been.

He stepped up onto the porch and couldn't fight back a grin when the door immediately swung open. No waiting for locks to be snapped back, which meant Caleb *had* definitely been watching and that he wasn't afraid to open the door to him. That knowledge sent a thrill through him.

"I think you lost something." He extended his arms to offer Loopy back to a smiling Caleb. The man looked entirely too good with that happy expression in place.

"Thank you." Caleb took the poodle, cuddling him briefly before setting him on the floor. "I didn't know he was such a talented escape artist, I swear. He never got out where we lived at before..." Caleb's smile died and his vivid gaze darted around a moment until he settled it back on Jesse.

"Before you moved here," Jesse finished for him, needing to ease Caleb's discomfort. The slight lessening of tension in Caleb's shoulders told him he'd succeeded. "Maybe he just really, really likes me." *Like I want you to.*

Caleb relaxed even more, but his smile wasn't quite as bright this time. "Yeah, that might be the reason he seems to run straight to your place."

Jesse nodded and tucked his hands into his back pockets to keep from reaching for Caleb. He was aware the pose spread his chest, thrusting it forward and putting his pecs on display in the tight T-shirt he wore. Caleb's gaze dropped to Jesse's chest.

The hitch in his breath was faint, but Jesse heard it, and it was all he could do not to whoop and throw his fist in the air. Caleb was definitely checking him out and liking it. Jesse did some checking out of his own. *Yeah, Caleb likes what he sees.* Either that or Caleb had just gotten a spontaneous erection courtesy of Loopy, who had returned and was jumping and yipping at his feet.

Jesse didn't think it was due to the dog. He really hoped it wasn't because of the dog.

"Sooooo…" Jesse waited for Caleb to look at his face once again.

Caleb's slow grin had Jesse's stomach doing funny things, like attempting a cartwheel or trying to duplicate the feeling he got when parachuting out of a plane. Caleb was still staring at his chest, and Jesse could feel that look, could feel his nipples pebbling, his dick perking up as well.

Jesse glanced down at his chest. *Well, no wonder he's staring and grinning. Those damn things are about to poke a hole in my shirt.*

Resisting the temptation to slap his hands over his nipples, Jesse cleared his throat. The noise seemed to snap Caleb out of his pokey-nipple-induced haze, and he finally looked at Jesse.

Caleb's cheeks were flushed, his lips looked even more tempting, and his eyes… Jesse could lose himself for days in the colors there.

He thought Caleb might stammer out an apology, so it surprised him when Caleb only darted a glance back to his chest and shrugged as if to say, *Can you blame me?* There wasn't a trace of an apology in the move or in Caleb's expression.

"I could fix the fence again," Jesse offered, thinking his voice sounded awfully husky to be speaking such nonsexual words. "Do it better this time, since my first repair job didn't hold."

"If you don't mind," Caleb replied, and damned if his voice didn't sound every bit as sex-laden.

Better, in Jesse's opinion. Low and thick and throaty, it teased him with promises of what Caleb would sound like when he was horny and lusty and ready to fuck.

"Yeah, I can." Jesse took his hands out of his pockets because the tight stretch of the denim across his dick was more than he wanted Caleb to see just yet. He waved toward his trailer and hoped Caleb's gaze followed the movement. Jesse didn't know what he'd do if Caleb noticed his hard cock and gave it an appreciative look. He didn't want to test his restraint and he didn't want to terrify the man he intended to have.

A retreat was definitely in order. "Let me just go grab some of my tools. I think I have some newer wire I can use to repair the fence." Jesse didn't wait for a reply. He turned tail and hurried away, hoping he could get his unruly dick under control before he returned.

Caleb shut the door, pivoted then flopped against it hard enough to knock the breath from his lungs. He glanced down at Loopy, who was still in a heightened state of excitement.

"Holy shit, Loopy! No wonder you were licking him all over!" Caleb rubbed his palm against his aching dick, groaning at the tendrils of pleasure that shot out from the hard length. "God, I'd like to lick all over Jesse's body." Just the idea had a shiver working over him.

Loopy yipped and spun around in a circle before darting to the back of the house.

"You little shit," Caleb muttered as he scrubbed harder at his dick. "You *know* he's going to be out there, don't you?"

Caleb closed his eyes, letting the images of Jesse's broad chest and taut nipples play through his mind. He wished he'd been brave enough to look down and see if Jesse had been sporting a hard-on as well, but had been afraid to in case he was wrong and Jesse wasn't gay after all. The last thing he needed was a pissed-off cop giving him a beatdown.

Still, those nipples and that preening pose had seemed to imply his neighbor was gay and interested. Jesse didn't seem the type to be fooling around, but Caleb's judgment wasn't quite what it could be. Hell, his head was screwed on so wrong that he couldn't trust himself to read anything into Jesse's actions, good or bad.

That realization didn't do anything to wilt his erection, however, and Caleb was close to doubling over with the need for relief. He moved away from the door, then turned back to it and snapped the deadbolts into place. No way did he want to risk having Jesse see him this horny and desperate.

And on the off chance he got brave enough to open the back door and actually converse with his neighbor, Caleb *really* didn't want to get busted with the mother of all erections. He glanced out of the peephole and made sure Jesse wasn't on his way over yet.

Caleb didn't see Jesse outside. He thought that there was enough time to take care of his embarrassing problem. As hard and horny as he was, it'd only take a few strokes, and it might save more than his pride.

That was what Caleb told himself as he rushed into the bathroom to jerk off.

He was wrong. He didn't even get two full strokes in before he was moaning and coming so hard he saw stars.

Chapter Five

Caleb wasn't surprised to find another mutilated bird on his porch. Between Loopy's frequent escapes, and Mix's — the murdering feline — increased offerings of gutted wildlife, his pets were keeping him on his toes. Literally, he thought, as he stepped out onto the porch and edged around what he thought was a dove. Hard to tell when he didn't want to look it.

When he glanced across the street, he was even less surprised to see Jesse sitting in his usual spot. Over the last few weeks since that embarrassing day Jesse had found him having a meltdown, Jesse had become a regular fixture in his life. They even talked almost regularly. Caleb looked forward to mail-check time every day, just so he could exchange hellos with Jesse and visit with him for a few minutes. It was always nice to see him.

For one thing, Jesse was much less squeamish when it came to disposing of the porch offerings left behind by Caleb's cat. He'd also repaired the fence and filled the holes Loopy dug to make his back yard escapes.

Caleb was grateful. More than that, he was developing a *thing* for his handsome neighbor. That little familiar thrill sparked in his chest every time he saw Jesse waiting, his skin glistening with sweat that also darkened his T-shirts in patches. Those dampened spots called to Caleb, made his mouth water with the need to taste the salty skin under the thin material. It was getting harder and harder to resist doing just that.

He didn't bother trying not to smile as Jesse stood and nodded. Caleb knew what that nod meant. His pulse escalated and he tipped his chin in his Jesse's direction.

Despite the fact that Jesse had been escorting him to his mailbox and back for almost three weeks, Jesse always waited for that sign, never walking over until Caleb let him know it was okay. It was that patient acceptance that made Caleb feel like he wasn't a completely broken man.

It also made him wish the mail ran on Sundays too. He used to love Sundays because he didn't have to go to the mailbox, but now Sundays dragged and Mondays had become good days.

Caleb stood on his porch and watched the long-limbed star of his pornographic fantasies saunter across the street and down the sidewalk. Jesse had been unbelievably kind, never trying to push Caleb for anything. Their little walk was usually filled with one-sided conversation from Jesse, idle chatter about his job or funny stories from his past. Never anything too heavy and never prying, just a subtle offering of himself so Caleb had slowly begun to feel safe.

Jesse's lips stretched out in a sexy smile that Caleb had spent too many hours missing. That wide mouth had been smiling around a certain part of him in a lot of fantasies of late, and that part reacted instantly to what it perceived as an offer. Caleb wasn't surprised —

once his dick had decided to work again, it seemed to be hard more often than not.

He tugged the edge of his T-shirt down past his groin nonchalantly, or so he thought, until one of Jesse's black eyebrows rose up over the top of his glasses. Caleb's skin heated with embarrassment. Any hope he'd had of remaining calm and cool evaporated. He felt like a bumbling idiot.

"Looks like Mix left you another present." Jesse leaned forward, peering over Caleb's shoulder. Jesse's familiar and welcome scent—sweat, cloves and a woodsy odor he couldn't quite identify—was particularly strong this close. It went from Caleb's nose to his lungs and straight to his dick, which gave an appreciative twitch.

"Yeah, he either really loves me or has serious sociopathic tendencies." Caleb let himself take one last, hopefully unnoticed, sniff before Jesse moved back.

Jesse seemed unaware of the effect he was having on Caleb, which might not be a bad thing, especially if he wasn't interested. Caleb would just play it cool. He almost laughed at that thought. He and cool were never going to happen.

"Maybe both," Jesse admitted. "It just seems strange that Mix has increased the frequency of gifts for the last two weeks or so—except on Sundays."

Caleb's heart thumped heavily, this time with unwarranted fear. He was messed up and paranoid, and it looked like he might be sharing those things with Jesse. The cat was the only explanation for the bird carcasses. Caleb had seen Mix take down and kill a bird on more than one occasion. Sometimes he thought Mix just waited until he looked out of the window, then put on a violent show for him.

"I figure he's just a really smart, bloodthirsty cat who happens to honor the Sabbath." Caleb shrugged, not wanting to dwell on the cat's hunting skills. "I've heard stories about pets doing things that imply they have a concept of time and schedules—waiting for their owners to get off a train or bus at a set time of day, stuff like that."

Jesse's smile was reassuring. "I'm sure you're right. I've never had a cat before, so I don't know what's normal for one."

Caleb laughed and shook his head. "I don't think there's one set definition for what's normal for a cat. They're all pretty unique."

"I'll take your word for it." Jesse's smile widened, and Caleb really wished he could see the man's eyes.

He was coming to hate those dark glasses.

"You want me to take care of this real quick before we go to the mailbox?" Jesse asked. "It's kind of messy."

Jesse usually did the disposals after Caleb returned to his house. The lurch Caleb's stomach gave at the 'kind of messy' along with the promise of a few more minutes of Jesse's company had him accepting his neighbor's offer. "That'd be great. Thank you."

Jesse jogged back across to his place. Caleb stood there and enjoyed the view. The man had a perfect ass—full, firm cheeks that shifted and taunted with each stride.

Staring at Jesse's butt was definitely *not* helping to dispel Caleb's erection. He thought about thumping the daylights out of his dick, but Jesse was already coming down his steps, a trash bag in hand. It *felt* like Jesse was watching him. Caleb's skin prickled with a sensual awareness, and there was a vast amount of tingling going on in parts of him that really didn't need the extra sensation. He was dangerously close to spurting in his jeans and he was afraid to look down to see if there was a telltale damp spot proclaiming his horniness. If that zing of sizzling heat at his groin was anything to go by, Caleb was very much afraid—and hopeful, though he didn't really want to go there—that Jesse was looking at that exact spot.

"I'll just…" Jesse's voice was rough and hesitant as he waved the bag.

Caleb couldn't look directly at him, not right then. He was pretty sure Jesse was gay, but if he wasn't, Caleb didn't want to see disgust or anger in his expression. Or worse, pity. Caleb tucked his right hand in his pants pocket and fingered the slip of paper with Jesse's phone number. He kept doing it while Jesse took care of bagging and disposing of the bird.

Ever since Jesse had so casually given him the number, Caleb had kept it with him like his own personal security blanket. The only time it wasn't on him somewhere was when he showered. Even then, he kept the paper on the closed lid of the toilet, within easy reach. Stupid, really, when he'd memorized the number right off the bat. But that little slip of paper made him feel protected. Anything capable of doing that was worth clinging to. He wondered if Jesse had kept his number, or if he'd programmed it into his cell, then tossed the paper in the trash.

"Can I ask you something?" Jesse's voice startled Caleb out of his musings. He noted the wrinkle that had formed on Jesse's brow, the slight downturn of his lips. Jesse looked like he regretted asking that much already, but Caleb trusted him. He hoped it wasn't a question about his hard-on.

"Sure," Caleb agreed. "You always do the talking. I guess I can try to answer a question." They began their walk down to the mailbox.

"You don't have to," Jesse said. "It's not bad or anything. I'm just curious."

Curious. The word caused Caleb a moment's concern, but he brushed it aside. Jesse wouldn't grill him about anything that might upset him, not yet.

"What do you do for groceries?" Jesse asked as they stopped by the mailbox.

Caleb couldn't help being surprised.

Jesse's neck turned a dull red, the color quickly spreading over his cheeks and settling at the tips of his ears.

"I mean, you have to have food. I wondered when I was at the store earlier, because you don't..." Jesse stopped and caught his bottom lip between his teeth.

Caleb's surprise left him as that plump lip served as a release for Jesse's chagrin. He hadn't realized he'd been holding his breath until it whooshed out when Jesse let his lip pop free.

"I guess it made me wonder," Jesse said. "Then I thought you might need something. If you did, I could get it, whatever it was, when I go to the store next time. If you want."

Jesse was nervous, his words coming out rapidly, and for some reason that made Caleb feel a little more secure, a little more trusting.

"My sister does the shopping for me, usually once a week or so. She brings it in the morning." Several times he'd been out of something or craved a specific food and had had to wait. He didn't want to inconvenience Kezabeth any more than he already was by asking her to make another trip.

Jesse nodded and looked relieved and embarrassed. "Oh, okay, I—"

"Did you think I was starving or something?" Crap, he wasn't *that* skinny, was he? Caleb tugged his sunglasses down his nose, wanting to see Jesse's reaction without the dark tint.

"No! I just was trying to be helpful." Jesse sighed and gave Caleb a crooked grin. "I didn't know what to think, which is why I'm asking. You could be stocked up for the next decade for all I know. There *are* a few people here like that."

And Jesse thought he was one of those weirdos? Well, okay, so he was weird, but only recently so, for the most part. "No, I—" Caleb stopped and gathered the mail, giving himself a moment to think. He didn't feel like such a freak doing his little lean-and-grab routine in front of Jesse, not like he had the first couple of weeks and certainly not like he had when Jesse used to watch from across the street. Jesse never said anything to make him feel like he was crazy. That was all on him.

Caleb shut the mailbox lid with more force than necessary. It threw his balance off, and he started to tip forward, his feet refusing to leave the sidewalk. He flailed his arms for balance, then felt a big hand grip his wrist and pull him back.

"I've got you." And Jesse did, because his arm was around Caleb's waist, his broad chest providing a stopping point for Caleb's back as he rocked on his heels. The panic that had flared was incinerated by something else, something that centered on the hard bulge pressing against Caleb's lower back. Tendrils of heat curled from that thick, denim-covered cock, slowly at first, then it seemed to race from Jesse's body to Caleb's balls, up his dick, and past his belly. The heat spread farther, working throughout his body until a needy whimper slipped from his lips.

"I'm sorry," Jesse muttered, cursing as he stepped back, one hand on Caleb's shoulder to keep him steady. "I didn't mean to grope you."

Caleb glanced over his shoulder and winced. That looked like a very large and very painful erection Jesse was sporting, and he would know — about the painful part, anyway. After an internal debate, he turned slowly and let Jesse see he wasn't the only one affected. There were a lot of things he was afraid of, things he'd never worried about before. But showing this big, kind man how much he wanted him wasn't as difficult as Caleb had feared it would be. And, he couldn't have refused to acknowledge the attraction he felt for Jesse any longer, not when Jesse was looking pretty damn terrified himself.

When Jesse had noticed Caleb's erection as he'd walked toward the man's porch, lust had hit him with the force of a kick in the gut. He'd squashed it. Just because Caleb was turned on didn't mean it had anything to do with him. The guy could have been watching straight porn before he came outside. That thought had stopped Jesse's dick from becoming fully erect right then and there.

Now, however, when he was hard and aching and feeling more than a little like a pervert for drooling over such an emotionally injured man, Caleb wasn't cursing him or having a breakdown. No, the cute little bugger faced him, the bulge behind his zipper quite evident. This time Jesse was certain it was there because of him. But what the hell could he do about it? It wasn't like he could drag Caleb off to either of their beds.

"Jesse?" Caleb took off his sunglasses and hit Jesse with all the sultry need shining in his eyes.

Jesse shook his head in bewilderment. "I don't know what you want me to do with these." He gestured at their erections. "You're not ready for me to come inside and…"

"And I'm a freak who can't leave," Caleb finished when Jesse faltered. "I know. Forget it."

"God damn it," Jesse muttered before he could stop himself, reaching for Caleb as he tried to rush past. "Stop, okay? Quit putting words in my mouth." He was pleased that he was able to keep his voice low and calm, that none of the anger seeped out. He cradled Caleb's elbow in his hand.

"That isn't fair, Caleb. I've never said anything like that, have I?" He hadn't thought it either. Actually, he hadn't dared hope Caleb would be attracted to him, which was why the evidence that he *was* had thrown Jesse off his stride. "Caleb?"

Caleb's shoulders drooped, but he looked Jesse straight in the eyes. "No, you haven't, ever. I... It's just me. I know I'm a mess."

Jesse wanted to hold the hurting man in his arms, but his own set of fears held him back. Different from Caleb's, certainly, but every bit as restrictive.

"I don't think you're a mess, just hurt. It takes time to heal from any kind of wound, whether it's a physical or emotional one." It didn't make Caleb a coward either, which was exactly what Jesse knew himself to be at that moment.

Caleb exhaled a shaky breath, then nodded once. "I'm sorry. You didn't deserve for me to be bitchy like that."

Jesse didn't blow off Caleb's apology, knowing it was important to Caleb that he accept it rather than claim he hadn't been hurt. "Apology accepted." Then he found himself at a loss, torn between wanting and fear. He reluctantly let go of Caleb's elbow and stepped off the sidewalk so Caleb could walk past him.

Caleb took two steps, paused then turned around. His expression had Jesse's softened cock filling and pressing uncomfortably against his jeans, the thin material of his boxers doing nothing to protect his swelling shaft. Caleb's lips parted, a bare breath slipping free, his arousal clearly evident. How could Caleb think he didn't want him?

Easy, jackass, you're too scared to do anything out here in broad daylight. Jesse might not be a native of El Jardin, but he'd lived here long enough to know most residents wouldn't be happy to discover one of their police officers was gay. 'Tolerance' wasn't a word used there to describe anything other than how a plant would or wouldn't fare in the heat. Caleb was either incredibly naïve about small-town attitudes, or he didn't care what people thought.

Except, Jesse thought as he watched Caleb's lustful expression crumble, he seemed to care about what *he* thought. Even if he was getting the wrong idea about why Jesse was hesitating. That wouldn't do.

"Caleb, can we maybe talk about this on your porch?" Jesse hadn't noticed any neighbors out, but that didn't mean they weren't watching all the same.

Caleb turned away from him but didn't walk off. "Is there really anything to talk about?"

Jesse nearly laughed at the question. Why did Caleb think he was sporting the hard-on from hell? He risked stroking a finger down Caleb's arm, pleased when he didn't flinch at the touch. In fact, Caleb almost seemed to lean into it.

"You do this to me, all the time." Jesse rubbed his thumb over Caleb's wrist before brushing his palm over his own erection. "And I mean, *all* the time. I'll be sitting through a briefing, and thinking your name makes me sprout wood. Driving patrol, eating lunch, writing up reports—hell, that's just at work. I walk around with a stiff dick thinking of you most of the time I'm off too."

He couldn't quite bring himself to admit that Caleb was the star of his beat-off sessions, but it should have been obvious. And maybe it was, because Caleb's lips twitched before spreading into a slow, sinfully sexy smile that fried a few of Jesse's brain cells. Suddenly, what the neighbors might see didn't seem so important.

Caleb was confused by the mixed messages. Jesse seemed to want him, but he wasn't *doing* anything. Except asking for them to continue their discussion on the porch. Another glance at the big erection Jesse was sporting, and Caleb found himself moving.

His shoulder bumped against Jesse's arm. Caleb didn't think he'd done it on purpose, but he couldn't be sure. It dawned on him that they had reached the porch. No, he was standing there, ogling his neighbor Police Officer Martin, and probably drooling as he did it. *Idiot.*

Caleb managed to drag his gaze up from that tantalizing proof of Jesse's attraction, aware of the way his own body was tensing and tightening, tingling with need. Jesse was everything Caleb had ever wanted in a man. He was huge and strong, gentle despite that thickly muscled body. More than that, he made Caleb feel *safe*, something he hadn't felt in too long.

Caleb's lungs constricted painfully as the air around them seemed to thicken with lust. He finally made himself look into Jesse's eyes.

"Can I...?" Caleb's voice suddenly failed as he raised his arm, his hand less than an inch from Jesse's chest. He wanted to stroke that firm flesh, test the resiliency of the sculpted muscle barely concealed under the cotton shirt with his hands, lips, teeth and tongue. God, Caleb *wanted.*

The shudder that rocked through Jesse's body was answer enough. Caleb moved his hand the necessary few inches and stroked the soft cotton. He felt the heat rolling off Jesse's body through the thin shirt. That heat seemed to work its way under Caleb's skin, filling him and stealing his ability to think. The lack of cognitive skills had to be the reason why he let his hand trail down to Jesse's belt, then lower still, until he was cupping the thick length of Jesse's cock through his jeans.

"Caleb." Jesse's breath stirred the hair pinned by Caleb's sunglasses. "We can't—"

Caleb jerked his hand back violently, his muscle control shot to the point that he ended up smacking himself in the stomach. Of course they couldn't. It was beyond stupid to think they could, or that Jesse *would*. No one in their right mind would want to hook up with a mess like him.

Humiliation washed over him, wilting his erection and threatening to send Caleb spiraling into the dark place in his mind that terrified him. He stumbled over the first step as he spun around, and barely managed to keep from crashing into the door.

"Caleb, wait." Jesse spoke in that soft, calming manner he'd used when he'd found Caleb feeling so broken, and it made Caleb feel even worse. Like Jesse thought he would break again.

"Not this time," Caleb muttered as he groped at the doorknob. "No fucking way!" The anger pushing at him made him clumsy as he grabbed the doorknob and twisted. For the first time since his life had been turned upside down, Caleb felt something stronger than the fear that had seemed to be his constant companion.

He shoved the door open so forcefully it slammed into the wall with a loud *crack* Caleb found very satisfying. Until that damned door bounced back and nearly clocked him in the face. He barely had time to fling his arm up and prevent that from happening. Ignoring the pain that shot through his arm, Caleb didn't spare Jesse a backward glance as he cleared the doorway.

To his complete surprise, Caleb didn't get that far. One foot in, and he went flying back out of the door. He was stunned for half a second before he realized Jesse had grabbed a handful of his shirt and was using that hold to keep him from making his escape.

No, not an escape. Caleb preferred to think of it as a dignified exit. *Except for the whole humiliation and door-slamming thing.*

Glaring at the big hand fisted into his shirt, Caleb bit off a sharp curse. "Let. Go." Part of him was surprised by his lack of fear. The rest of him was just pissed. "Now."

"No." Jesse tugged and Caleb nearly toppled down the steps. Only Jesse's other hand gripping his hip kept him from going down in an ungainly sprawl. Jesse held him there, inches away from that big, warm body. "Do you trust me?"

Amazement doused the flames of his temper when he met Jesse's patient, open stare. Not at the understanding and desire that gleamed in Jesse's eyes, which might have floored him at any other time, but because, despite being touched — manhandled, even — Caleb didn't feel the slightest twinge of fear.

What he did feel was a consuming need for the sexy cop that blotted out everything else. Caleb let his gaze drift to Jesse's slightly parted lips. The sight of a pointed pink tongue poking out from between those slick lips had Caleb's dick jerking. *I need that.* And Caleb knew the answer to Jesse's question.

"Yes, I trust you." He had no concern about Jesse hurting him, not on purpose.

Jesse's response was a softly uttered, "Good," as he tugged Caleb closer.

His lips parted as Jesse bent down, and Caleb's senses exploded. Caleb was surrounded by him—his touch, scent, those brown eyes burning into his, the sound of their mingled breaths and Caleb's rapidly beating heart.

And his taste, God! Caleb groaned, his tongue sweeping over Jesse's and setting every nerve in Caleb's body on fire. Jesse tasted dark and sweet, with the bitter tinge of coffee and something else, something Caleb suspected was as simple and complex as any puzzle he'd ever tried to figure out.

Caleb ground his aching dick against Jesse's thigh while simultaneously sliding his hands under the back of Jesse's shirt. Muscles tensed and rippled under Caleb's hands as Jesse nipped his bottom lip. The stinging pain that followed was swept away by Jesse's tongue before another nip had Caleb's fingers digging deep into the taut flesh beneath his hand. Jesse arched in, a rumbling sound emanating from him into Caleb's mouth. He rubbed and pressed his body against Jesse's, eager and needy in a way he'd never thought to be.

Jesse wrapped his arms around Caleb, the strength in them so great it made Caleb's head spin. Locked tight against Jesse, all Caleb could think was that he wanted more and wanted it badly. Held firmly, he felt safe. He would have laughed with pure joy had Jesse not been devouring his mouth.

He supposed that was why the sound of the door slamming shut didn't register at first, but when it did, the sensual spell snapped.

Shutting the door was a risk, but Jesse hadn't had any choice. If anyone had driven by and seen them, it would have cost him his job. That was what he'd wanted to explain to Caleb a few minutes earlier, but the man hadn't given him a chance before lunging away. Jesse kept his arms around Caleb, whose eyes appeared dreamy and heavy-lidded, his lips red and swollen from their kisses.

Watching the lust seep out of Caleb's green eyes, feeling the stiffness of his gaunt body, when seconds before he'd been so pliant and warm, made Jesse ache for the man. He ignored his sense of disappointment, the near-painful throbbing of his cock.

"I was trying to tell you we can't do this outside." Jesse needed Caleb to understand that. "This town isn't particularly concerned with political correctness. Most people would have a problem with anyone going at it like that outside, gay or straight." More so with gay than straight, but still a solid truth. Jesse wasn't ready to step out of the closet yet.

Caleb's cheeks turned ruddy, and he shook his head. "You're right. I'm sorry. I didn't think, I just—" He shrugged. "And you were right there. The only thing I could think about was getting closer." Caleb's voice dropped to a breathy whisper that sent a jolt straight to Jesse's dick. "I thought about getting my hands on you. My mouth on you." Caleb shook his head, as if to dislodge the need he was stirring up inside them both.

Despite the way Jesse's body throbbed with a demand for satiation, Caleb wasn't ready. Not when he'd stiffened with fear because of a shutting door. He didn't want to say or do the wrong thing, didn't want to hurt this gorgeous, wounded man, and somehow he was sure that would happen if he didn't give Caleb time to think about this. *Hope to God it doesn't backfire on us both.*

"I couldn't think much myself," Jesse offered.

The tips of Caleb's lips tilted up and eased some Jesse's tension.

Jesse was struck silent for a few seconds by that promise of a smile. "We got carried away and went from zero to sixty in a matter of seconds."

Caleb's smile bloomed, and Jesse felt like someone had kicked him in the gut.

The man was stunning, not that he'd say so. Not yet. "You're pretty irresistible." That wasn't supposed to come out either, but when Caleb's smile caused his eyes to sparkle, Jesse was glad he'd blurted out that powerful tidbit.

"Irresistible, huh?" Caleb relaxed subtly, in small degrees, until he was once more pliant and leaning into Jesse. "You're kinda sexy yourself." Caleb's cheeks pinkened, but he kept his gaze steady, and Jesse thought he might have to tack *adorable* on to his description of the man.

Wait. Kinda sexy? Not to be vain or anything, but he knew he was attractive. He worked hard to keep in shape. Jesse was about to work himself up over being only *kinda* sexy.

Caleb's laughter snapped him out of his inner rant. The sound was sweet and Jesse could easily get used to it. Addicted to it, even. He grinned and pecked a chaste kiss to Caleb's lips, wanting to feel that laughter against his skin. "You're a tease, aren't you?"

Caleb's laughter turned into a snort. "Not really. Not usually." His brow furrowed and his lips pinched together. "Maybe you're special or something."

"I'm not even going to ask what that *something* might be." Jesse planted another quick kiss on Caleb's lips, wondering why he felt the need to taste his laughter and his frown. "Look, I have to go on shift in a little while, but I want you to think about this. Me, in here with you."

"Yeah?" Caleb blinked slowly, confusion causing his frown to reappear. His eyebrows scrunched, nearly touching above his nose, where his skin bunched into a wrinkle.

Adorable. There was no other word for Caleb.

"What do you mean?" The question held a hint of suspicion. Caleb hadn't tensed again.

Jesse had to tread carefully. "You kind of froze on me when we came in the house."

Caleb turned his head and unsurprisingly to Jesse, stiffened in his arms. "Yeah, I guess you wouldn't want to have me flip out on you. Again." He brought his hands up and pushed at Jesse's chest.

Not gonna happen. Jesse didn't want to frighten Caleb, but letting go of him seemed wrong. Instead he brought one hand around and cupped Caleb's chin, pulling gently until Caleb was forced to face him again. The hurt in Caleb's eyes was tempered with a large dose of self-loathing. Either one alone was enough to make Jesse's heart ache, but the one-two punch of both nearly took him down onto his knees. He couldn't stand it, couldn't let Caleb think he'd turn his back and walk away.

"Don't put words in my mouth." Not when there were so many other things he would rather have Caleb put there. Jesse batted that dirty thought aside. "I can handle it if me being here with you makes you uncomfortable at any time. We'll work through it. I won't just walk out that door and never come back. I can't."

Jesse did his best to keep his expression open and earnest, his voice calm and steady. Inside, he was damn near quaking with fear. What was he doing, making that kind of commitment? And to Caleb, who would need for him to follow through on his promises? What the hell had happened to his brain, making him say such things? The realization he'd said it, and meant it, freaked him out more than anything he'd faced.

But the hopeful look that chased those dark shadows from Caleb's eyes was more than worth it. *That* look firmed Jesse's resolve to do whatever he could for Caleb and then some.

"I mean it, Caleb." Jesse brushed Caleb's full lower lip with the pad of his thumb.

Caleb reached up with his other hand and caught Jesse's wrist, not stopping him, only holding on. His long, tapered fingers looked delicate, the nails short, and— Jesse frowned.

"Uh. Where's your mail?" Jesse already had a hand back, reaching for the doorknob. Caleb's eyes rounded, and his lips repeated the gesture to form a pretty O. "You dropped it outside?"

"I... Maybe?" Caleb grinned sheepishly and shrugged. "I guess so."

Jesse tugged the door open, and sure enough, Caleb's mail was scattered on the porch. A surge of pride spun through him, a giddy feeling that he had such an effect on Caleb. *Of course, if I'd been the one holding the mail, God only knows what would have happened to it!*

Jesse stepped out and stooped over to pick up the mail. *Kezabeth Cortez? Who the hell is Kezabeth Cortez, and why is her mail coming to Caleb?* Jesse remembered the woman he'd seen outside with the two little girls. *Caleb's sister, then?*

Jesse handed over the mail and bit his tongue to keep from asking questions. He wanted to pry, but he also wanted an explanation given freely. Disappointment welled in him as Caleb took the mail and turned away, then walked over to set it down on his coffee table.

"Thank you. I'm glad the wind didn't kick up and blow it everywhere."

"Yeah. I hope that was all of it." *Who is Kezabeth Cortez?* The question wouldn't go away, yet Jesse refused to ask it.

If Caleb's hunched shoulders were any clue, he knew Jesse had noticed the name on the envelopes, and was waiting for Jesse to mention it. Whether from stubbornness or something else, Jesse kept his mouth shut. An uncomfortable silence filled the room. Would the man break?

"So, I guess you'd better get ready for your shift, huh?" Caleb asked.

Apparently he was going to blow Jesse off. That didn't sit well with him. Jesse didn't care to be dismissed so casually. "I thought, if you were awake, I'd stop by when I take my break."

Caleb turned to face him, his green eyes searching as Jesse struggled to keep his expression bland. He didn't want Caleb to know how much he wanted to stop in.

"Sure, that would be great." Caleb locked his fingers together in front of his groin. "What time? I'm usually awake most of the night."

Jesse had had enough of the stilted conversation and uneasy silence. He walked over to Caleb and pulled him into his arms, smiling at the gasp that slipped through his kiss-swollen lips. Jesse pressed their bodies together as Caleb worked his arms from between them and rested his hands on Jesse's hips. Caleb felt so fragile, his back bony and slight.

"It varies, but if it's a slow night, I try to break around two." Jesse slid a hand down to cup Caleb's ass and lifted him so their lips met easily. He'd meant it to be a gentle kiss, a promise of sorts, but as soon as Caleb moaned into his mouth, Jesse's plans to be smooth vanished and the kiss became a heated mashing of lips, tongue and teeth. By the time he broke the kiss, Jesse's body felt fevered and his cock was back to being painfully erect. He forced himself to release Caleb and step back.

"I'll see you later, then." Jesse winked and left while he could still make himself leave Caleb alone. He wondered how much longer it would be before he found it impossible to walk away from him when Caleb had that hungry look on his face.

Chapter Six

Caleb slid the deadbolts in place after Jesse had left. Then he stood there, staring at nothing, wondering how in the hell to pass the next several hours. His skin felt tingly and tight. Caleb wondered when the last time anyone—any *man*—had affected him so much. No one came to mind. He'd already developed more of a relationship with Jesse than he had with anyone in the past.

Caleb crossed over to the couch and plopped down on it. He tried to figure out what it was about Jesse that made him so irresistible, made Caleb not even want to try to keep a distance from him. *How could Jesse kiss me like that then just...leave?* Caleb was sure they could have both gotten off in ten minutes or less. *Way* less on his end.

The ringing of his cell phone snapped him out of his funk. He got up then jogged into the kitchen, where the phone lay on the microwave. A glance at the caller ID had him grinning as he opened the phone. "Hey, sis, what's up?" Maybe she would stop by for a bit and bring the girls. That would sure occupy him for a while.

"I wanted to call and see how everything was going," Kezabeth replied.

No, you wanted to call and make sure I hadn't had another meltdown. "Everything's great." Caleb hadn't had another episode since the one that had ended with Jesse walking him to the mailbox the first time. He shouldn't have told her about his falling apart then, but he'd been scared he was losing his mind, and talking to his sister about it had given him a temporary measure of peace. At least he hadn't mentioned Jesse. Kezabeth would have grilled him six ways to Sunday if he had. He sighed and walked back into the living room. The couch seemed to call his name once more, so he sat down and got comfortable.

"No more problems?" Kezabeth's tone was asking more than her question.

"Why don't you just come out and ask if I'm fucking nuts yet, Kez? Ask what's on your mind." That came out bitchier than he'd intended.

"Well, isn't *someone* in a shitty mood today? What happened? Did you get a nasty call from your agent or something?"

Kezabeth wasn't nearly as bitchy as he was, but her question made him shudder. The idea of Macy Ferris pissed off and on his butt was beyond unpleasant.

Caleb hadn't felt anything other than pain, fear or numbness for the past couple of months. "No, I'm..." *What? Horny? Confused? Frustrated? And I can't find my lube!* Those were answers he was too smart to give. "I think I'm bored." Which totally surprised him. "Are you and my lovely nieces coming over today?" So what if his voice carried a heavy dose of begging. He was *bored.*

Kezabeth's sigh was answer enough, but she spoke anyway. "Mom and Dad swung by and took the girls for a couple of weeks. I would come over, but I have an appointment with Dr. Samuels in an hour."

"Is Remy going with you to this one?" He knew Kezabeth might not want to talk about her husband... Then again, she might need to.

"No. We're still doing individual counseling until Dr. Samuels feels we're ready to tackle c-counseling as a c-couple."

"I'm sorry, Kez. I shouldn't have brought it up." He was such an insensitive dick sometimes.

"No, Caleb, it's okay." Kezabeth sniffled once before she seemed to get herself under control. "I love him so much. I know we can get past all this. It just takes time."

"Remy's a great guy. I know he loves you and the girls very much." Caleb didn't doubt it, but the guy did have some problems. Then again, who was he to judge? "Anyone would be all shook up after shooting a kid like that. Tack on the media screaming about police officers abusing their power and crap, and it's no wonder Remy is..." He faltered, realizing there was no good way to complete that sentence. To say *falling apart* would not make Kezabeth feel any better.

"It wasn't his fault." Kez stated it clearly, defiantly.

Caleb wondered if Remy had any idea how lucky he was to have someone who believed in him so thoroughly. "I know that, sis, but *he* needs to believe it." When a fourteen-year-old drug dealer pointed a gun at a narcotics officer, there were many people at fault, but not the officer. The fact that the gun hadn't been loaded didn't matter. That couldn't be discerned in the split second when Remy had thought he and his partner were going to die. The public outcry and the slaughtering of Remy's career by the media were the price he'd paid for doing his job.

Kezabeth sniffled, then said, "*You* need to believe that what happened to you isn't *your* fault."

Caleb's gut clenched. He did *not* want to talk about that, because he *was* at fault, at the very least for being a naïve fool.

"Look, Kez, I need to go. I have to work. Lots of work waiting for me." Or he'd do something, anything besides continue this conversation.

"You always do that, Caleb. You always change the subject or completely evade it, and you can't keep doing that! Dr. Samuels—"

"Dr. Samuels is your psychiatrist, counselor, or whatever you want to call him. He sure as hell isn't mine." A tic began in Caleb's left eyelid, a sign of irritation that only his sister was able to rouse in him. "I hope you aren't wasting your money talking about me."

"Jeez, you're my brother, and I love you. Of course I talk about you! All I was trying to say was…" Kezabeth sighed so loudly that her breath sounded like a mini tornado rushing through Caleb's ear. "You know what? Never mind. I'll come by and see you tomorrow, okay?"

The better to lecture him in person, no doubt. "Yeah, that'd be great."

Caleb finished the call and looked around as his mind went right back to thoughts of Jesse. Doubts crept in and he tried to push them aside, but it was a long time before Jesse would be knocking.

* * * *

It was a slow night. Jesse didn't know whether to be grateful about it. On the one hand, if things continued this way, he would be able to take break on time. On the other hand, time dragged as he waited for it to be two a.m. With his luck, dispatch would receive a call at ten minutes to two.

Then again, his luck must be pretty good. He'd had a double armful of sexy male heat, although it had been hours since then.

By break time, Jesse had the Dodge Charger pursuit vehicle he drove while on duty parked at his place. A half minute later, he was striding across the street to Caleb's house. He'd barely knocked on the door one time when the deadbolts slid back. Then the door was open and Jesse had a quick impression of warm beige walls and artsy prints. Before he could really look around, Caleb moved to stand in front of him.

Jesse took in the nervous smile and the wary flicker of Caleb's eyes and knew something was wrong. He wanted to reach out and pull Caleb close, hold him and soothe away whatever tormented him.

The idea that Caleb might have experienced another episode made Jesse's stomach churn. No one should have to go through that kind of hell. As he studied Caleb, noting the tension and exhaustion that seemed to envelop him, along with the way Caleb kept his gaze averted, he was certain Caleb had indeed been through the fires of hell once again.

He had the fleeting thought that he should ask first, but his legs were already moving, his arms reaching for Caleb, as if his body knew better what to do than his brain did.

"Tell me." Jesse pressed Caleb tightly to his chest and kicked the door shut.

"Locks," Caleb muttered and tried to free himself.

Jesse wasn't ready to let him go. He turned them both around and took one hand off Caleb long enough to set the deadbolts into place.

"Tell me." Jesse wanted to hold Caleb closer, but the feel of his knobby spine under Jesse's hands reminded him how delicate Caleb was, and in more than just the physical sense.

A shudder ripped through Caleb, then his hands were gripping Jesse's back, fingers digging into hard muscles. Caleb turned his head and rubbed against Jesse's chest, murmuring so softly Jesse couldn't make out the words.

"Caleb, tell me what happened, please." He slid his hands down to Caleb's protruding hipbones, which were more proof of his frailty.

"Bad night."

Yeah, well, he had already figured that much out. He didn't know if he should press Caleb for more or let it lie. Which would be better for Caleb? Jesse wished he knew. *Should I ask?* Uncertainty was something he wasn't used to, and he found he didn't particularly care for it. In fact, he decided it sucked ass.

"Caleb." Jesse tried to lean back so that he could look at him, but Caleb had a surprisingly strong grip and showed no signs he was willing to let go of Jesse. "Did you — ? Was it — ?" Oh shit, how did he ask Caleb if he'd had another meltdown? And why hadn't he thought about that before opening his damned mouth? *Fuck it!* "Are you okay?"

Jesse felt Caleb's laughter rather than heard it, the vibrations spreading from where Caleb was pressed against his chest. Caleb tipped his head up and snared Jesse with his bright gaze and his up-tilted lips.

"Yeah, I am. Better than okay, actually." Caleb snaked his hand up to clasp the back of Jesse's head and pull him down for a hard kiss that ended as quickly as it began. "Come on. I set out stuff for subs. I hope that's all right."

Jesse let Caleb lead him into the kitchen, noticing small details such as the golden color of the hardwood floors and the burgundy leather couch and lounger. The house exuded a comfortable, lived-in feeling Jesse was aware of even though his mind whirled with questions.

An assortment of lunchmeats and cheeses was laid out on the island. The pretty blue, beige and burgundy tiles on the island were repeated in the kitchen. The cabinet doors were painted to match the burgundy, the base of the cabinets a complementary beige, and the deep blue color repeated on the countertops. Jesse was almost glad Caleb couldn't see his kitchen in all its 1970s paneled glory.

On the table, condiments and various vegetables were neatly aligned and ready to be slapped onto sub sandwiches. Two plates were laden with buns, pickle spears and chips. Jesse realized Caleb was waiting for him to say something.

"This is great, thank you. I don't have a lot of time, so you've made a great meal." He wanted to sit with Caleb, to ask what had happened during the hours since he'd left. Somehow he didn't think what little time remained from his break would be enough. Instead, Jesse reached for the plates, nearly dropping them both when Caleb echoed his thoughts.

"You said you don't have much time, so maybe—" Caleb grinned as Jesse managed to save the plates from hitting the floor. "You could stop by again after work?" The faintest traces of color appeared on Caleb's cheeks as he looked down at the plate Jesse set in front of him. "We'd have more time, and we could...we could talk then."

Judging by the way that faint color bloomed into a neck-to-earlobes flush, Caleb had more in mind than just talking. Jesse's dick snapped to attention and he stifled a groan. *And here I thought the first half of my shift dragged by!* He squirmed in his seat, trying to make some room for his erection where there really wasn't any. There were better things to focus on, however. *Like Caleb.*

"I wonder what you were thinking that caused you to flush." Jesse reached out and trailed the back of his knuckles over Caleb's cheek. He wished Caleb wasn't looking down, so he could have seen his sparkling eyes. Even so, the way Caleb's lashes cast shadows high on his cheekbones, and with his skin tinted by that bashful blush, Caleb was something else, something beautiful to behold. "I'd like you to talk to me, Caleb, to feel you can. After that, then I'd like to see about doing whatever you were thinking of that caused that blush to climb all over you."

That had Caleb's gaze shooting up to his, and the heat in his expression nearly stole Jesse's breath. A slow, sexy smile stretched Caleb's full lips. Jesse's heart skittered as moisture seeped from his cockhead.

"Fuck. Caleb. You can't— You can't look at me like that." Jesse stood and pulled Caleb to him. The lack of resistance on Caleb's part, the eager, open willingness as he melted into Jesse's arms, dragged a groan from Jesse that he shared while plundering Caleb's mouth. Caleb met him stroke for stroke and nip for nip, rocking his hard dick against Jesse's thigh.

"Christ," Jesse muttered as he lifted his lips. Everything in him screamed for him to stay here, to finish this and sate himself in Caleb's warm body. "Caleb, I can't. We can't, not right now."

Caleb stiffened briefly but then relaxed and chuckled as he looked at Jesse. "I know. You need to get back to work, but you'll come over when you're done, right?"

"Oh yeah." Jesse dropped a chaste kiss on Caleb's swollen lips and forced himself to let go. He stepped back and raked Caleb with his gaze, lingering on the bulge at Caleb's groin and the wet spot that was spreading over the faded denim of his jeans. "I'll definitely be back."

Jesse had just enough time to run into his place and swap out his pre-cum-dampened uniform pants for a clean pair. Doubts assailed him when he caught a glimpse of himself in the bathroom mirror.

"What am I doing?" Jesse took in his flushed features and kiss-plumped lips. He wondered if he was taking advantage of Caleb. God, he hoped not. He wanted to believe he was a better man than that. Truthfully, he wanted Caleb so bad it hurt, but fucking wasn't all he wanted with him. *Does that make it all right?* Jesse wished to hell he knew.

Chapter Seven

He tried to hold out and wait until Jesse finished his shift, but at the rate his cock was throbbing, Caleb knew he'd blow his load as soon as Jesse touched him. That would be embarrassing, and he wanted whatever happened between them to last for longer than ten seconds. Caleb waited until he figured Jesse had less than an hour left, then took care of his aching erection. He was faintly amused by how loud his heartbeat pounded in his ears before it dawned on him that the pounding was actually coming from the front door.

"Shit!" Caleb bolted up, trying to stuff his dick back into his pants, his heart racing frantically, but not with fear. *Oh no, not fear at all, thank God.*

"Just a minute!" Caleb ran to the bathroom and tossed his shirt in the hamper before grabbing the soap, then washing his hands. Snatching a clean T-shirt from his bedroom, he shouted, "I'm coming!" He hoped Jesse could hear him.

Caleb couldn't bite back a nervous giggle as he pulled the shirt on. He'd just come and it had been fan-fucking-tastic, all because he'd been thinking about — no, fantasizing about — his neighbor.

And all of a sudden, Caleb felt as nervous as a virgin, shaky and breathless with a tinge of excitement and fear thrown in.

The burn of a blush rose over his chest and neck. It would no doubt spread to his hairline by the time he got the door open. His fingers did tremble, and he felt hot all over when he looked through the peephole and saw Jesse outside. Caleb unlocked the deadbolts as fast as his shaking hands would let him. Then he opened the door.

Caleb sucked in a sharp breath at the picture Jesse made standing on the porch step in his uniform. He apparently hadn't paid nearly enough attention when Jesse had stopped by a few hours ago. The dark blue shirt fit snugly across Jesse's broad shoulders. The short sleeves encased bulging biceps and triceps like a second skin. Caleb could see the hard ridge of pecs under the starched cotton material. He just knew that shirt had to be covering a spectacular set of abs. A thick leather belt circled Jesse's lean hips and was threaded through the belt loops of his gray-blue uniform pants. As Caleb watched, the front of those pants tented in a very impressive manner.

"Caleb." Raspy and deep, Jesse's voice snapped Caleb from his visual feasting.

Crap. He'd been caught staring. His mom would have whapped him for his bad manners.

Jesse frowned and swatted at a June bug. "I hate these damn bugs."

Caleb swallowed his embarrassment at his brazenness. After all, they'd both been clear about what would happen when Jesse returned. "Come in, please." He stepped back and gestured for Jesse to come in, making sure to lock the deadbolts afterward. Taking a deep breath and hoping he wasn't a brilliant shade of red, he faced Jesse and cursed silently. Jesse could at least pretend not to be amused at Caleb's discomfiture.

"Want to have a seat?" He felt so nervous suddenly. Maybe taking the edge off had been a mistake after all.

"Sure." Jesse headed for the recliner Caleb had just masturbated in. He nearly protested, but the idea of that big, sexy body sitting in the same spot turned him on in ways he had never imagined. Besides, he wasn't going to tell Jesse what he'd just done there. He sat on the couch and fidgeted with a hole at the knee of his jeans.

"So—" he began.

"I saw—" Jesse said at the same time.

Caleb laughed, wondering if he was the only one feeling the sexual tension in the room. Yeah, he had been aware of the fact that Jesse had gotten hard, but the man was sitting there, acting like it never happened. *What the hell, seriously?* He tipped his chin, signaling Jesse to go ahead with what he'd been about to say.

Jesse shifted his weight before finally leaning forward and draping his forearms across his knees. He eyed Caleb intently, concern evident in his brown gaze. "Earlier you looked upset. Tired and… I don't know. I just wanted to make sure everything was okay." He shrugged and looked at his feet in a way Caleb found entirely too endearing.

"I don't sleep much most of the time. I have nightmares. Flashbacks sometimes, like the other day. Like earlier. I deal with it." God, Jesse really *would* think he was a basket case. Well, he kind of was. Caleb didn't flinch away from Jesse's questioning gaze.

"It isn't because…" Jesse's Adam's apple bobbed in an enticing way that made Caleb forget all about his nervousness. "Was it anything I did?"

It took a few seconds for the question to register, but when it did, Caleb immediately let out a sound of protest. He reached for one of Jesse's hands before he'd even thought about it.

"No." Caleb shook his head vehemently. "Don't think that, okay? Just don't." One person feeling guilty and messed up was enough. Caleb squeezed Jesse's hand. A tingle of heat flared in his groin when Jesse turned his hand over and intertwined their fingers. How could something so innocent be so seductive?

"I thought maybe I pushed too hard, maybe I shouldn't have mauled you. I don't know." Jesse's dark eyebrows knit together, nearly touching as he frowned. "Maybe I shouldn't have made you walk to your mailbox that first time, even though I hope that's actually helped."

Caleb shook his head again. "Jesse, I know I can't stay locked up in here forever. I know that *rationally.*" Caleb's lungs felt constricted, as they did every time he thought about *why* he was now so afraid. His voice dropped to a strangled whisper as he continued, "But something inside me was damaged."

He couldn't do this after all. Caleb started to stand and found himself held tight in Jesse's strong embrace. He despised his own weakness and the shudders that racked his body.

"It's okay. You don't have to talk about it, not right now," Jesse murmured, rubbing his back.

Each caress from Jesse chased some of the tension from Caleb's clenched muscles. He felt safe with Jesse, and was angry that he still couldn't he talk about what happened. Caleb was so frustrated with himself that he wanted to kick and scream.

Shame for not being a better man, a stronger man, filled Caleb, and he pulled out of the embrace. He stepped back and met Jesse's gaze, determined to quit being the same damaged person he'd been for the past couple of months, even if it was done one small step at a time. He'd had pride once upon a time. It was time for him to get it back.

"I want you." Those three words were the hardest to get out. Caleb read the hesitation in Jesse's expression, and wondered if he'd blown his chances by admitting to the nightmares and flashbacks.

Jesse stepped closer to Caleb, then closer still until they were touching from thighs to chests. The nudge of Jesse's stiff cock pressed against Caleb's belly. Caleb's cock was heavy and aching as though he hadn't just come minutes ago.

"Caleb, I don't want to take advantage of you." Jesse's voice was soft and full of concern.

Instead of being offended, Caleb melted somewhere inside, a warmth spreading through him from Jesse's consideration. It combined with the desire that had been riding him for days and fed his determination to have this one man.

He looked at Jesse, saw his need reflected in him, and found a wantonness inside. Caleb rubbed his dick against Jesse's thigh, remembering the hesitation and desire that warred in his gaze. Caleb could get rid of the former and stoke the latter. He placed his hands on either side of Jesse's belt buckle, then tucked his thumbs under Jesse's waistband there. Caleb tipped his head up, watching Jesse intently.

"Take advantage of me? Do you know what I was doing while you were banging on my door, Officer

Martin?" Caleb's voice came out in a throaty purr he'd never imagined himself capable of. *Must have released my inner slut, woo hoo! And it looks like my police officer is loving it.*

The heat burning in Jesse's molten eyes ratcheted up several notches as he shook his head. Caleb freed a hand and reached up to cup the back of Jesse's neck. He used that grip to encourage Jesse to lean down until their lips almost brushed. Eyes locked on Jesse's, Caleb gave his hottest smile.

"I was fucking my fist as I buried my fingers in my ass, thinking about how it would feel to have you deep inside me." Caleb would have been scared of the predatory look that came over Jesse had he not deliberately stoked the man to the breaking point. "I came so hard I thought it would be hours before I was ready to go again. But" —Caleb slid his hand down to Jesse's and dragged it over to his straining erection— "here you are, and here *this* is, aching and needing just because you showed up." He couldn't resist thrusting against Jesse's big hand, groaning when Jesse cupped him and squeezed.

Labored, shaky pants reached Caleb's ears. He realized the sounds were coming from his soon-to-be lover. He rotated his hips again, murmuring encouraging words as he felt Jesse's hesitation, prepared to beg if that was what it took.

Jesse took his hand off Caleb's cock and stepped back. He opened his mouth to protest, but the slut took over again. "Right there" —Caleb pointed at the recliner— "just minutes before you sat down, I was *right there* thinking of you, fucking myself and calling *your* name as I— Oomph!"

Tackled and devoured. He couldn't think of any other way to describe it. Jesse had backed him against the wall and sealed their mouths together before Caleb knew what had hit him, and *holy fuck*, it felt good!

He reached up and dug his fingers into Jesse's shoulders as Jesse slipped his hands between Caleb's ass and the wall. Jesse gripped his cheeks firmly, then lifted him until his cock rubbed against Jesse's.

Caleb moaned into the warmth of Jesse's mouth, moaned again when a slick tongue teased the roof of his mouth. He ground his dick almost frantically with Jesse's, the friction from the movement drawing his balls tight as he heard an answering sound from his lover. He nipped at Jesse's tantalizing lower lip, sucked it into his mouth and licked at it.

Jesse responded by thrusting his hips so hard that Caleb was surprised they didn't put a hole in the wall.

"Again." Caleb murmured the words against Jesse's lips, let out a whimper as their hips pumped. It wasn't enough, no matter how good it felt. Jesse must have agreed, because he lowered Caleb's feet to the floor and stepped back abruptly, then tugged off his shoes and socks before reaching for his belt.

Caleb stared transfixed as Jesse unbuckled the leather belt and started removing weapons and other cop stuff. Jess set the belt and all the accoutrements attached to it on the entertainment center, then unfastened his pants in a mesmerizing dance of efficiency.

"Damn it, Caleb, get your jeans out of the fucking way!" The order was laced with sexy, frustrated need and had Caleb hurrying to free his cock, not caring that he fumbled with the buttons and trembled as he tried to get his pants open. All that mattered was seeing Jesse's dick, touching it and feeling it pressed against his own.

"Oh fuck." Caleb's eyes widened as Jesse's fat shaft was freed from his underwear. Jesse was definitely well-endowed. Caleb couldn't stop staring at the thick length as it bobbed while Jesse kicked off his pants and underwear.

"Caleb."

The rough growl of his name was hot enough to make Caleb's dick twitch and draw his attention from Jesse's glistening cockhead to his commanding mouth. Caleb had dropped his hands to his sides instead of working on getting naked, but another set of bigger hands, sexier hands were at his waist as Jesse grabbed at his jeans.

"Yeah," Jesse muttered, then Caleb's pants were being shoved down, his cock springing free of the confining denim.

Caleb grinned at Jesse's sharp inhalation and knew the cause. Hopefully, the effect would be that Jesse would spend a lot of time wondering if he was going commando after this.

He waited impatiently for Jesse to move or speak, to do *something* instead of simply stare. It was thrilling to see the raw lust in Jesse's expression, but he needed more than just a look.

"Push them down or let me, Jesse. I want to feel you." The words were met with a flurry of motion as Jesse bent slightly and removed the jeans. Caleb stepped out of them and whipped off his T-shirt. He reached for the buttons of Jesse's uniform shirt, managing to get it unbuttoned while Jesse slid his hands all over Caleb's body, touching him in a way he'd been aching for. A whimper born of frustration slipped from his lips as he pulled Jesse's shirt open and found a white undershirt.

Too impatient to deal with removing it, Caleb shoved the offending material up to Jesse's armpits and latched on to a brown nipple. The taste of Jesse's skin and the scent of his big, warm body had Caleb moaning as he scraped his teeth over the taut peak. He brought one hand to the other nipple and pinched it as Jesse rumbled his approval. Two calloused hands clamped onto Caleb's ass and pulled him in tight, squishing his cock against Jesse's muscled thigh.

Jesse ground his dick against Caleb's stomach, smearing a sticky trail of pre-cum across his skin. Heat seemed to radiate from the wet trail and lit up Caleb's nerve endings as he moaned around the nub he was tonguing.

"Fuck!" Jesse tightened his grip on Caleb's ass. "Hold on to my arms."

Caleb obeyed without question, flicking Jesse's nipple one last time before releasing his tasty treat and grabbing on with a firm grip right above Jesse's elbows. His world swirled crazily as he was spun around and lifted easily, his back pressed into the wall once again. Jesse stepped in and pinned him in place, that rumbling sound coming from deep in his chest again and working its way through him in a way that had his dick throbbing.

"Ahh, shit, Jesse, that's—" Caleb's need to tell his lover how hot that sound was came to a halt when Jesse took advantage of his open mouth and melded their lips in a fierce kiss. Teeth clicked together as they each sought dominance. A growl from Jesse had Caleb almost coming on the spot as he ceded control. Something about putting his trust in Jesse did things to him, physically and emotionally, that he was afraid to examine too closely. Luckily, Jesse thrust his cock against Caleb's again and the ability to think was shot to hell.

Caleb scrabbled to get his hands between them, trying to wrap them around both of their cocks. Sweat from their bodies as well as pre-cum provided the lubrication as he fisted their hard lengths.

Jesse stopped plundering his mouth long enough to lick his way to Caleb's ear. "Put your legs around my waist, babe."

Caleb's heart pounded at the endearment, although he told himself it meant nothing, just pillow — or, in this case, wall — talk. Jesse's grip on his ass tightened as those muscular arms held him securely off the ground. Caleb reluctantly let go of their cocks and grabbed Jesse's arms. He wrapped his legs around Jesse's lean waist and started to move, only to find himself pinned securely in place.

He needed more. "Jesse, please, let me..." Caleb trailed his hands down to Jesse's sides, waiting for the slightest chance to slip his hand between them. Jesse pivoted his hips, bringing their dicks together in a way that had Caleb's vision blurring and ears ringing.

"Caleb, *now!*" Jesse's voice was low and strained. The words were followed by a sharp nip to Caleb's neck.

Caleb gripped their cocks with both hands just as Jesse's nip turned into a sucking bite. Caleb jerked from shoulders to fingertips, and his back bowed against the weight of Jesse's body. The hands on his ass cheeks squeezed hard and pulled him even closer. Caleb wanted to stroke slowly, to learn the texture and every minute detail of Jesse's fascinating length, but his body was demanding a fast and furious rhythm.

Jesse kept sucking on the sensitive skin of Caleb's neck, and Caleb knew it was just about over for him. His fingers tightened as he pulled harder. Another minute, and his balls drew up tight. Twinges of pleasure started at the base of his spine before shooting outward to nerve endings he'd never known existed.

"J-Jesse." Caleb could hardly get the name out. He was too busy panting and working their cocks frantically.

Jesse pivoted his hips in short, rapid-fire motions. He clenched Caleb's ass. Another of those sexy rumbles worked free.

Caleb tensed his thighs, and his strokes became erratic. He couldn't arch any more, couldn't thrust. All he could do as his world exploded into brilliant bursts of light was turn his head to the side while a keening noise slipped from his lips. His entire being narrowed down to the pulsing in his balls, the feel of hands and skin and cocks, the excruciating ecstasy when streams of musky spunk shot from his cock.

Jesse stopped sucking on Caleb's neck. A deep, guttural sound came from Jesse as he tipped his head back.

Caleb tried to focus, wanting to see the sheer beauty of Jesse's expression. He squeezed their cocks together harder, pulled on their compressed lengths, and was rewarded with the sharp scent and heated moisture of Jesse's cum. He felt each pulse, but kept his gaze on Jesse's face. Caleb wanted to shout to the world that he had put that fiery yet dazed look on the man's face.

Lips parted, drawn back almost into a snarl, eyes heavy-lidded, and the skin stretched taut across the planes of his cheeks—the man was a perfect image of what an orgasm should look like. Muscles bunched and strained under tanned skin as Jesse thrust again and again, digging his fingers deeply into the globes of Caleb's ass.

Caleb didn't ever want it to end. He wanted to have Jesse pressed against him, cock pulsating in his hand and beside his dick for as long as he could.

"Can you... Can you hold on to me, babe?" Jesse asked.

Breathless but still sexy as sin. Caleb had no idea how Jesse did it. And that endearment—why did it light him up so much inside? *I'll worry about that later.* He brought his hands up, then held them out to his sides. He looked at one, then the other.

"Uh, Jesse?" Caleb bit his cheek, trying not to laugh as Jesse looked at him in confusion. "You sure you want my hands on you?"

Jesse frowned at Caleb. "They were just on me, so— Oh." His frown turned into a smirk, and he winked at Caleb. "I really wouldn't care, but I think you might have trouble with your hands all, uh, slicked up. I wouldn't want to drop you."

Laughing, Caleb unwound his legs from Jesse's waist. "What a coincidence. I wouldn't want to be dropped. Not that I think you would...drop me, I mean."

"No." Jesse gently gripped Caleb's upper arms. "I wouldn't. I would, however, love a shower... If that's okay?"

That note of uncertainty in his voice did more of those things to Caleb's insides that he didn't want to think about, not yet. He shot Jesse a cocky grin instead.

"As long as you don't mind some company. I kind of need a shower myself. Maybe a nap too." He pushed away the shyness over the last part of his statement. The idea of having Jesse lying beside him in bed, holding him... Caleb gestured with his sticky hands toward his stomach and chest. Jesse's gaze followed the movements, then settled on Caleb's neck. Jesse's eyes darkened. Those amber bits in the brown irises become more pronounced. Caleb started to reach for the spot he thought Jesse was looking at, but caught himself before his cum-coated fingers touched his neck. He glanced down and saw Jesse's cock jump, growing semierect.

"I don't suppose you have any condoms?" Was that his voice sounding all wistful and horny? Caleb wouldn't have believed it, except he *felt* all wistful and horny.

Jesse's expression went from lusty to disappointed. "No. I'm guessing you don't either?"

Caleb shook his head, trying for his most mournful look. "Sure don't. Guess this means we'll just have to get creative, huh?"

"Creative. Fuck yeah, we can be *creative* all you want." Jesse leered, his eyes heating back up. "But come the end of my shift tomorrow, I'll be knocking on your door with everything we need for some good old-fashioned fucking, if that's all right with you."

A grin stretched his lips wide and had to work to keep himself from pumping the air with his fist and shouting, *Oh yeah! Score!* Instead, he tried to have some decorum.

"That, Mr. Jesse Martin, is more than all right. That is absolutely perfect."

Chapter Eight

Jesse pushed his basket to the checkout counter, scanning the area for any familiar faces. He'd been good and kept his hands to himself for the most part when he'd walked Caleb to his mailbox earlier. There'd been another dead bird, a dove this time. At the rate the poor birds were being slaughtered, he wouldn't be surprised if rumors about Caleb being a bird-sacrificing devil worshipper began spreading.

That propensity for gossip was why he'd driven in to Las Cruces, specifically to avoid running into anyone he knew. Granted, the lube and condoms were buried in the basket under food and other necessities, so they weren't easily noticeable, but still. Any of the checkers in El Jardin would note every item and make sure to pass the info along to his or her buddies. That was just the way it was in his town.

While the supplies he'd purchased weren't necessarily proof of his sexuality, they *were* reasons to talk. Talk would lead to scrutiny, and before long everyone would probably figure out that he was gay. He wasn't ready to deal with that being known just yet.

Jesse put all the items he was going to purchase onto the conveyor belt. He stood with his hands in his pockets as he watched the cashier scan each item without looking at it. For once he was glad to have someone rude waiting on him. Well, if what she was doing could be called waiting on him. So far, Jesse didn't think the girl had even bothered to look at him, and she hadn't even bothered to greet him. He was totally okay with that.

He swiped his card and signed the screen when the appropriate line appeared. Tipping his head to the cashier, Jesse wheeled the basket to his car and put everything in the trunk. He couldn't push back the anticipation caused by knowing those there were two particular items in his possession. His cock hardened as he imagined pushing deep into Caleb's warm body, the tight, scorching heat as his inner muscles clamped down on Jesse's heavy length.

After their shower session that morning, he knew how snug Caleb's body was. At one point he had worked three fingers deep into the man's tight hole. He'd felt certain his fingers would bear singe marks from the fiery channel as he had concentrated on stretching the resistant little ring.

"Shit." Jesse unlocked the door and eased into the seat. No matter how he tried to adjust his cock, it was obvious he would have an uncomfortable drive home.

* * * *

"Well, you're grinning like a madman, Caleb!" Kezabeth's eyes were lit with joy as she studied him.

Caleb *was* pretty damned happy, and seeing the worry gone from his sister's eyes only added to his elated state. "Yup, I sure am. And I was expecting you hours ago!" He reached through the doorway and pulled Kezabeth inside. The startled squeal she let out when he wrapped her in a big hug and spun her around made him laugh. It had been too long since he'd felt anything other than fear and pain. He felt so much happiness it was almost overwhelming. Caleb let Kezabeth study him after he set her back on her feet. She needed reassurance too, after everything that had happened.

He didn't want to go darting outside, but he finally felt hopeful that one day he would be able to do so without a twinge of oppressive terror. Jesse had given him that hope. Recovering was his responsibility, but it was nice, more than nice, to have Jesse's help. And it was nice to have access to Jesse's glorious, sexy body. Caleb felt his grin widen.

"I got here as soon as I could. Better late than never and all that crap." With her hands on her hips, Kezabeth was the spitting image of their momma preparing to grill answers from them. "Caleb Marshall Tomas, what have you been up to?"

Caleb tossed a hand in the air and slapped the other hand over his heart. "Nothing, I swear!" He wiped the grin off his face and tried his best to look innocent.

Kezabeth's eyes glittered and her lips twitched as she struggled not to smile. "I'm supposed to buy that innocent act? Even when you've got your fingers crossed up in the air?"

He dropped his hands to his sides and laughed. "You weren't supposed to notice that, sis. You were supposed to be focused on the hand on my chest or my brilliant smile or my twinkling eyes."

"Oh, puh-lease!" Kezabeth poked him in the ribs, digging her finger in so he yelped and jumped back. "Like I'm that stupid! Now hit the couch and dish!"

Kezabeth sat on the couch then pulled Caleb beside her. Her smile faded to a frown. "What's that?" She pointed a pink-tipped nail to his neck.

Shit! Caleb slapped a hand to the side of his neck. He knew exactly what that was. Judging by the way Kezabeth's frown deepened, she did, too—and she didn't approve.

"Would you believe I burned myself with a curling iron?" Humor never hurt. In this case, it didn't help either.

Kezabeth grabbed his arm and studied the purple hickey.

Caleb let his mind wander to the cause of that mark. It had started out innocently enough—if Jesse chasing a drop of water with his tongue could be considered innocent. Surely it was only natural he would suck the water up once he caught it. He was lucky she hadn't noticed the other one yet, where Jesse had marked him *before* the shower.

She snagged the collar of his T-shirt with slim fingers and tugged. She shot a look at him. "No, I don't think the curling-iron excuse is going to work here, brother mine." Kezabeth tugged on the collar again, stretching it as she peeked down his shirt. "Sheesh, not even a vacuum cleaner could do that."

"Hey!" Caleb swatted at her hand. "Cut it out!"

Kezabeth got that look in her eyes, the one Caleb always called the Evil Little Sister Look.

"Aw, come on now, Cale." Kezabeth plucked at his shirt—collar, hem, sleeves, anywhere she could grasp. "What are you hiding under there, hmm?" Kezabeth poked him in the ribs again as he tried to catch her hands.

"Wouldn't you like to know?" Caleb teased back, and for a few minutes, there was nothing between them but laughter and the type of teasing only siblings could get away with.

By the time they got it out of their systems, they were both holding their sides and gasping for breath. Kezabeth leaned back and eyed him seriously. "Is it the guy across the street?"

Caleb arched an eyebrow. "Why would you think that?"

Kezabeth rolled her eyes. "Puh-lease."

Caleb couldn't *wait* until his nieces started rolling their eyes and *puh-leasing* Kezabeth. He'd bet she would learn just how annoying those two things were. And he'd swear her eyes made a complete three-sixty in their sockets. Caleb didn't care if that was impossible. He figured she had done it so often that her eyeballs could do three-sixties in seconds.

Kezabeth poked him again. "I have been here enough to notice him pretending not to notice you while you pretend not to notice him back."

"Twice you've been here when he was outside, and I wasn't staring at him or anything." Boy, his protest sounded weak to his own ears. No way would his sister buy it. "Okay, I was. He was. So, yeah."

"Caleb." Kezabeth leaned forward, resting her forearms on her knees. "Do you think you're ready for this? I mean, I know the man is sexy, but afterward, when y'all are done screwing around? What happens then? Or is it maybe going to be more than a fling? Can you deal with a relationship right now? And can he deal with the, ah… Have you told him what happened?"

Caleb felt more like a freak than ever, though he knew that wasn't Kezabeth's intent. The truth was, he didn't know Jesse that well, although their shared mailbox trips had given him an insight into the man. What he did know was his lover was patient, understanding and hot as fuck, with a mouth that could suck a golf ball through a garden hose.

He studied his toes as he thought about his answer. It might not be enough for his sister, but all he could do was be honest with her. "I don't know that we have a relationship exactly." Caleb looked up and met Kez's probing gaze. "What we have is explosive, combustive, and I don't want to resist it." He reached for Kezabeth's hand and cradled it between his. "He knows I'm fucked up. How could he not after watching me *not* watch him?"

A flicker of anger crossed her face. "Then how do you know he isn't just taking advantage? What if he just thinks you're, you know, easy?"

He couldn't stop the laughter that burst from his lips. "God, Kezabeth, we haven't even— And I've never been a slut. Even so, I want to climb him and ride—"

"Caleb! Sheesh!" Kezabeth smacked his shoulder. "I don't want the details. Well, not all of them." She grinned. "Especially if you haven't had sex yet. You don't have enough info for me, bro."

"We've had sex, Kez. It doesn't have to be *that* kind of sex or it's not sex at all. I'm sure there are *other* sexual things people can do that are...well, sex." Caleb snorted. "You have two daughters, Kez. There is no way you're that naïve. I could tell you plenty, but I won't."

Kezabeth opened her mouth, a sharp retort ready, Caleb was sure. He didn't know whether to groan or be grateful for the knock on the door. When Kezabeth's eyes lit up with an unholy curiosity, Caleb groaned. She knew, as did he, who stood on the porch.

The sugary grin she gave him as she stood was all the warning he got. Caleb bolted off the couch and lunged for her, barely managing to fling an arm around her waist and pull her behind him.

"I don't think so, you evil woman." Caleb gave her a gentle shove as he looked out of the peephole. The light reflected on Jesse's dark hair and made his brown eyes sparkle. "Just a minute," Caleb called out as he unlocked the deadbolts. He pulled the door open and accidentally elbowed his sister in her chest.

"Oomph! Damn it, Caleb!" Kezabeth cried.

"Everything okay, Caleb?" Jesse was in his uniform and he looked so edible that Caleb's mouth watered.

Caleb glanced back at his sister and snickered at her stunned look. So he hadn't gotten around to Jesse's profession. It was worth the bitch-out he'd get to see that look. Her hand still groped her breast.

"I think everything is fine, but, Kez, you should maybe let go of your boob?" Caleb almost felt bad when she blushed bright red.

"You're the boob," she muttered. "Turd."

Caleb decided it would be wise to let those insults pass. He turned back to Jesse and felt his heart stutter at his lover's smile.

"Let me guess, you must be Caleb's sister? You have that whole sibling-rivalry thing going on." Jesse's lips twitched as if trying not to laugh.

Kezabeth shot Caleb a baleful look. "Not if he keeps trying to knock my chest through to my shoulder blades." Kezabeth nudged him aside and jerked the door open wider. "Would you like to come in, or does my brother always leave you out under the porch light for bug bait?"

Caleb's cheeks heated. "Sorry. Please, come in." Now he sounded like a stuffy prick, and he knew how much Jesse hated those stupid bugs.

Jesse stepped in and placed a hand on Caleb's hip. Caleb looked up at him and saw need and laughter in his warm brown eyes.

"Why don't you go have a seat, and I'll lock up. Okay?" Jesse whispered in his ear. He gave Caleb's hip a little push then reached back and began locking the deadbolts.

"Soooo." Kezabeth turned the simple word into a multisyllable warning as she watched Jesse walk to the couch. "I'm guessing you're the one who painted my big brother with all those pretty purple hickeys."

Caleb was going to strangle her.

Chapter Nine

Jesse knew by her expression that she was going to take aim at him. He kept a straight face as she delivered her opening salvo. Caleb looked like he was ready to pop a vessel. Or his sister.

Jesse offered his hand. "They are rather pretty, aren't they? The purple brings out the green in his eyes." He didn't bother to hide his grin as Caleb's sister goggled.

Caleb snickered.

"Jesse Martin, ma'am." He held out one hand. "Pleased to meet you."

"Kezabeth Cortez. Please, no *ma'ams*." She shook his hand and studied him from head to toe and back up again before releasing his hand.

The humor in her eyes was tinged with a heavy dose of concern.

Jesse thought he was going to like her just fine. "Thank God you have a sense of humor."

"God knows, it's the only thing that helped me through my childhood." Caleb patted his sister on the head, earning him a poke in the ribs.

"Cut it out, Cale, or I will bring out the elbow." Kezabeth bent her arm and waved a pointy elbow.

Caleb snorted but stepped closer to Jesse. "As long as it isn't the dreaded knee."

"Come on, kids. Let's all play nice." Jesse laughed. "And definitely no knees."

"So…" Caleb took Jesse's hand and pulled him to the couch. They sat beside each other, fingers entwined, bodies touching at hips and shoulders. Caleb glanced at the clock. "Your shift starts soon, doesn't it?"

Nodding, Jesse gave his hand a slight squeeze. "I'm fixing to go in, just thought I would stop by." He didn't have any intention of telling Caleb he'd been more than a little curious about the car in his driveway, though the knowing smile implied he'd it figured out. Jesse let his gaze drop to the love bite on Caleb's neck, and his cock twitched. He had done that in another half dozen or so spots as well. The possessive need to mark his lover was a new one, and it both startled and amused him.

"Ahem. Still in the room," Kezabeth pointed out, and Jesse felt the tips of his ears heat with embarrassment. No doubt he was making a great impression by drooling all over her brother.

"You could always leave," Caleb teased as Jesse looked at her.

Kezabeth shot Caleb a blank look. "I could always crash on your couch for a couple of days, so be nice."

Caleb gave an exaggerated shudder, but his voice was warm with affection when he spoke. "You know I love you, Kez. You can crash here anytime. The girls too, of course."

The smile Kezabeth sent her brother was brilliant and disarming and so like Caleb's that Jesse's breath hitched. He could imagine those two little girls wearing the same smile and getting whatever they wanted.

"Thanks. I may have to take you up on your offer sometime, you know." Her smile dimmed. Jesse could almost see the laughter and joy seep out of her, and he wondered what was going on in her life that could affect her so adversely.

Caleb leaned across Jesse and patted his sister's knee. Something passed between the siblings that made Jesse feel like an interloper. He stood and pulled Caleb up with him.

"I have to get back to work. Do you have a pen and something to write on?"

"Sure, I can grab something really quick." Caleb frowned and studied him intently. "You have to go already?"

Jesse reached out to smooth the lines on Caleb's brow and hoped Kezabeth didn't mind. He simply had to touch the man.

"I do, but I'll be off in another" — Jesse looked at his watch — "ten hours, barring any emergencies."

"Will you come over when you're off?"

The timid question sent a spark of heat straight to Jesse's groin. The need to reassure Caleb was nearly overpowering. Jesse cupped Caleb's chin and tipped his head up. If his sister minded this, she'd just have to deal with it. He brushed a soft, chaste kiss over Caleb's lips. The heat in his lover's beautiful eyes nearly undid him when he raised his head from the kiss.

"I'll be here," Jesse promised, whispering the words low enough that he hoped only Caleb heard them. He didn't care if Kezabeth knew, but the lust in his voice might be more than she wanted to hear.

Caleb flashed his heart-stopping smile at Jesse. "Good. I'll be right back."

Jesse watched Caleb dash into the other room, looking sexy as hell. He turned back to Kezabeth and laughed when he found her fanning herself with her hands.

"I'd say I'm sorry, but…" He shrugged.

Kezabeth propped her hands on her hips and gave him another once-over. "Don't hurt my brother."

Points for being direct, Jesse mused. "I have no intention of hurting him. That much I can promise you." It was not just a statement and he hoped Kezabeth realized it.

She stared at him and tapped one foot on the floor before nodding. "I think you mean that. I hope you do."

"I do. Your brother is…" Jesse was saved from getting mushy when Caleb rushed back into the room, pen and notepad in hand.

Caleb looked from Kezabeth to Jesse and back again. "Kez, are you grilling my lover?"

Warmth rushed through Jesse at the way Caleb didn't hesitate to claim him. Kezabeth only arched an eyebrow and rolled her eyes.

"Pest," Caleb teased as he turned and handed the pen and notepad to Jesse. He wrote his name, address and phone number on the sheet, tore it out, and extended it to Kezabeth. The startled looks on their faces had Jesse gnawing on his cheek to keep from chuckling.

"Kezabeth." Jesse met her gaze. "You call me if there's anything you need."

She took the paper and tucked it into her jeans pocket. "Yeah, okay. Thanks."

"It was nice meeting you." Jesse reached out to shake her hand again.

Kezabeth snorted as she took it. "I don't know if I'll buy nice, but it was at least amusing."

Jesse laughed. Kezabeth was direct and funny. He was glad Caleb had her. He would be willing to bet she was protective as hell over her loved ones.

"Okay, I'd better go." Jesse put a hand on Caleb's hip and steered him to the door. "Call if you need anything before then, okay?"

"I will." Caleb reached up and pulled Jesse down for a kiss that wasn't chaste at all. The teeth tugging at his bottom lip and the tongue stroking the roof of his mouth had Jesse's cock hard as steel when the kiss ended. He had to fight the urge to adjust himself as he felt Kezabeth watching him. He planted a quick peck to Caleb's forehead, then left while he still had the willpower.

Jesse groaned when he got in his car, glaring at his erect dick. Damn it, it was going to be a long night. The radio on the equipment console crackled. Dispatch came through with a call for a domestic disturbance. Looked like he wouldn't be checking in at the station first after all. Responding to the call, Jesse felt the chill that always worked down his spine when a domestic dispute was reported. Those calls were often extremely volatile, having the potential to become deadly without the slightest warning. He hesitated to flip the toggle switches for the lights and sirens. He didn't want to alarm Caleb or Kezabeth. It'd be better to wait until he'd driven a few blocks away. They would probably still hear the siren, but at least it wouldn't be blaring right outside Caleb's door.

Jesse pulled away from the curb and headed to the address he'd been given. It was the first time he'd heard of any problems from this particular residence. He hoped there wouldn't be more calls there after this, but feared there would be. It seemed like domestics were always repeated because the offenders never stopped.

* * * *

Caleb and Kezabeth looked at each other when they heard the siren. The sound brought the reality of Jesse's job screeching to the forefront of Caleb's thoughts. He hadn't considered anything other than the man himself. Now Caleb suddenly found himself trembling.

"Cale, honey, he'll be okay." Kezabeth sat beside him on the couch and put her arms around him. Resting her head on his shoulder, she held him until the trembling stopped.

"I guess his job didn't seem real until now," Caleb explained. He'd been so wrapped up in how Jesse made him feel, in the laughter and desire in the man's warm brown eyes. "I only thought about what we do, what I want to do, you know? And I feel like a shallow, selfish prick."

"Aw, Caleb, don't be so hard on yourself. You two can't have been, ah, messing around for too long."

Caleb shot her an irritated look. "It's not just messing around! We talk and laugh, and he helped me when I couldn't g-g-go outside..." He was too close to crying. Again. That weak, whiny person that had taken over his body since he'd been attacked was back and screwing with his head.

He tugged on Kezabeth's arms and pushed up, fighting humiliation at his weakness. Jesse had been a police officer for some time. It was evident in the way he carried himself that he was confident and secure in his job as well as his life. What was Jesse doing, messing around with someone like him?

"Stop it, Caleb!" Kezabeth stalked to him. She pushed him hard enough that his back hit the wall, surprising him out of his pity party. "You've let what happened to you take over your life, and I'm telling you it's time to stop!" Kezabeth stepped closer and brought up her finger. "You won't get help."

Caleb watched her finger poke him in the chest.

"You won't talk about it." Another poke. Kezabeth's eyes were bright with anger. "All you want to do is stay here, hidden away. What happened to the man you used to be, Caleb? Is one violent event in your life going to keep you from ever being that man again?"

Caleb leaned in, almost nose to nose with his sister. "Yes!" He stepped forward as Kezabeth moved back, following her until they stood in the center of the living room. "Yes, yes, yes! That *violent event* damn near killed me, Kezabeth! You weren't the one left lying broken in a puddle of blood, struggling to breathe and terrified the last thing you would ever see was the boot coming at you from the fucking psycho that almost fucking killed you!"

The anger died from her eyes. Tears gathered and leaked down her cheeks as she shook her head. "No, I wasn't, but—"

"There is no but, Kezabeth!" Caleb couldn't control the anger that surged through him—it terrified him and elated him to feel something other than fear. "That was *me* it happened to! Each blow, each punch and kick, it took a piece of me until something shattered inside me." Caleb's anger left as rapidly as it had arrived. "I don't know how to fix that. Sometimes I don't think anyone *can* fix it," he whispered brokenly.

Kezabeth was wrapping him in her arms again before the last word left his lips. "We can, Cale. We can do this. You just have to want to."

Caleb started to say that was the stupidest thing she'd ever said. Of course he *wanted* to get better. Didn't he? Did he want to give up the safe feeling it gave him to be locked away from the world? Right now he didn't know. He thought about Jesse and the sirens. Something bad was happening not too far away. This was a small town. Who knew what emergency call Jesse had received?

"Caleb?" Kezabeth's voice was quiet, as though she was afraid of upsetting him again.

Caleb hugged her, feeling her tears soaking through his T-shirt. "I'm sorry. I shouldn't have yelled at you. You've got your own share of problems, and you're helping me out, too."

"No, no, I think maybe it's good that you got angry. You've held it inside for months, you're entitled to be angry. You are," she added when he shook his head. Kezabeth wiped her nose on his shirt and grinned. "You can get past it. I know you can."

Caleb looked down at the nasty glob of mucus his sister had left. "Well, one thing's for sure. You certainly know how to take my mind off it. That's just…that's nasty!"

Kezabeth's laughter echoed in the living room as he carefully pulled off the shirt. Her eyes gleamed with triumph, and the smirk she wore made Caleb want to kick his own ass.

"You devious little creature!" Caleb faked a lunge at her. She gave a high-pitched whistle and pointed.

"Thank you, yes, I am! It was gross, but it got your shirt off, and I count five—no, make that *six* more hickeys on you. And you two haven't even had sex yet!" She broke out in gales of laughter, hands pressed to her sides.

"Kez," Caleb growled, then gave up and joined her, thinking she did have a point. If he and Jesse ever did fuck, Caleb might just be covered from head to toe in pretty purple marks. The idea of Jesse sucking up marks all over his body had Caleb's cock filling embarrassingly fast.

"Go fix us a drink, you pest." *Before you notice something else to tease me about.* Caleb gave her a push toward the kitchen, holding his dirty shirt in front of his cock in what he hoped was not an obvious manner. The glint in her eyes made him doubt his success. Being the wise man he was, he spun on his heel and dashed to the bathroom, grinning as his sister's laughter followed him down the hall.

Chapter Ten

Jesse was beyond tired and seriously worried about the state of humanity. Some days were just like that. He saw cases of cruelty and hatred that he couldn't understand. The domestic call earlier had been between a husband and wife at first. The woman had been beaten, her nose broken and her eyes nearly swollen shut. Once her husband had been led away by Monroe, who'd been Jesse's backup, Jesse had talked to her about pressing charges. She hadn't wanted to. He'd heard the reasons before—it was a mistake, he loved her, she loved him, she deserved it. When he'd asked why she'd called nine-one-one, she'd said she hadn't.

That was when a boy had peeked out of the bedroom doorway. Jesse had spotted the black eye on the kid and had wanted to go outside and drag the kid's dad out of Monroe's car and beat the holy hell out of him. Instead he had walked into the bedroom where that boy had been hiding, then he'd shut the door, and talked to the kid—Steven.

Steven was a ten-year-old boy, much smaller than his age. Judging from his hollowed-out cheeks and gaunt expression, Steven wasn't fed regularly, but the burn marks and bruises on his exposed skin said he *was* abused regularly.

Jesse had called CPS, Child Protective Services, and had stayed with Steven in the filthy bedroom until a protective services investigator arrived. Jonas Ryan, the only CPS investigator for the town, quickly but thoroughly conducted his interview and asked Jesse to escort him and Steven from the property. He had, and had been called every bad name he'd ever heard, and several he hadn't, by the battered wife who was responsible for many of the bruises and scars on Steven's body.

It wore him down, mentally and emotionally. He had never programmed himself not to be affected by such violence, and he didn't know if he ever could. Jesse needed to find some way to cope with it. Spying the black duffel bag on the passenger-side floorboard, he thought he just might have a way to get past the anger.

The drive home seemed to take longer than usual, even though he only lived three miles from the station. By the time he pulled into his driveway, he'd managed to avoid hitting two cats and narrowly missed getting T-boned at the stop sign on the corner of his block. Caleb's driveway was empty. Kezabeth must have gone home. Caleb's house was lit up like the Fourth of July and the porch light teemed with June bugs. That last bit made him shudder. Something about those peanut-shaped bugs creeped him out. Maybe it was the fact that they never failed to dive-bomb him, or the way they crunched when he stepped on one.

His stomach heaved at that image, and Jesse shut off that train of thought. So he got the heebie-jeebies from those annoying bugs—that didn't mean he was less of a man, especially if no one else ever knew about it.

Jesse grabbed the bag with the lube and condoms and got out of the car. He rushed up the steps and unlocked his door. Once inside, he set the bag on the coffee table. His uniform was shed on the way to the bathroom. He would pick it up later. Much later, hopefully.

The water hadn't had time to warm up when he stepped in the shower, and he bit back a yelp. He looked down at his cock. The cold water hadn't affected him at all. *Guess the water's no competition, not against the image of Caleb spread out, taking my dick into that tight, silky ass.* Jesse shook his head. If he didn't stop right there, he might just come the second he slid the washcloth over his erection.

It had to be one of the quickest showers ever, but he was clean and one step closer to getting where he wanted to be. Jesse swiped the towel over his head and body, then wrapped it around his hips as he left the bathroom.

"Clothes," he muttered as he yanked open dresser drawers. He eyed his underwear, thought about how Caleb hadn't been wearing any yesterday, and groaned as his cock jerked. Maybe he should sneak across the street in his towel. He could stand on Caleb's porch under that bright light with those nasty bugs bouncing off him, and everyone in the neighborhood see him. *Not a good idea to let his dick do the thinking.*

Jesse grabbed a pair of boxers, then went to his closet and looked over the choices. Jeans, jeans, more jeans. His favorite pair were soft and worn down, with holes in the knees and a few other places. He let his hand hover over the hanger. Should he dress up, or would Caleb not care if he showed up in comfortable clothes?

Jesse shook his head and picked a newer pair of jeans. Maybe his holey jeans would be fine for casual fucking, but this felt like *more*. And he didn't want to think about that too much. He pulled out a dark blue polo shirt and practically leaped into his clothes. He debated over the shoes but finally decided dock ones would be best, as he could skip socks and kick them off easily. Ready at last, he picked up the bag he'd had setting on the coffee table. Then he turned off his porch light and stepped outside. Jesse locked the door and headed across the street.

As he knocked on the door — right above the sign that he wanted to take down and toss into the trash — he realized the buzzing and bumping from the June bugs weren't bothering him as much as usual. The sound of deadbolts sliding open had Jesse tensing with need.

Caleb opened the door and smiled, his green eyes lighting up. Jesse thought he would do a hell of a lot more than tolerate June bugs for the man.

"Come in." Caleb stepped back, making room for him to slip through the doorway. Jesse itched to grab him and kiss his smiling lips, but waited until the door was shut and the locks were set. He looked Caleb up and down — tousled auburn hair, big flannel shirt over a baggy T-shirt, and...torn jeans, the tattered edges pooling over bare, narrow feet.

What did the torn jeans mean?

"Jesse?" Caleb's voice was barely audible. "Is something wrong?" Caleb's smile slipped.

"No, I was, ah, thinking." *Thinking that maybe I'm overdressed, or I'm wanting more from this than you are.*

"Because you're frowning like something's wrong," Caleb said.

Well, shit. That wasn't how he'd intended to start this night off. "Sorry, I think I'm a little nervous."

"Oh. That's kind of sweet, really." Caleb's smile came back, and Jesse's doubts disappeared.

"I don't know about sweet." He held up the bag and shook it. "Sweet would probably be a dozen roses and a box of chocolates instead of a dozen condoms and a tube of lube."

Caleb chuckled and grabbed the bag. "That depends on who is defining sweet. I'm not big on roses. Chocolate, of course, is the food of the gods. But this?" He opened the bag and pulled out the contents. "These right here, my sexy neighbor, are a promise of something sweeter and hotter than anything else you could show up with. Come on." He dropped the condoms and lube back into the bag and grabbed Jesse's hand. "Let's get to the bedroom and get naked."

Like Jesse would be dumb enough to argue with *that*.

That frown worried Caleb, even though Jesse seemed over whatever caused it. Caleb glanced down at his clothes as he led his lover down the hall, then cast a quick look at the man. New jeans, nice tight polo... A step up from his usual casual clothes. Okay, maybe a couple of steps up, and maybe Caleb's ratty jeans gave Jesse the impression he hadn't been looking forward to this...a lot.

If that was the case, the man was in for a surprise.

Caleb let go of Jesse's hand as soon as they reached the bedroom. He stripped off his shirt, eager to feel skin on skin.

Jesse stared at him, and Caleb felt that faze like an actual caress.

He shivered, then unbuttoned his jeans. He watched Jesse's eyes widen in appreciation. Jesse *did* like the commando thing.

"Fuck, Caleb." Jesse reached for him, but Caleb stepped back, stumbling a bit with his pants pooled around his ankles.

"Wait." Caleb put his hand up to slow Jesse's approach. "It occurred to me that you might think I was dressed kind of sloppy, but I swear there's a reason."

Kicking his jeans aside, Caleb lowered his head and looked up at Jesse through his lashes. He'd never been a tease, but he found he liked it. The sharp intake of breath from Jesse said he liked it too, or at least wasn't unaffected by it.

"And that reason is…"

Caleb couldn't hold back a smile. "Well, it seemed that something loose would be better with this." He turned and watched Jesse over his shoulder, shaking his ass. *Maybe just a little more teasing.*

"Caleb, God." Jesse's voice sounded strangled, as though it was a struggle to get out each word. "That's so fucking sexy." He came forward and spread Caleb's butt cheeks, tapping the butt plug hard enough that Caleb gasped.

Caleb felt his eyes drift shut as the plug was twisted in half circles over and over. Thank God he'd finally found his box of toys. "Wanted. To be ready."

"Yeah, great idea." Jesse pulled the plug halfway out and thrust it back in.

"Shit!" Caleb fumbled for the edge of the dresser. In the mirror Jesse was watching him. He pumped the plug in and out. Caleb stared at their reflection, the sight of his nude body with his lover fully clothed behind him was so erotic his balls drew tight. The plug rubbed against his prostate and Caleb moaned.

"Jesse. Gonna come… Want you," Caleb gasped as the plug was pulled out, the sudden emptiness making him feel bereft. Jesse reached around him and set the toy on the dresser.

With quick movements, Jesse had his jeans unbuttoned. He looked at Caleb and stroked a hand down his ass. "Stay right there, just like that."

A shiver went through him as he realized Jesse was going to fuck him right there, where they could both watch in the mirror. He heard the ripping of the condom wrapper and closed his eyes, letting the need and hunger build. The sound of the lube cap being opened, the spluttering of that thick liquid being poured out seemed especially loud. The cool liquid hit his skin, sliding down his crease. Then Jesse's fingers were there, rubbing and penetrating him in a series of hard thrusts.

A whimper escaped from his lips when Jesse pulled his fingers out, leaving him empty and aching. The rasp of denim against the backs of his legs, the heat of Jesse's big body and his strong hand gripping Caleb's hips made him open his eyes and seek out his lover's dark gaze. He felt the nudge of Jesse's cock against his hole then Jesse locked his arm around his stomach and thrust hard.

Despite having been loosened some by the plug, there was still a bit of discomfort as Jesse's fat tip breached his body. There was a burning, stretching sensation as Jesse slowly, steadily filled him. Caleb closed his eyes and reveled in the feeling of being stuffed full, relaxing into it rather than tensing up.

"Caleb. Watch." Jesse pressed his hips closer. He dropped his arm from around Caleb's middle and grabbed his other hip instead.

Caleb blinked until his vision cleared. The idea of locking stares with Jesse while they fucked scared him. He didn't know why. His heart beat faster and he thought he might have a panic attack, but when he finally dragged his gaze upward, everything settled inside him. Jesse's mouth was tipped in a sexy smile and his eyes were warm and filled with something that might be tenderness. And Caleb needed him to *move*.

"S'go." He'd barely gotten the words out before Jesse canted his hips and pumped with slow, deep thrusts. Caleb pushed back into each one, his gaze on Jesse's in the mirror. He squeezed his inner muscles, needing more even. His balls tingled, snuggling against his body.

"Caleb" was all the warning he got before Jesse's fingers dug deeply into his hips. Jesse pounded into him, hard thrusts that brought Caleb to his toes even as he continued to slam his hips back with shameless eagerness. His eyes kept trying to drift shut—he couldn't see, his vision having gone blurry within seconds of Jesse reaming his ass. Each driving penetration from Jesse's thick cock drew moans and whimpers from him. His muscles clenched and his hands were white-knuckled from his hold on the dresser. The feeling of Jesse taking him like this, burying his cock hard and deep, his balls slapping against Caleb—it sent tiny explosions of heat through every nerve ending in his body.

He tried to speak, to let Jesse know he was going to come, but his voice failed. Jesse fisted his dick and began stroking in time with his thrusts. It was too much. Caleb's arms and legs wobbled as he came so hard it was painful, strings of spunk shooting from his cock onto the mirror.

Jesse growled and let go of Caleb's spent cock, then wrapped his arms around him to keep him from falling. He ground his hips against Caleb and moaned, a low, rough rumble that made Caleb want him all over again even as Jesse's cock swelled inside him. Caleb clamped his muscles down hard and was rewarded with another one of those sexy-as-fuck moans. He could easily become addicted to that sound. He might even already be addicted, because he wanted to hear it as often as possible. And God, he wanted to feel Jesse splitting his ass open again, and the man wasn't even done yet.

Jesse heaved with one final thrust and brought his lips to the back of Caleb's neck. He felt every pulse of release from Jesse's cock. The man filled him like no one ever had. Shivers raced down Caleb's spine, goosebumps raised up on him as Jesse licked and nipped the sensitive skin. And still, Jesse kept him pinned with his warm brown gaze. Caleb struggled to find the word for how that made him feel — owned, claimed, maybe both. But he also felt oddly safe. He had a vague thought he should be worried about such feelings, but then Jesse's teeth nipped a particularly sensitive spot.

* * * *

The feel of warm, taut flesh rubbing against his cock woke Jesse up from hazy dreams. He blinked away his disorientation, his mind spinning as he tried to work out where he was and whose body was pressed against his. The room was sunlit despite the blinds and heavy drapes over the windows. Jesse's eyes cleared and he looked at the auburn-topped head that rested on his arm. A slow smile spread across his face. *Caleb.*

Memories of burying his dick inside Caleb's snug channel chased off Jesse's lingering sleepiness. He trailed a hand down his lover's chest. And let it drift lower, rubbing lazy circles around Caleb's concave stomach before drifting over to a prominent hip bone. Jesse rubbed that blade of a hipbone again absently while he considered his feelings for the man sleeping beside him. Caleb brought out all sorts of protective instincts Jesse hadn't known he possessed. He wasn't typically drawn to men who were so obviously wounded, had never felt the need to swoop in and rescue anyone like he did with Caleb.

All of Jesse's former boyfriends had been regular guys—okay, maybe bland, to a certain extent. When those relationships ended, Jesse had walked away relatively unscathed, his heart and soul still intact. But something about Caleb led him to believe that might not be the case if they became involved on more than a physical level. Whatever walls he'd built around his heart were already crumbling where the Caleb was concerned. It was intimidating, and if he were to be completely honest, a little exhilarating as well.

A low humming sound from Caleb had Jesse stilling his hand. Caleb arched his back, pushing his ass firmly against Jesse's shaft. A narrow hand found his and tugged it from Caleb's hip to his cock. Jesse gripped that hard length and pumped it leisurely, enjoying the way Caleb's hips rolled as he fucked his hand.

Jesse let his lover get warmed up then he pressed his lips to Caleb's ear. "Wanna fuck me?"

Caleb's eyes flew open, and his whole body tensed for about one second then he was nodding and reaching for a condom and lube. Caleb's cock pulsed in his hand. Oh yeah, Caleb wanted, and he'd better let go of Caleb's dick before he hurt himself. Grinning, he opened his hand and rolled onto his back. It had been a while since he'd bottomed. It would probably be better for him to get on his hands and knees, but then he wouldn't be able to watch Caleb's face, and he liked to watch his lover's green eyes spark when he came.

The crinkling noise of the condom wrapper being torn open brought his attention back to Caleb.

"Let me." Jesse sat up and accepted the condom. He took his time rolling it down the thick, pretty cock, drawing a moan from his lover with his careful ministrations. Once Jesse had the rubber on, he reached lower and cupped Caleb's balls, rolling them in his palm and pressing his fingertips to the soft skin behind them.

"Enough." Caleb grabbed Jesse's wrist, surprising him with his strength. Jesse kept thinking of Caleb as delicate, and certainly he was in some ways, but that thin body held a lot more strength than anyone would guess unless they knew Caleb well.

Caleb popped the cap off the lube, and Jesse stuck out his hand. "I'll stretch myself."

"Oh, but I…" Caleb hesitated, looking from Jesse's hand to his cock. "I want to."

Shaking his head, Jesse grabbed the lube and poured some into his hand, trying not to let that look of disappointment stop him. "Next time, I promise, but right now I want you in me as fast as possible. You'd want to take your time, make sure I'm comfortable, and be way too cautious." He handed to lube back to Caleb.

"Of course I would! Why is that a problem?"

"Because…" Jesse lifted his leg and smeared the lube around. "You'll start off with one and work your way up as I stretch, and it will take too long, whereas I…" He couldn't stop the hitch in his breath as he pushed two fingers past the tight ring of muscles. Caleb's eyes widened as he watched Jesse prepare himself roughly. "I just want you in me."

Jesse pumped his fingers in and out, scissoring them and forcing his body to take a third. The burn felt good because he knew it meant he was one step closer to having Caleb fucking him, and he wanted that with something that bordered on desperation.

"*Now!*" Jesse pulled his fingers out, and Caleb knelt between his thighs.

"Stop topping from the bottom," Caleb muttered, but his green eyes were lit with laughter and need. "Roll your hips to the side."

Jesse arched his eyebrows but complied. He twisted his hips until he was almost lying on his side. Caleb placed his hand on the back of Jesse's thigh, pushing the top leg toward Jesse's chest. He straddled Jesse's bottom thigh, his balls warm and weighty against Jesse's leg. Jesse shivered as Caleb slid his fingers up and down his crease, lightly teasing at his hole with each pass.

Caleb moved up a few inches, pressing in the fat, flared head of his dick, breaching Jesse and making him suck in a breath to keep from hissing. There was no way he wanted to do anything that might make his lover stop. He willed himself to relax and bear down, embracing the burning invasion as Caleb rocked back and worked more of his cock into Jesse's ass.

"Fuck. Your ass is squeezing my dick so hard." Caleb's voice was strained as he paused and looked up from where their bodies were joined.

Jesse hooked his arm under his bent knee, hitching his leg higher. "Caleb, *just fuck me already!*"

Caleb let go of Jesse's ass and leaned forward, slapping his hands on either side of Jesse's body. His eyes glittered with determination as he dropped his head low. "Shut up and let me."

Jesse was aware of the fact that he was doing his best goldfish imitation, his mouth opening and closing as surprise at Caleb's clear demand for domination struck him. It also turned him on. Jesse snapped his mouth shut and nodded.

"Good." Caleb's lids dropped until his eyes were nearly closed.

A quick thrust had Jesse biting his bottom lip. Caleb shifted and grabbed his bent leg with one hand. The other hand gripped Jesse's shoulder, then Caleb was moaning as he pushed his dick in to the hilt. Jesse tasted blood and realized he'd bitten his lip, but it wasn't enough of a distraction to block out the burning pain as his inner muscles adjusted to accommodate Caleb's thick rod.

"Shit!" Caleb was panting, his body trembling with the effort to hold still until Jesse was ready for him to move. "Relax! I can't move no matter how much I want to, your ass is holding me so tight."

Jesse took a deep breath and the pain receded. Pulses of pleasure rippled through his channel, and this time Caleb's moan was joined by his. The feel of Caleb grinding his hips against him, one sharp hipbone digging into Jesse's ass, had him reaching for his cock. Caleb's eyelids flickered, then he was drawing back, sliding his dick almost all the way out before plunging back in.

"Oh fuck, yes!" Caleb fucked him, hard, fast and deep.

Jesse stroked his cock, gripping it tight and pumping his fist in time with Caleb's thrusts. The dual pleasures, being fucked inside and out, had Jesse's toes curling as his balls drew up, the tingling in his spine spreading throughout his body.

"Caleb. Gonna come." Jesse's lids grew heavy, but he kept his gaze locked with Caleb's.

"Yeah, I have to feel you come on my cock," Caleb bit out through clenched teeth. He looked almost fierce as he worked his dick in Jesse's ass. Jesse's one coherent thought was that he'd had no idea Caleb would be such an intense top. Then he was yelling as his cock pulsed and wet heat shot over his hand and stomach. His muscles clenched. He watched in dazed fascination as Caleb flung his head back, the tendons in his neck protruding in a way that made Jesse's mouth water. A strangled sound sprang from Caleb as Jesse's cock swelled deep inside him.

As Caleb filled the condom, Jesse thought of something that scared him more than anything else ever had. He wanted to feel Caleb's cum shooting into his ass, wanted to feel each burst of spunk warming the inner muscles that embraced Caleb's cock. That was something he'd never done, not even as an inexperienced, horny teenager, and while he'd wondered about it, there had never been anyone who he felt strongly enough about to try it.

That he was considering it now scared the shit out of him. There wasn't the time to deal with it either. Jesse closed his eyes as Caleb thrust one last time, afraid his lover might look down and see more than he wanted him to. He had a lot of things to think about. Maybe he would be able to share those things with Caleb, but not now, not yet. Not until he had dealt with them first.

Chapter Eleven

Caleb woke up, aching in places that had been neglected for too long. The sore muscles brought a smile to his lips as he rolled over and reached for Jesse. His hand smacked into the mattress and his eyes flew open. Caleb was alone. Why that made him feel like shit was beyond him. He was used to waking up alone.

Flopping back on the bed, Caleb flung a forearm over his eyes and tried to figure out why it bothered him to do so this time. He actually *hurt*. Because, damn, it felt like something was pressing down on his chest when he thought about Jesse slipping out without even waking him to say goodbye. Caleb sat up again. Jesse's shirt was tossed on the chair, but everything else of his was gone. And there wasn't a note in sight.

So Jesse had been in such a hurry to get out that he'd left his shirt. *Does he regret what we did together, the times we had sex? We didn't sleep much, we were too busy fucking.*

And it had been ball-scorchingly hot every time. Caleb was pretty sure he'd be getting hard just thinking about it if he didn't feel like the world's biggest loser. He started to lie back down and bury his head under the covers when a clanging noise came from the direction of the kitchen.

"Oh. Dumbass!" Caleb flung back the covers and got out of bed. He grabbed a pair of cotton PJs that were sticking out of the dresser drawer. He tugged them on and hurried down the hall, muttering about what an idiot he was for jumping to conclusions. No matter what he told himself, he couldn't press down the bubble of happiness that kept trying to rise up and spread out. A chant—*Jesse didn't leave me, Jesse didn't leave me*—kept flitting through his head. Caleb reached up and tapped his forehead.

His smile faltered. "He might not have this time, but if he hears that shit, he will." Caleb forced aside the needy voice and turned into the kitchen.

Jesse waved a spatula at the stack of mail on top of the island. "Who's Alexander Wyatt?"

Caleb glanced at the mail, then back at Jesse. Black tendrils of smoke wafted around the man, and Caleb had the ridiculous thought that Jesse must be really angry. Then reality hit and Caleb dashed around the island to the stove.

"Move!" Caleb pushed at Jesse, and Jesse spun around, extending an arm out to shove Caleb away from the stove.

"Shit!" Orange flames licked around what might have been bacon. Jesse cursed again as he grabbed the handle of the skillet. "Get me a lid!"

"Yeah." Caleb spun on his heel and jerked open a cabinet. He yanked out a big cast-iron skillet and turned to Jesse, nearly smacking him in the shoulder with it. "Here, this should do it."

Jesse grunted as he took the skillet and placed it over the burned bacon, smothering the fire. Black smoke rolled out from the edges, but the fire was out. Caleb breathed a sigh of relief, trying to think of a joke to break the tension, until he remembered why there *was* tension in the first place. He looked up and sure enough, Jesse was staring at him, his big arms crossed over that muscular chest, spatula still in his hand. Caleb studied his lover's face, trying to figure out if he was angry or what, but couldn't get a read on his mood.

Crossed arms could be a sign of defensiveness? Caleb was sure he'd read that somewhere, but he didn't know why Jesse would be feeling defensive. Maybe he was remembering it wrong, and someone who crossed their arms over their chest was trying to close himself off. Shit, he didn't know.

"Caleb?" Jesse's calm voice cut through Caleb's mental rant.

Caleb's gaze wandered to the stove. He thought about how he'd felt when he'd woken up and thought Jesse had lit out and how happy he'd felt to discover he was wrong. And Jesse was here, in the kitchen.

"You were making us breakfast," Caleb murmured.

"Yeah, I thought you'd worked up an appetite," Jesse replied.

"I thought you'd left." Caleb looked into Jesse's eyes. Happiness washed over him again. "Saw your shirt, thought you'd woken up and realized what a mess you'd fucked around with." Caleb shut up as Jesse's expression was clearly readable.

Jesse was angry, bordering on furious. Caleb took a step back as Jesse uncrossed his arms and dropped the spatula, but he wasn't fast enough. Jesse laid his hands on Caleb's shoulders and dug in.

"Do. Not." Jesse's fingers squeezed harder, holding Caleb captive as surely as his stormy brown gaze. "Talk like that about yourself again. Do you understand me?"

Caleb was turned on and ticked off at the same time. His dick liked the rough handling and the orders, but his big head—the one that was supposed to keep him out of trouble—was having some issues. He grabbed Jesse's wrists and jerked, but nothing happened.

Irritated beyond reason, Caleb glared at Jesse and considered kicking him in the shin. "What are you going to do, duct tape my mouth shut?" Caleb waved his hands before bringing them to the insides of Jesse's elbows. If he had to, he'd dig in his thumbs.

Jesse's eyes turned molten. "I wouldn't do it, Caleb, because I will turn you over my knees and paddle it until your ass is nice and pink—which is exactly what I'll do the next time I hear you ripping yourself."

Caleb's heartbeat sped up. His cock swelled, threatening to peek out of the elastic waistband of his pajama bottoms. He checked to make sure it hadn't happened, and leered at Jesse when he noticed the erection.

"As far as deterrents, I think you might have picked the wrong one." Caleb stroked his palm over his cock and watched Jesse's pupils dilate. Maybe Jesse *wasn't* the one in control here after all. Caleb slipped his hand down his PJs and fisted his cock. He got in a few good tugs before Jesse cursed and grabbed his hand, taking over and effectively putting an end to Caleb's teasing.

"Who is Alexander Wyatt?" Jesse asked.

This time when Caleb stepped back, Jesse let him go. Caleb released his softening dick and planted his hand on his hip. He considered his options and decided some things might be worth the risk.

"Can I ask you something before I answer? Without this reverting to a juvenile version of 'but I asked you first'?" Caleb watched as Jesse nodded instantly. Jesse's lack of hesitation somehow made him feel better.

"What's going on between us?" God, that was harder to say than he'd expected, and now he blushed. "I mean, I did think you left, but you didn't, and I'm not... I haven't been able to have a relationship in years, and I don't know if that's where we're heading, or if it's just a case of convenience, or...or if I should shut up, but I can't answer your question if I don't know I can completely trust you. You see what I mean?" Caleb sucked in a long breath, clamped his mouth shut and bit his traitorous tongue, which seemed to want to spill his secrets to this man.

Jesse shook his head and chuckled, amusement evident. "What, exactly, did you want me to get from that?"

What, indeed? Caleb fingered the waistband, staring at the floor. "It's just that I need to know what's happening here." He gestured with his hand between them. "What you're asking — the answer is a matter of trust."

Utter silence filled the kitchen and Caleb glanced up at Jesse. A frown marred his handsome face.

"Have you done something...illegal?"

That was the last question Caleb had expected. He didn't know whether to be amused or insulted. Caleb settled on neither. Instead, he stepped closer to Jesse and rested his hands on his bare chest, never breaking away from Jesse's worried stare.

"The only bad things I've done" — Caleb leaned in and stood on his toes, then brushed his lips against Jesse's — "were with you. I bet quite a few of the things we did are illegal in several states."

Jesse cupped his ass and lifted him up enough so Caleb had to hold on for balance. "And you need to know what's going on between us before you can answer my question?"

"Yes." Caleb breathed the word against Jesse's lips, wondering if that *yes* was an answer to more than one question. Jesse's mouth crashed down on his, his slick tongue stroked into Caleb's mouth, sending bolts of heat shooting to Caleb's cock. He moaned into Jesse's warm mouth, licking and sucking, his body reacting as though it hadn't been sated several times already.

When Jesse lowered him back down until he could stand flat-footed, Caleb leaned his head against the man and held on.

"I think you melted my knees," he muttered against Jesse's bare flesh, and couldn't resist licking a drop of sweat that rolled down the tempting skin. The salty taste did little to satisfy the need growing in Caleb.

"Caleb." Jesse kneaded Caleb's buttocks, encouraging him to rub against Jesse's thickly muscled thigh. "I don't know what we have, but it isn't a one-night stand, and it damned sure isn't convenient. I would never sneak off on you. Even if I got called in, I would wake you and tell you."

Most of that speech warmed Caleb's heart, except that one small part. "What do you mean, it damned sure isn't convenient?" He didn't pull away from Jesse like his first impulse told him to—he'd learned not to jump to conclusions.

"I mean—" Jesse released one of Caleb's cheeks. He slid his hand over Caleb's back then up to his neck before curling long fingers under his chin to tip his head up. "I mean that this is a small town with plenty of small-minded people." Jesse's chocolate-brown eyes shone with sincerity. "You were hurt before, and I don't want anything like that to happen to you again."

Caleb fought back a shudder, because *he* didn't want anything like that to happen to him again either. Saying the whole thing sucked ass was a major understatement.

"What does the one have to do with the other? What happened had nothing to do with my sexuality." Caleb snorted at the thought. "I didn't have any sexuality! I hadn't been with anyone for at least a year at that point." *Please don't ask.* He wasn't ready, not yet.

For a moment he was afraid Jesse would push it. He could see the man working to suppress the need for answers. When he nodded, Caleb let out a breath. He took Jesse's hand and led him into the room behind the kitchen. His office was compact and unusually neat. Caleb hadn't been able to concentrate on his work since he'd been hurt. If he had been capable of working, the large wooden desk would have been covered in papers and notepads, books and pens scattered across its now gleaming surface.

Instead, everything was tidy. That in itself made Caleb feel like a failure. Jesse's hand rested on the small of his back. The comfort of the gentle touch chased away the voice in his head that said he was weak and damaged. Caleb pointed to a bookshelf at the other end of the room, studying Jesse's face for any indication he already knew who he was.

"There, on that shelf, is Alexander Wyatt." Jesse looked at the thirteen books that lined the bookshelf, hardbacks and paperbacks of each title. "And here." Caleb tapped his chest, drawing Jesse's gaze back to him. "Here's Alexander Wyatt. I'm author Alexander Wyatt."

It was what Jesse could describe only as a true *what the fuck* moment. So his lover was a reclusive writer. Jesse walked over and picked up the first book. *Science fiction.* He opened the book and scanned the inside cover for details about the story.

"Holy shit." Jesse hadn't realized he'd spoken the words until Caleb issued a nervous laugh.

"Is that a good holy shit or a bad holy shit? Because I always have trouble differentiating between the two." Caleb's voice had a slight quiver to it that had Jesse closing the book, then putting it back in its place. He faced Caleb, wondering why the man was so secretive about his identity.

"Is your name really Caleb Tomas?" Jesse watched Caleb's head bob up and down. "You use Alexander Wyatt as a pen name, right?" More nodding. Jesse was reminded of the bobble head plastic dogs that were all the rage a few years ago—everyone and their mother had seemed to have one of the things in the back window of their cars.

He cupped Caleb's chin again and forced him to meet his gaze. "Why are you so nervous?" Then a thought hit him, and Jesse figured he was on a roll. "If you want who you are—who Alexander Wyatt is—to stay a secret, do you think having mail delivered here in your pen name is a wise idea?"

Caleb's eyes widened owlishly, and he shook his head, slipping his chin from Jesse's grasp. "Oh no. All that mail"—he waved a hand in the direction of the kitchen—"that goes to a PO box. Didn't you notice?"

Well, no, frankly he hadn't gotten past the name before Caleb walked into the kitchen.

"Kezabeth picks it up for me and either hand delivers it or packs the letters into one of those big manila envelopes, then she mails it here in her name." Caleb grinned and bobbed his head again. Jesse gave up and put his hand on top of Caleb's head.

"Um, why did you do that?" Caleb's eyes crossed and he looked back at Jesse.

"You keep nodding your head."

Caleb's brow knitted in confusion. "What the fuck does that have to do with anything?"

"I can't take you seriously when your head bobbing reminds me of those little plastic dogs in car windows."

Irritation gleamed in Caleb's eyes, and he reached up and swatted at Jesse's wrist.

"That is messed up, Jesse." Caleb glared at him, his lower lip protruding the slightest bit. "I'm not some damned plastic Chihuahua!"

Jesse couldn't seem to look away from that plump bottom lip. "They weren't all Chihuahuas, and of course you're not. I know for a fact that you are one sexy as fuck man, not a Chihuahua." He watched Caleb struggle to hold on to his anger and decided to help him out. "One sexy as fuck man who has a sexy as fuck pout." Jesse rubbed Caleb's lower lip with the pad of his thumb, until Caleb nipped at him.

"I do not pout!" Caleb tried to look angry but ended up laughing. "Not much anyway." The laughter vanished, and a worried look replaced the joy. "So you really hadn't heard of me?"

Jesse felt insulted Caleb would even question the fact, but he let it go. Because Jesse hadn't heard of him, or because he thought Jesse *had* heard of him and was lying about it? Jesse wished he knew. "No, I hadn't. Sorry if that insults you. I don't have the time to read. Will you get all offended if I tell you I generally prefer to read nonfiction?" God, he hoped not. Then he would have to admit there had been too many times where he just got lost trying to read science fiction, which made him feel like a fool.

"No, I guess not." Caleb tapped his chin as he studied Jesse. "It might even be a good thing, since I won't have to worry about you going all groupie on me."

"All groupie?" Jesse swept his gaze down Caleb's thin form, then back up to his lover's eyes. "I think I might just go all groupie on you, but for a totally different reason."

Caleb pinkened and Jesse couldn't resist leaning down to kiss the man. The rumbling sound Caleb's stomach made had the kiss ending as they both laughed.

"Come on." Jesse looped his arm around Caleb's narrow hips. "Let's get some food in you. I promise not to burn it this time."

"Sounds like a plan." Caleb shoved his hand down the back of Jesse's jeans to tease the top of his crease. "After that, you can get something else in me too."

Jesse wondered how Caleb would feel about a glass of milk and a piece of toast. It was the quickest thing he could think of to feed him. He started to suggest it—he would have only been half joking—but his fingers brushed across Caleb's sharp, bony hip, and he caught himself before he spoke. "Okay, but you have to eat a good breakfast because you'll need it to keep up with me."

He leered at Caleb when he snorted. Jesse winked, but he promised himself he would do whatever he needed to in order to take care of this man by his side.

Chapter Twelve

It was annoyingly quiet in the house. Loopy wanted to go out back and bark at...everything, apparently. Caleb put the pup outside again, then returned to the living room. He sat in his favorite spot and scrolled through the offerings on the channel guide and wondered once again why he paid for satellite TV. It gave him more options of what not to watch. Despite the near-oppressive silence, there wasn't a single thing on that tempted him to turn up the volume. Caleb glanced at the time on the TV screen—it'd been less than half an hour since Jesse left. The residual feelings of happiness were fading fast now that he was alone again.

"That's pathetic." Caleb tossed the remote on the couch and stood up. Depression threatened to darken his mood, and it irritated the hell out of him. Why should he feel so lonely when he'd been alone so many times before?

Caleb walked to the back door and unlocked it, thinking Loopy might be ready to come in again. He opened the door and stuck his head out, letting loose a shrill whistle. Loopy ran for the door, yipping and jumping as he made his way inside the house. Caleb grinned at all the canine joy bouncing at his ankles. "Just let me lock up."

Once Caleb had taken care of that, he grinned at Loopy. "Come on, boy." Caleb squatted and patted the wiggly poodle. He wasn't successful at avoiding the occasional lick to his face, but the fluff ball always made him feel better. Caleb didn't know how anyone could feel down when shown such adoration, and he adored Loopy right back. He even loved his prickly, bird-murdering feline. Maybe one day Mix would let Caleb pet him and feel that soft gray fur. Purring sweetly one minute and hissing the next, Mix was an amusing contradiction.

An obnoxiously loud rock song blared from the kitchen. Caleb rose and tried to get to his cell phone as quickly as possible. Trying not to trip over Loopy made him have to listen far too long. He breathed a sigh of relief when he saw the caller ID, before pressing a button to answer.

"Hello, Kez, what's up?"

"Hey, Cale, did you forget I'm doing grocery day this afternoon instead of tomorrow?"

Caleb *had* forgotten. He suspected the change had something to do with her being protective and him having a new lover. What she didn't know was she'd probably have encountered Jesse just as much if she came in the mornings.

"Yeah, I did. Sorry." He walked over to the refrigerator and pulled the door open. A quick inventory told him he at least needed bacon. Caleb stifled a grin. Looked like everything else was running low as well. Caleb shut the door then checked the freezer. The selection of frozen dinners made Caleb feel like a pathetic loser. He closed the freezer, moved over to the pantry and sighed when he glimpsed its contents. Cans of soup and packages of ramen — was it any wonder he skipped so many meals?

"Kez, I think I need about everything." He had a vision of serving Jesse a bowl of soupy noodles for dinner. "Um."

"Yes?" Kezabeth's voice sounded slightly mocking. "Is there something else you need me to get? Say, condoms or —"

Caleb's face erupted in lava-like heat. "God no!" He couldn't suppress a shudder at the idea of his sister purchasing anything having to do with his sex life. That was just wrong on too many levels.

Kezabeth's laughter had Caleb pulling the phone away from his ear. "Oh, come on. I'm only trying to make sure you practice safe sex!"

"Who needs practice?" Caleb could have smacked himself. He did *not* want to have this discussion. "Can we move on?"

Kezabeth wouldn't let it go. "What are you going to do if things between you and Jesse get, er, deeper?"

Caleb couldn't hold back a snort of laughter. If *things* got any *deeper* the next time he and Jesse fucked, he would be in serious trouble. His lover's dick was definitely size proportionate, and he was at least six-four. "Maybe you should rephrase that question. Or, better yet, drop the whole subject!"

"Jeez, you perv! You know what I meant! I'll grab some —"

"No!" Caleb would never live it down if she did. And it was just *wrong*! "Jesse took care of it!" This time he did smack himself on the forehead. Groaning, he closed his eyes and waited.

"Does this mean I should buy extra food?"

Caleb's eyes shot open. That wasn't the type of question he'd been expecting. Maybe Kez would let it go, but he doubted it. More than likely, she was waiting until she could torment him in person. What had she asked? *Oh.*

"Yeah, and maybe some real food." Caleb searched his mind for meals he knew how to cook. It didn't take long at all, and that fact made him resolve to spend some time online, looking up recipes. "Hamburger stuff. And steaks?"

"Okay, I'll keep in mind that you might be having a guest over. Often?" It wasn't a very subtle probe, not that she did subtle very well anyway.

"Yeah, let's go with that." Would Jesse be here often? Caleb didn't know, but he hoped so. It wasn't like he and Jesse had really firmed up what they had going on, other than that it wasn't a one-night stand.

"I should be there in a couple of hours." There was a note in Kezabeth's voice that set off little alarm bells in Caleb's head. "When I get there, there's something I want to talk to you about. Promise me you'll keep an open mind."

"Kez, can't you tell me now and get it over with?" If not, he would worry until she got here and told him.

"No, I think it would be best to talk to you in person." Kezabeth sighed heavily. "Please, it's nothing to worry about, I promise, but I'd prefer to wait until we can sit down and speak face-to-face."

Somehow he didn't find her words very reassuring, but he wouldn't get any more out of her. Kez was at least as stubborn as him.

"I'll see you in a bit. Be careful."

Caleb hung up the phone and turned to find a pair of adoring canine eyes watching him hopefully. He smiled and reached for the box of dog biscuits on the counter, feeling a little less worried. It was impossible to dwell on whatever his sister wanted to discuss when the house was suddenly filled with happy yips and a wagging tail.

"All right, all right." Caleb opened the box and laughed at the chaos that ensued. "Follow me, Loopy." Stepping gingerly to avoid trampling the poodle, Caleb headed into the living room. There might not be a damn thing on TV, but he had enough company to keep him busy for a good while.

* * * *

"Heard your new neighbor's queer."

Jesse froze at the sneering voice, then forced himself to relax. Monroe was the newbie on the force, hired six months ago. The man's arrogance and swagger along with his obnoxious mouth had grated on Jesse's nerves from the moment they had met.

More than once, Jesse'd overheard the man make a racist comment or express some other bigoted, idiotic opinion. He thought Monroe was putting on an act, trying to come off as tough, since he was a wet-behind-the-ears rookie. Jesse hoped that with time, the attitude would fade somewhat. Now, however, he realized the man was an asshole and unlikely to ever be anything else.

Jesse shot a glance over his shoulder at Monroe. "Where'd you hear that?" It had to be just more gossip. No one here knew anything about Caleb or their relationship. Normally he wouldn't have even bothered to find out, but this concerned Caleb, and therefore, him.

Monroe shrugged, giving him a sly look. "Doesn't matter, does it? He's a damn fag. Probably got hisself beat for it too. That same rumor has it that you're his new best friend. I wonder what I'd see if I drove by there a little before three tomorrow?"

A chill started working its way through Jesse, but he squashed it. He knew there would be talk, that someone would notice him and Caleb and the regular walks to the mailbox. Still, hearing the smarmy implication there was something going on, especially from a coworker who already annoyed the crap out of him, made him more than a little pissy. His temper spiking, he stepped over to Monroe and leaned in close, enjoying the way the man went from smug to wary.

"You know" — he kept his voice low and silky, the anger buried deep — "a lot of people had plenty to say about you too when you moved here. Still do, actually."

Jesse took a step back, pleased with the way Monroe's skin went ruddy with anger. As for Monroe's veiled accusations, Jesse wouldn't address those at all. Obviously people already knew about their friendship. He wouldn't explain it to anyone, least of all this asshole.

Monroe's blue eyes blazed with hate. "Who the fuck's been talking shit? And what are they saying?"

Shaking his head, Jesse shrugged then headed for the door, needing to get away before he said or did something he probably wouldn't regret. The fury in the man's gaze was like a laser burning into the back of his head.

Jesse paused at the door and turned enough to look at Monroe. "Now, Monroe, I told you before, back when you were talking shit about Rodriguez. I don't do gossip." He pushed the door open and walked out of the police station. Jesse didn't bother biting back a grin at the curses that reached his ears before the door slapped shut. Maybe, if he got lucky, the captain would hear Monroe and pop him into an anger-management class or two. Not that it would help. As far as Jesse knew, there was no cure for being an asshole. Then his grin faltered as he realized Monroe's comments had made it risky to swing by Caleb's tonight.

"God damn it!" Jesse stopped by his Charger and tried to rein in his anger. It wouldn't do anyone any good if he beat the shit out of Pat Monroe. By the time he'd calmed down, Jesse had concluded two things. One, he couldn't risk stopping by Caleb's tonight, not with the threat of Monroe spying on them.

And second, he wouldn't let anyone keep him from Caleb, not permanently. If he had to choose between Caleb or his job, what would he do? Jesse hoped he never had to find out, but Monroe's spiteful nature was almost an assurance that he would.

* * * *

"You're serious?" Caleb looked at Kezabeth, then back down at the business card in his hand. He flipped the card around and around between his thumb and forefinger, watching the writing disappear and reappear with each turn, wondering if there was a snowball's chance of this working.

Kezabeth scooted closer and took the card away. "You're going to bend it all to hell, and yes, I'm serious. What can it hurt to try it?"

Caleb shook his head. He didn't know what it would hurt, except maybe to get his hopes up for nothing. "It sounds like some kind of scam."

"Oh, puh-lease." Kezabeth's eyes rolled. "You can do almost everything online nowadays. Why not this?"

"I can think of quite a few things you can't do online." Caleb waggled his eyebrows at Kezabeth and yelped when she pinched his thigh. "What the hell? You're pinching me because I pointed out you can't get a haircut or surgery or —"

Another pinch had him snapping his mouth shut.

"I am so sure that's what you were referring to, you perv. And maybe you can't exactly do those things online, but you can schedule them online." Kezabeth tapped the business card against her knee. "Will you please at least think about it?"

Caleb leaned back on the couch and closed his eyes. He was tired, and not just physically. He rubbed at his temples to ease the pounding in his head.

"Let me get you some aspirin." Kezabeth patted his knee. A few seconds later, Caleb heard her digging around in her purse. More like a suitcase. "Here."

Caleb cracked an eye enough to see her hand in front of his face. The two white tablets might help ease his migraine, if he was lucky. Caleb popped the pills in his mouth, swallowed them dry, and cursed himself for not bothering to get his prescription refilled. God, he was so fucking messed up! But did he have to be?

"Okay, I'll try it." Caleb put pressure on his temples when Kezabeth's happy screech set that spot to throbbing harder. "Kez, please."

"Oh shit, Caleb, I'm sorry." Kezabeth tugged on Caleb's shoulder, urging him to lie on the couch. "Stretch out here and try to sleep for a while. I promise I'll wake you if I hear from Jesse. You've got a few hours before his break."

Caleb grunted as he turned on his side, burying his head in the throw pillows. Something swished over him, then a light blanket landed on him. Loopy settled against his back, a familiar, comforting presence. His sister leaned down and gave him a kiss on the cheek.

Kezabeth sighed and kissed his cheek again. "Would you mind if I stayed here tonight? I'd like to be here if you need me. The girls are with Mom and Dad still. I promise not to interfere with your sex life."

Caleb shuddered and shot her a dirty look. "I don't care if you stay, but don't ever say 'sex life' to me again." He shuddered again and shut his eyes. "Thank you for staying and for trying to help me."

"You're welcome, Caleb. You're going to be fine, just fine." She patted his shoulder then wandered into another room. Caleb thought about what she'd said and about the words printed on the business card. It would be nice if Kezabeth was right, but God, he was so afraid to hope anymore.

Chapter Thirteen

Banging on the door woke Caleb. He sat up slowly, relieved not to feel the awful throbbing anymore. He glanced at his watch. *Two-thirty a.m.* His heart seemed to skip a beat until he realized Jesse never banged on the door.

"Kez, wait!" Caleb pushed off the couch and stumbled over to the door, grabbing her hand before she could work through the locks. Loopy danced and yipped with agitation — that was not his happy bark. "That's not Jesse."

"Then who — ?" Kezabeth tried to push him aside, but Caleb planted his feet and looked through the tiny hole. A shiver crawled down his spine. The man wore a uniform like Jesse's, but he gave Caleb the creeps.

"I don't know who it is, and I'm not sure I want to find out," he whispered in his sister's ear, then peeked at the man again. Kezabeth nudged him aside and looked through the peephole. Caleb scooped Loopy up before he tripped somebody. "Hush, Loopy, calm down."

"He doesn't look very friendly." She didn't bother to keep her voice down. Kezabeth looked again and frowned at Caleb. "Maybe you should let me answer the door."

Caleb started to tremble. Opening the door to Jesse a few weeks ago had been hard enough, and Caleb had been drooling over the man for weeks. This other man, though, he was unknown.

Caleb experienced an almost suffocating sense of panic. He nodded to his sister, feeling like a complete wuss, and went back to sit on the couch where he would be out of the stranger's view once the door was open. Loopy settled beside him only long enough for Caleb to relax his grip then the poodle was off the couch and skittering back to the door, barking like mad. Caleb let Loopy have his way. There was no reason to disabuse the dog of the notion he was a Rottweiler.

Kezabeth mouthed, "It will be fine," before she unlocked the deadbolts. Caleb started to stretch out on the couch, but fear kept him upright and ready to spring. Where or why he'd need to jump up and run was beyond him, but when he got like this, logic ceased to matter.

The last lock slid free. Kezabeth opened the door wide enough to peer out. Loopy thrust his head out and stopped barking, his body stilling as he began to growl.

"Can I help you, Officer?" Kezabeth reached down and scooped Loopy into her arms. "Hush now, killer."

Caleb snickered at her syrupy-sweet voice. Anyone who knew his sister would have gone on alert at that tone. Even Loopy stopped growling.

"I wanted to stop by and introduce myself. Make sure everything was all right. I'm Officer Pat Monroe."

Caleb cringed at the nasally voice. He noticed the stiffening of Kezabeth's back and shoulders.

Apparently she didn't have a good feeling about the man either. Maybe next time Loopy went on canine alert, they should just refuse to answer the door.

"So you stop by at two-thirty in the morning to say hi?" Sarcasm dripped from her voice.

Caleb would have laughed, except he was fairly certain Kez would be getting pulled over and ticketed by this particular cop any time he saw her behind the wheel from now on.

"The lights were on, ma'am."

That asshole sounds angry. Caleb found himself torn between trying to shrink into the couch cushions and getting up to slam the door in Officer Pat Monroe's face.

"The lights were on because I suffer from insomnia, not because I'm expecting guests." Kezabeth opened the door a little wider and leaned out, pointing at the sign. "I prefer not to be disturbed."

"You know, some people would be a lot nicer to a police officer who knocked on their door, no matter what time it was." There was no mistaking the venom in the man's voice — all pretense of friendliness was gone. "*Some* people might think it was a mistake to be so fucking rude to a cop."

That got Caleb off the couch and to the door. He pulled Kezabeth out of the doorway and faced the man. "Put Loopy in the back, please." The dog was growling again. Soon he'd be pawing at Kezabeth's arms. Caleb waited until Kez was out of the living room before glaring at the asshole on his porch.

"Why are you here?" Caleb locked his knees to keep from them trembling as he studied the man. This was one face he didn't think he should forget, or trust. He wouldn't have thought it possible, but the officer's lips pinched even tighter. *Man, this is one unattractive dude.*

Caleb felt an absurd urge to giggle and clamped his jaw down firmly.

"I told that woman why I was here. What other reason would I have?" The man swept Caleb with a beady-eyed glance.

"Something other than the bullshit you're feeding us." It made no sense whatsoever for a cop to bang on his door in the middle of the night unless something was wrong. "How stupid do you think we are?" Caleb narrowed his eyes at Monroe. "Maybe a call to the chief of police would clarify whether this type of behavior is normal."

The hatred in the police officer's eyes made Caleb's stomach churn. Monroe looked like he was more than capable of violence. The fact that he would like to inflict some on Caleb seemed obvious, and this time he couldn't hide the fine trembling that started in his fingers and spread throughout his body.

Caleb also couldn't stop himself from flinching when Monroe leaned in.

"I wouldn't do that if I were you, pretty boy. Bad things might happen to you and that pretty lady behind you." Monroe's gaze flicked over Caleb's shoulder, which was all the warning he got before his sister lost her temper.

"That's enough!" Kezabeth grabbed Caleb's arm and jerked him aside. She stepped up to Monroe and pointed her finger. "We are not some naïve newcomers who can be intimidated or bullied by some…some small-town newbie cop with a chip on his shoulder!"

"H-how did you — ?" Monroe turned a brilliant shade of red as he sputtered.

Caleb watched in morbid fascination as his sister bent closer to a surprised Monroe. "*You* don't know who you're messing with, Officer Monroe. My husband is a *detective*, a very *respected* detective. I've seen guys like you come and go. And believe me, you *will* go. *Now!*"

Caleb didn't think he had ever seen anyone so angry.

Monroe glared over Kezabeth's shoulder, straight at him. Caleb held his stare until Monroe glanced at Jesse's place. Then the obnoxious police officer faced Caleb once again.

A smile that scared the hell out of Caleb spread on the officer's thin lips. Monroe raised an eyebrow and nodded, the smile turning into an evil-looking smirk before he turned and walked back to his cruiser.

Kezabeth and Caleb watched until he drove away.

"That man is a complete and utter asshole." Kezabeth slammed the deadbolts in place. "You need to tell Jesse."

"No!" Caleb grabbed Kezabeth and spun her around. "No. That cop, he knows somehow." Caleb shook his head. "No, that's not possible. He can't know, but he suspects, and this is a small town, as Jesse pointed out to me." He hadn't given it much thought before, but now he wondered if Jesse had meant *he* didn't want people to know he was seeing Caleb. It had sounded like Jesse was concerned about the repercussions for Caleb's sake, but what if Caleb had misunderstood?

And if he cared about Jesse, then Caleb knew what he had to do.

"Oh no. I do *not* like that look at all." Kezabeth slid an arm around his waist. "Whatever it is you're thinking, unthink it, because it sure doesn't make you happy."

"Kez."

"Caleb." Kezabeth steered them into the kitchen. "Sit down and eat. Think it over. Don't do something you'll regret. And don't go making decisions for Jesse. He can decide for himself what risks he's willing to take."

Sure, that was true, but Caleb didn't want Jesse to have to take *any* risks, not because of him. And how was he supposed to eat?

Caleb's eyebrows shot up as he looked at the meal his sister had prepared. How the hell had he slept through all this? Homemade enchiladas covered in a thick layer of cheese. *Yum.* There were beans, rice, nacho chips and queso. And she'd made more than enough. Caleb spotted the dinner plates. Yup, there were three, as well as three sets of silverware and three glasses.

"I don't think Jesse's stopping by tonight anyway." Caleb pulled out a chair for his sister, then sat down when she did.

"Yes, he will," she argued. "He said he'd be by after work." She dished up enchiladas, unaware Caleb's mouth had dropped open. She looked up at him and grinned as she slid the enchiladas onto his plate. "What?"

Caleb tightened his hands on the arms of his chair. "When did you talk to Jesse? Why didn't you tell me this earlier? And why didn't you wake me up?"

"I didn't talk to him. I texted him, which is why I didn't wake you." Kezabeth put a scoop of rice on his plate and reached for the beans. "I thought he should know you were incapacitated for a few hours."

Caleb groaned and rubbed at his forehead. "When did all this occur?"

Kezabeth shrugged and moved the bowl of queso and the bowl of nacho chips between them so they could share. "About five minutes before Officer Asshole appeared at your door. I really didn't think telling you I'd texted Jesse in front of that jerk was a good idea." She gestured to the extra plate. "But obviously, I expected him for this meal. That's another reason why I texted him too. He replied that he wouldn't be by to eat with us, but he'd definitely be here after his shift ended."

"Why in the world did you think Jesse needed to know I had a migraine, for Christ's sake?" He cut into his enchiladas, then stopped. "You do realize I'm a man? That being gay doesn't make me effeminate?"

Kezabeth looked up from her plate and scrunched her eyebrows. "What are you talking about? Of course I know you're a man! Jeez! And you're really not effeminate, so what are you babbling about?"

Caleb scowled. "What do you mean, *I'm not really effeminate*? I'm not effeminate at all! Men don't go whining to their lovers that they have a headache! It's just... Kez, we've only fucked—um." *Shit!* Caleb blushed and shoved a forkful of food in his mouth as Kezabeth squealed with laughter. Maybe he should keep his mouth full so he couldn't say anything else humiliating.

"Jeez, Caleb, you're priceless, you know that?" Kezabeth swiped at her eyes and shook her head. "I kinda figured you and Jesse had already done that particular deed."

Caleb nearly choked on his food, which sent Kezabeth into another round of laughter. Caleb glared at her and tapped his fork on his plate. "What is it with you and my sex life?"

Kezabeth's eyes widened. "I didn't ask about your sex life! All I said was I'd figured y'all had already bumped uglies."

"I know what you said." Caleb pointed his fork at her. "I just don't know why you said it."

"Why are you so embarrassed? It's not like I want details, because believe me, I don't. Not any more than you'd want details about my sex life." Kezabeth looked away, blinking away the tears.

Shit! He hadn't meant for her to get upset. Caleb was well aware that bringing up Remy would upset Kezabeth. He truly believed they loved each other and would find a way to work out their issues. If they didn't, it might shake his whole belief in love, because he'd never seen anyone else, other than his parents, who seemed so devoted and in love. At least, that was how Kez and Remy had been before the shooting.

Caleb reached for Kezabeth's hand. "Kez, do you want to talk about what's going on with Remy?"

Kezabeth sniffled and shook her head. "I can't. Not right now, okay?"

He patted his sister's hand and studied her closely, wondering how he hadn't noticed before that she was hanging on by a thread. Caleb forgot about his irritation with her — it seemed downright petty when she was only trying to help and, now that he was looking for it, when she was clearly suffering a great deal.

"It's fine, but if you ever do need to talk about it, let me know." Caleb patted her hand one last time when Kezabeth agreed and appeared ready to move away from the subject. He'd make sure he gave her something guaranteed to distract her.

"So." Caleb shifted slightly in his seat, not entirely comfortable with turning to his sister for advice, but willing to brave nearly any topic to keep her from tumbling into a funk. "Why don't you tell me what you think I should do about Officer Asshole and my lover?"

Kezabeth's eyes gleamed and she leaned forward, elbows on the table and chin propped on her hands. "Well, first off you need to at least *try* to get some help. Then you need to have a little faith in Jesse, don't you think?"

Caleb wondered if Kezabeth had any idea how much it scared him to take the step to get help. Her other suggestion was much easier. Caleb had more than a little faith in Jesse.

"I don't want anything to happen to him because of me, Kez."

Kezabeth shifted closer and drilled him with an intense stare. "Shouldn't it be his choice what he's willing to risk? You don't have the right to decide that for him, do you? I mean, I understand not wanting Jesse to be hurt, but there are different kinds of pain, and if you push him away on the pretext of keeping him safe, how much pain are you causing him then?"

Caleb sighed and rubbed at his forehead. "I know. You're right as usual. Try not to be all smug about it if possible."

Kezabeth's arms came around his shoulders, and her forehead rested against his temple. "I won't, I promise. Will you at least give Dr. Gregg a chance too?"

"Yeah," Caleb said, dread and hope both welling inside him. "I think I can do that."

It was a long while later before Kezabeth went to sleep, and he could sit on the couch and think. And worry. And wonder. The white business card lay on the coffee table. He picked it up, studying the web address.

"Well, why the hell not now?" He read the card again, this time tracing each line with his fingertip.

Dr. Justin Gregg, DO, LPC
Member of APA
Most Insurances Accepted for Online Therapy &
Psychiatric Services

A website, fax, phone number and email address were also listed. Caleb didn't think it would make a damned bit of difference, but who knew? He'd been wrong before, and it had nearly gotten him killed. If he was wrong to try this, it wouldn't cost more than a few hours and okay, possibly several hundred dollars. He could afford it, and maybe it would help, but for now he decided to hold off on telling Jesse about it. Better to wait and see the results first.

Caleb hurried to the office. If he hesitated much longer, he would talk himself out of even giving it a shot. He had his laptop powered up and Dr. Gregg's website open within minutes. The site itself was done in what Caleb could only assume were supposed to be soothing shades of blue, nothing dark. Was that some psychological tool, to present a subject that might be intimidating in a calm, peaceful manner? If he clicked on a link, would chirping birds and unicorns appear?

Caleb snorted and reined in his sarcastic thoughts. The idea of getting psychological help was scary, that was why he was being so snarky about it. He also knew it wouldn't help him at all if he didn't adjust his attitude. Two deep breaths helped to center himself and calm his mind.

"Let's see." Caleb scrolled over the links, then clicked the one about online therapy. After reading carefully, he clicked the link that listed the types of sessions available. He didn't think email sessions would cut it, but IMs might. The prices were listed also. The more sessions he ordered, the cheaper they were. Knowing what a mess he was, Caleb selected the largest package, which was twenty, one-hour long video chat sessions for just over two thousand bucks. He dug his wallet out of his back pocket and entered in his credit card information.

"That's done," he muttered. "What's next?"

Next was another link, this one to a form Dr. Gregg requested be filled out and emailed to him with a request for appointment times. Caleb clicked and blinked at the number of questions. The form was broken up into sections, each with numerous boxes to be checked or ignored.

"It's a freaking psych evaluation." Caleb realized there would be a lot of checked boxes and very few unmarked ones, except in the part that asked about addictive substances and self-injury. Those would all be blank. There were several under the categories of depression and anxiety that he'd need to check if he was going to be honest.

Fuck it. It's already paid for. Caleb dutifully checked all the boxes that applied. He attached the form to the email he would send Dr. Gregg, then wrote a short introduction in the body of the email. Next he gave a bare-bones accounting of what had happened to him. Doing so rattled him, and he blinked past a wave of dizziness. For a moment, Caleb considered just giving up.

"No." He forced himself to finish with a few of the changes brought on since he'd been hurt. It wasn't complete by any means, but it was the best he could do right now.

Something had lifted inside him — some oppressive weight was shifting, and he wanted out from under it. He wanted to have a normal life, to be able to go not only outside, but anywhere without feeling like he would shatter into a million inconsequential pieces. He wanted to live without the constant fear that had been his companion and tormentor for months. He didn't want his sister to have to open his door for him because he was too terrified of a stranger on the other side. If doing this Internet-therapy thing would get him there, then he would do it. Fuck his pride — that hadn't been any help anyway.

Chapter Fourteen

Jesse stood on Caleb's dark porch. There were no lights on inside either. Should he knock, or was Caleb sending him a message? Or was he still asleep and Kezabeth had turned off all the lights when she went to bed? It wasn't like he could go home and wait for Caleb to come over. All he wanted to do was make sure his lover was okay, and yeah, maybe he wouldn't mind holding him for a while, falling asleep with that thin body pressed against him.

"Damn it!" Jesse tapped his foot, considering his options. The obnoxious sign was askew. He reached out to right it. Why did he bother? He hated that sign. Still, he straightened it. Maybe he'd just knock gently on the door, see if anyone answered.

Movement at the window to his left caught his attention, the blinds twitching as though someone pushed them aside to look out. Jesse tapped on the door and breathed a sigh of relief when Loopy's excited yips sounded behind the heavy panel. Deadbolts flicked open. He counted those sounds, and when the last one clicked, Jesse waited for the knob to turn. When it didn't, he hovered between uncertainty and impatience. Impatience won out.

Leaning against the door, Jesse knocked again. "Caleb? It—"

The door swung open so fast that Jesse had to scramble to keep from pitching forward. Caleb placed a steadying hand on his chest as Jesse grabbed the door frame. His other hand cradled the excited poodle.

"Sorry." Caleb's voice quivered. "I didn't know you were leaning against the door."

Jesse felt the soft touch from Caleb's hand on his chest all the way to his cock, which had become uncomfortably hard. "It's okay, baby." He wondered if the worried look on Caleb's face was really there—it was hard to tell with only the light coming from a streetlight.

"Are you going to let me in?" He reached for Caleb's hand, which was still rubbing small circles on his chest. Jesse tugged until Caleb was cupping his erection, unable to stop himself from grinding against Caleb's hand when he squeezed Jesse's dick through his pants.

Caleb set Loopy down, smiling as the dog barked and spun in a circle before bounding down the hall. Once the poodle was gone, Caleb leaned forward to lick a line from Jesse's collarbone to just under his jaw.

Jesse stepped inside, then locked the door. He spun on his heel, moving forward quickly and forcing Caleb to back up. A startled gasp left Caleb's lips when Jesse reached out and slid his hands under Caleb's arms and lifted him. Jesse pushed Caleb against the wall, holding him up first with his hands, then by pressing his chest against Caleb's.

"Put your hands on my shoulders and your legs around my waist."

As soon as Caleb complied, Jesse filled his hands with Caleb's ass, grinding their cocks together as he sighed and did what he'd been dreaming of since leaving hours ago. Jesse slanted his mouth over Caleb's, taking advantage of his parted lips.

He kissed Caleb with every bit of need and frustration that had been building inside him, spearing his tongue into the warm recess of his mouth. Jesse knew the kiss was bordering on brutal, but there had been a quiver in Caleb's voice when he'd opened the door, and the desire to know why that was so tugged at him, stirring up something he hadn't felt before. When he realized it was the need to claim and dominate, Jesse nearly lifted his lips from Caleb's in surprise. Since when had he become some wannabe Dom?

Since you felt Caleb's hesitation when he opened the door. Since the quiver in his voice made you think he might be reconsidering having anything to do with you. Fuck.

Jesse gentled the kiss, even though Caleb hadn't protested—had, indeed, been moaning into Jesse's mouth while he'd nipped, licked and owned Caleb's mouth.

But apparently his lover wasn't having any of the gentler treatment. He bit Jesse's bottom lip hard enough that Jesse's eyes shot open in surprise. Caleb's hands tightened on his shoulders. His fingers dug in deep enough to make bruises. Caleb squeezed his legs around Jesse, mashing their cocks together as Caleb wriggled his hips, squirming as he tried to get the friction he needed.

Something inside Jesse exploded in a burst of blinding need. He locked his arms around Caleb and stepped away from the wall, making his way to Caleb's office through the darkened house. It was a wonder he managed not to trip and kill them both, but need and determination guided him as surely as a light would have.

Jesse took one hand off his lover just long enough to open the door and turn the light on. Jesse ignored Caleb's grumbling and kicked the door shut, blinking as his eyes adjusted to the sudden brightness. Jesse cupped the back of Caleb's head and took his mouth again, sucking that plump lower lip before sweeping his tongue across the roof of Caleb's mouth. Jesse swallowed Caleb's desperate-sounding whimper and continued to plunder until Caleb was begging with his body and his words for more.

"What do you want?" Jesse tipped his head back and looked at Caleb's lust-flushed cheeks and kiss-swollen lips. Those two things, along with the way Caleb's eyelids seemed too heavy for the man to keep open, were doing all sorts of things to Jesse's cock and balls. He *wanted* so strongly that he felt a surge of fear, uncertain if he could control himself enough to make sure Caleb was ready for him. Then Caleb's eyes snapped open, and the smile that stretched over his wide mouth made Jesse's cock pulse and leak pre-cum.

"I want you to fuck me, hard and fast." Caleb nipped at Jesse's chin and ground his erection against Jesse's. "I want you to fuck me with all that angry desperation you were kissing me with before it scared you. I want— Oomph!"

God, Caleb didn't think he'd ever been so turned on. He really liked this side of Jesse, and could only assume he knew what had triggered it. Somehow Jesse must have picked up on the fact that he'd been considering breaking things off. Caleb grunted when his world tipped and his back was pressed onto the desk. Jesse tugged at Caleb's ankles, and Caleb dropped his legs from around Jesse's waist.

"Get your clothes off, baby." Jesse's voice was low and gravelly, sending a jolt through Caleb and he clenched his ass in anticipation. "This is going to be a fast, hard fuck."

"Yes, please." Caleb would have cringed at the neediness in his voice, but he was too far gone to care. He pulled his shirt off, then unfastened his jeans. Caleb lifted his hips and was shoving his pants down when Jesse grabbed two fistfuls of the denim and yanked.

There was a soft *thud* as Jesse tossed Caleb's jeans over his shoulder, then Jesse was grabbing his hips. Caleb was tugged forward until his ass was nearly hanging off the edge of the desk. He started to prop himself up on his elbows, but Jesse placed one big hand on his chest and pushed him back down.

Caleb closed his eyes and locked his fingers behind the back of his head to cushion it against the hard surface. Jesse spread Caleb's ass cheeks and licked the length of his crease. Caleb's eyes flew open and his head smacked the desk as he flung his hands out to claw at the desktop. "Fuck! Fuck, Jesse," Caleb moaned while Jesse's tongue swirled and prodded, but when Jesse scraped his teeth over the wrinkled skin, Caleb yelled and arched his back. He ground his tailbone as he tried to get more of what Jesse was giving him. Jesse clamped a hand on Caleb's hip, pinning him in place, and he went back to nibbling and tonguing Caleb's hole.

Caleb felt a slight burn as Jesse worked a finger inside him then Jesse's tongue licked into him as well. Some distant part of him realized he was babbling, spewing incoherent words and sounds he'd rather not be making. Then another finger was pushed inside him, stretching and burning, until Jesse moved his fingers and tapped Caleb's gland. Pleasure speared through him and his brain shut off. He didn't know what he said or if he said anything at all—the only thing he was aware of was Jesse.

His balls drew up tight as his cock pulsed, the tingling in the base of his spine spreading out to the tips of his toes and fingers. Suddenly, confusingly, he was empty, Jesse's fingers and sinful mouth gone. Caleb almost protested, until he heard the crinkling noise of a condom wrapper being torn open. That sound had him clenching in anticipation of the coming invasion. A *snap* of a cap had Caleb pushing up on an elbow to find Jesse squeezing a tube of lube. He couldn't help but arch an eyebrow in question.

Dark slashes bloomed on Jesse's cheeks as he smiled sheepishly and shrugged. "Thought about fucking you in your office, on this desk, all damned day. Didn't want to have to detour to the bedroom for the stuff."

"Oh…" *That was…thoughtful?* Caleb wasn't sure what it was, but it made his dick achingly hard and filled him with a warmth he didn't want to examine too closely. He looked into Jesse's molten brown eyes, and that warmth spiked to a five-alarm fire of desire. Jesse never broke eye contact as he lubed his cock and spread some of the thick liquid around Caleb's opening. Caleb moaned when Jesse's lube-slicked fingers pressed into him, pushing the lube into his passage to ease the way. Then Jesse grabbed Caleb's legs and set them on his shoulders.

The tip of Jesse's dick sought entrance into his clamping ring, and with a muttered curse, he was pressing into Caleb. Jesse locked his arms around Caleb's thighs and steadily drove his cock deep into Caleb's ass. He didn't stop until his balls slapped against Caleb and the rough denim of his jeans rubbed over Caleb's skin.

Caleb's vision cleared, and when he saw Jesse's face, a shiver racked his body.

"You're so fucking sexy," Caleb thought he managed to say.

Jesse gave him a cocky smile. "And you've got the tightest, sweetest ass." Caleb barely processed what he said before Jesse pulled his dick almost all the way out. "Grab the edge of the desk, baby, so I can fuck you like you want me to."

Caleb's fingers obeyed right before Jesse moaned and pounded into him. He'd wanted all that angry desperation, and Jesse was giving it to him. Jesse lifted Caleb's hips and his next thrust brought Jesse's shaft into direct contact with his prostate. His vision dimmed as colors exploded behind his eyes. A keening sound filled the small room as Jesse slammed into him again and again, stroking over his gland with each powerful thrust.

"Come on, baby. Gonna come soon. Can't last." Jesse's words were spoken between gasps and grunts as he reamed Caleb's passage. Those sounds were the spark that ignited his orgasm. Caleb's entire body jerked and his cock throbbed. The first jet of cum hit his chest and a roar filled the room as Jesse's fingers dug into his thighs. The roar that was ripped from his lover had Caleb's balls pulling tighter as another burst of seed shot from his dick. Wet heat splattered onto Caleb's chin and chest as Jesse's dick swelled inside him.

Another yell was torn from Jesse as he ground against Caleb's ass. Caleb's cock spurted more strings of cum as Jesse's climax shook him. His blurry gaze locked with Jesse's, and Caleb wanted to blink so he could see his lover clearly, but he couldn't bring himself to do so, to break the connection thrumming between them even for a split second.

Jesse let go of Caleb's legs, pushing them down so he could kiss Caleb, slowly and languorously. Caleb had to close his eyes then, unable to focus on Jesse without them crossing. He was glad he'd closed them when he felt them prickle with tears. Jesse was cherishing him with his lips and tongue, stroking and moaning as he made love to his mouth. Caleb felt like a wuss thinking such a thing, but he didn't know how else to describe it. Nobody had ever taken the time to kiss him like they cared. And the fact that he was kissing his lover back in the same manner was not lost on him at all.

Jesse made himself end the kiss, afraid if he didn't do so, they might still be on this desk in eight hours, lips sealed to one another because it felt that good, that right.

Christ, what's happening? Jesse wasn't sure, and it scared him, but not nearly enough to consider walking away from this man. He stood up and captured Caleb's hands with his. Then Jesse just stared, because Caleb sprawled out on that desk coated with his own spunk and looking thoroughly fucked was erotic as hell.

Tugging, he pulled Caleb up and held his hands until he was sure Caleb was steady on his feet. The drowsy, sated look in Caleb's vibrant green gaze made Jesse feel smug, even as he realized he was probably wearing the same look. He watched as a particularly large glob of cum slowly slipped down Caleb's chest. *I'd love to follow that trail of spunk, to taste –*

Caleb moaned and leaned toward him, and Jesse realized he'd spoken the words out loud. A chunk of white on Caleb's chin caught Jesse's eye, and his mouth watered. Would one small taste hurt? He started to bend forward.

Caleb swiped at the cum, rubbing it off and shaking his head. "No, Jesse. I'm clean, but you shouldn't just take my word for it." Caleb smiled and brushed the pad of his thumb over Jesse's bottom lip. "I wish…" Caleb averted his gaze, bending to grab his shirt off the floor before wiping the cool spunk from his skin. Jesse watched as color bloomed on his lover's cheeks.

"You wish what?" Jesse couldn't stop himself—he had to reach out and touch one of those ruddy stripes on Caleb's cheek. The feel of his lover's skin under his fingertips did funny things to Jesse's heart and wondrous things to his formerly spent dick. "Tell me, baby."

Caleb shrugged, and the color on his cheeks darkened, but he gave Jesse a direct look. "I guess I wish we could take each other's word for it. That's stupid, and I know better. But I don't think you'd lie to me." Caleb shook his head, his gaze boring into Jesse's. "No, I *know* you wouldn't lie to me." Caleb stepped back, a worried look chasing away the pretty blush Jesse found so fascinating. "How can I know that, Jesse? How can I believe it when we've only known each other for such a short time? Maybe I really *am* crazy."

"No." Jesse closed the distance Caleb had tried to put between them, taking his lover in his arms and holding him. He didn't like Caleb pulling away like that. He'd learned that the second the man did it. Jesse rubbed Caleb's back, aching for his lover and unsure of why he did so. "You're no crazier than I am, because I feel the same way, baby. I think we connected before we even spoke."

Jesse leaned his head back far enough so he could look at Caleb. "Didn't you see me blistering my ass on those steps every day, six days a week for over four weeks?" A memory niggled at him and he couldn't help but tease his lover a bit. "And how about that sign you put up right after I tried to come over and introduce myself? Caleb, I sat out there in the heat with an uncomfortable hard-on that never seemed to quit, just so I could get a glimpse of you."

Caleb looked stunned, his green eyes wide as one trembling hand reached up to skim up Jesse's arm. "You were sitting out there to watch me? And not because you thought I was weird?"

Jesse noticed Caleb hadn't addressed the sign, but he let it drop. It didn't matter—he had his man now, snotty sign or no.

"Sweetheart, you've fascinated me from the moment I saw you." Jesse was not, however, telling his lover he'd kind of resembled an old man when Jesse had first seen him. "And this"—Jesse brought one hand up and buried it in Caleb's auburn hair—"God, baby. When the sun hits this gorgeous hair, it's incredible with all the reds and golds that appear like magic. Don't you have any idea how fucking hot you are?"

Caleb snorted and rolled his eyes. He then looked totally mortified. "Oh shit. Did I just roll my eyes? I did, didn't I? Ugh! Kez is rubbing off on me!" A brilliant smile played over Caleb's mouth as he gave Jesse a sultry look. "You were really there to watch me? What do you think I was doing under the cover of those sunglasses? Do you know what a strain it was on my poor eyeballs to keep my head tipped down? I probably damaged something. And you're the fucking hot one— I'm the messed-up, scrawny one."

"Didn't I tell you I'd bend you over my knee if you kept dogging yourself?" A vision of Caleb's ass sporting pinkened handprints was all too appealing, until Jesse remembered how Caleb had looked when he'd first moved in. Busted and bruised, beaten to hell. He felt like a total shit for making the threat now.

"Hey, don't." Caleb cupped Jesse's jaw and pressed his erection against Jesse's thigh. "You wouldn't hurt me, and what you've threatened to do obviously doesn't scare me. On the contrary." Caleb thrust and rubbed his cock harder against Jesse. "It makes me horny as hell, which means I'm going to have to keep trash-talking myself until I can convince you to follow through on your promise." Caleb moaned softly as he continued moving his hips. "I mean, your threat."

Jesse groaned and gripped Caleb's hips, stopping him from thrusting again. Fuck, Jesse couldn't think when he did that! He rested his chin on the top of Caleb's head and closed his eyes. "I don't think I can do it, baby. No matter how pretty your ass would look covered with my handprints."

A shudder rippled through Caleb, and damned if Jesse didn't feel Caleb's dick jerk. *Fuck.* Maybe he could do it, eventually. "At least not yet."

"I think I understand." Caleb's voice was muffled as his face pressed into Jesse's chest.

"You do?" Maybe Caleb could explain it, then, because Jesse wasn't quite sure why he couldn't spank Caleb when they both seemed to want it.

"Yeah." Caleb pushed at Jesse, signaling that he wanted to move.

Jesse reluctantly let the man go and grinned when Caleb reached for his hand. "Let's get dressed. I'll feed you, since Kezabeth made enough dinner for an army." Caleb flicked a glance at Jesse before releasing his hand. "Then I'll tell you what happened to me and why I'm so fucked up."

Steeling himself for whatever Caleb was going to tell him wouldn't do any good, Jesse realized as his stomach churned. He'd wanted to know, or at least *thought* he wanted to know about both things. No, he needed to know, if he wanted a relationship with Caleb. Jesse just prayed he was strong enough to hear what his lover had to say.

Chapter Fifteen

He could do this, Caleb thought as he cleared away the dirty dishes. He bent over to load the dishwasher and nearly moaned at the memory of the fucking Jesse had given him earlier. Caleb wanted to feel Jesse for days, but even more he wanted Jesse inside him every day, and wanted to be inside Jesse as often as they both could manage it. He paused before turning to face Jesse, wondering when he had become such a slut. *Seriously*.

In fact, it had been well over a year since he'd been with anyone. He'd coped just fine until he was hurt. Then there'd been nothing going on down below the belt. Now it seemed all he wanted to do was fuck. He was a slut. No, that wasn't right either, because he couldn't think of anyone he wanted to fuck, or be fucked by, other than the man waiting for him to start talking. Steeling himself to do that very thing, Caleb faced Jesse.

Seeing Jesse's concern brought out the sudden need to feel the man's arms around him. Caleb walked over and placed his hand on one of Jesse's broad shoulders. He wondered about all the things he thought he saw in

Jesse's warm gaze. Jesse cared for him, he had no doubt. How much, Caleb didn't know. He was torn between wanting to find out and being too afraid. What if he was just someone Jesse wanted to save or, worse, someone Jesse felt sorry for?

"Stop it." Caleb heard the words, realized he'd muttered them out loud. "Well, shit! Now I'm censoring my attempts to make myself feel like crap. You should be happy."

Jesse smiled and slid his arm around Caleb's waist. "I am, baby." Jesse stood and kept his arm around Caleb. "Would it be okay if I held you while you talk?"

How in the hell had Jesse known Caleb needed that? He was going to ask, but when he looked into Jesse's eyes, Caleb had an epiphany — he wasn't the only one who needed comfort to get through this.

"I'd like that, very much. I was planning on asking you the same thing."

They paused outside the guest room long enough for Caleb to open the door so Loopy could hop in bed with Kezabeth then Caleb led Jesse to his bedroom. He tossed back the covers and proceeded to strip, glancing over and grinning when he caught Jesse watching.

"I want to be comfortable." Caleb cupped his semierect shaft and winked at Jesse, enjoying teasing his man.

Jesse stripped his clothes off and fisted his erection, arching an eyebrow at Caleb as he did so. "I'm not sure how comfortable *this* is going to be." Jesse shook his dick a couple of times.

"It was pretty damn comfortable riding it." Caleb squeaked and dove for the bed as Jesse lunged at him. He expected to be caught. Why hadn't he been caught? Because Jesse was standing at the foot of the bed, studying him. "What?"

"Are you stalling? You don't have to talk about what happened before you moved here if you're not ready." A muscle ticked in Jesse's jaw. "But I do want to know what the problem was when I showed up earlier."

"I'm not stalling." Caleb stopped and gave it some thought. Had he been stalling? *No.* Well, okay, maybe, but he hadn't meant to. "I'm sorry. I do want to tell you, it's just that at the same time I don't want to talk about it. Crazy, huh?"

What was he going to do, draw pictures? How stupid was that? Besides, he totally sucked at drawing. Caleb patted the bed. "Lay down by me and hold me like you said you wanted to. I think maybe I… Um." Caleb cleared his throat and smiled, though he could feel it wobbling, so it couldn't have been very attractive. "I'm more nervous about this than I thought."

"Ah, baby, come here." Jesse sat on the bed and pulled Caleb onto his lap. Jesse wiggled and scooted until he had his back against the headboard then he pressed Caleb's head to his shoulder, burying his fingers in Caleb's hair. Jesse's other arm was locked tight around him.

A sense of security flooded Caleb, and he would have wept with relief except for the fact that it was so good to feel safe like this—it seemed he'd been scared for his whole life. Caleb knew his life before the attack hadn't been the fear-filled experience it was now, yet the fear that had become so much a part of him those months ago when he had nearly died colored everything in his past just as surely as it affected almost everything in the present.

Caleb had already taken one step to prevent that traumatic day from controlling his future. As the steady beat of Jesse's heart thudded beneath his hand, Caleb felt the sudden surety that this step was every bit as important as the first, maybe even more so because of the man who held him in his arms.

"Are you sure you want to do this?" Jesse's breath ruffled his hair as soft kisses were placed on the top of his head.

Caleb was damned sure he was tired of being frightened. He wanted to get better. He didn't want to have any more meltdowns that left him a shaking, sobbing mess. And he was sure he owed Jesse an explanation. He was afraid, actually, that Jesse might just give up on him as being crazy unless Caleb could make him understand *why* he was the way he was.

Which would be hard, since Caleb didn't understand that himself. He took a deep breath and thought of where to begin. "I know you hadn't heard of Alexander Wyatt until earlier, but, ah, my books are really popular, sell very well." He wasn't bragging. It was just a fact. "Well enough that I had a nice home in a gated community. I thought that stupid gate made everything safe, kept the bad people out and the good people in." Caleb couldn't hold back a harsh laugh at his own stupidity or his erroneous judgment. As though a steel gate could divide good and evil.

"Hey, it's a natural thing to believe you're safe in your neighborhood when there's a gate and security. There was security, right?" Jesse stroked Caleb's back, helping him to remain grounded in the present instead of being pulled back into memories of that night.

"Yeah, there was, but security wouldn't hassle people who were known to live there."

Jesse tensed beneath him. He paused, stilling his hand for a brief moment before continuing to rub Caleb's back. "No, I guess they wouldn't."

"I had a habit of taking a walk when writer's block reared its ugly head. Not a big deal. It's something I've done hundreds of times, usually at night, since I'm a night owl. I know now how stupid that was, wandering around at night with my head lost in plot knots. Guess it's a miracle nothing had happened to me before then, really." Caleb couldn't suppress a shudder as he forced himself to continue. A sheen of sweat covered his body, despite the cool air in the bedroom.

"Hey." Jesse tipped Caleb's chin up and looked at him. No trace of pity shone in his eyes, for which Caleb was thankful. "You don't have to go on."

Caleb shook his head sharply. "Yes. I do. I can't *not* tell you."

He waited until Jesse nodded before continuing. "So, a few months ago, I was out walking like I'd done so many times before at my old place. I tended to get lost in my head on walks. It was one of the ways I worked past writer's block. Not always, but yeah, it could help. This was one of those nights. I had a nasty plot snarl and I'd finally figured out how to solve it. I was so relieved. I remember, I shook my head and realized I'd wandered right back to the house. My house, I mean. Not *right* back. I was actually across the street from it." He hated remembering it. "Then they were just there. Maybe they'd been following me. I don't know." Caleb couldn't hold back the shudders that rippled through him any more than he could slow the sudden pounding of his heart or ease the tightness in his chest.

He could see Jesse's lips moving but couldn't make out any words over the voices in his head. Caleb could hear the taunts, the threats, just as clearly as he had when it'd happened.

Ghost pains spread out over his body, muscle memory of fists and boots striking his flesh. He felt the sweaty hand clamped over his mouth and nose, cutting off his air, heard his screams as he was tackled to the ground and beaten. He fought against the arms holding him, his mind confusing the past and the present, but his struggles stopped when Jesse's voice filtered through the chaos, his breath as soft as his voice in Caleb's ear. Slowly, Caleb became aware of Jesse's hands sweeping over his back and arms.

"I've got you now. It's okay, Caleb. You're safe."

How many times Jesse had said those words, Caleb didn't know or care. All that mattered was that Jesse was there with him. He sucked in a stuttering breath as Jesse placed a sweet kiss on his lips. Caleb brought a hand up to cup the back of Jesse's neck and opened for the gentle sweep of Jesse's tongue. By the time the kiss ended, Caleb was calmer. The shudders slowed to sporadic shivers that were less demanding on his aching muscles.

"They wouldn't stop," Caleb forced out, needing to finish. "They just k-kept hi-hitting and ki-kicking."

"Caleb, you don't have to tell me. I think I know." Jesse brushed a kiss across Caleb's temple, his voice sounding as raw as Caleb felt.

"No, you have to understand." Caleb was determined to explain it, to tell Jesse why it was so hard for him to leave the house. "I k-kept looking, even when it felt like something broke inside me, when I felt bones break..." Caleb's voice hitched. "I was so close to my house, and all I could think was, *If I'd just stayed inside, behind that locked door, this never would have happened!*"

Jesse shifted and rolled to his side, nudging Caleb until he was stretched out and facing him. The compassion, the tenderness in Jesse's eyes, wrenched at Caleb's heart, threatening to bring forth the tears he'd managed to keep at bay. Caleb blinked until he forced the tears back—it was bad enough that he'd broken down in front of Jesse again. There was no way he'd let the man see him cry, not again.

"No matter how safe it might have been, I couldn't stay there in that house, couldn't look out the windows and see that spot where I'd almost died. I couldn't, especially when the police didn't have any leads—"

Anger washed over Jesse's features in a split second. "No leads? No one saw anything?"

"Not enough, or no one wanted to admit it." Caleb fought to keep his eyes open against the exhaustion and the lethargy that often followed the flashbacks. "Since I wasn't robbed, they figured it was some of the neighborhood kids. Bored rich kids. The police said it was planned, because they... They wore masks. Those creepy knit ski ones."

"Shit. Shit, Caleb, I'm sorry."

Caleb watched Jesse's eyes close, watched his lover get his emotions under control before he spoke again. "It isn't unheard of. Too many people think wealthy kids don't do shit like that. As if they're immune via money. Who's handling the case? Where did this happen?"

"Detectives Masterson and Benson, and my brother-in-law, Remy. He's a detective there and was riding the department in Albuquerque about the case."

Jesse's eyes snapped open, and he frowned. "Was? What do you mean he *was*?"

Caleb sighed and let his eyes drift shut. "Kezabeth's husband is on paid leave right now. Detective Remy Cortez?" He wondered if his words were really slurred or if he was too tired to hear them clearly.

"Oh shit. He's Kezabeth's husband?" Jesse sounded shocked.

Caleb cracked open an eye to glare at Jesse. "It wasn't his fault! The kid pointed a weapon at him and—"

Jesse cut off Caleb's heated defense of Remy.

"No, Caleb, I know. I do. There isn't a cop around who would blame him, but it's fucked up what the media is saying. And God, Kezabeth must be going through hell." Jesse shook his head. "I wish there was something I could do."

"You're doing a lot just by being here." He yawned, his jaw popping loud enough that he wondered it didn't come unhinged. "I have to sleep for a bit. I'll tell you about what happened this morning later on, or you can ask Kez. Will you stay with me until I fall asleep? Won't be long."

Jesse held him close, moving so his head rested on his shoulder. "Yeah, I can do that. I'd like to do that."

Chapter Sixteen

Jesse tried to sleep, but he was wound too tightly. Any time he let his eyes close for more than a few seconds, he relived the violent beating that had caused Caleb so much pain. Jesse finally had to slip out of bed, trying his best not to disturb Caleb.

He stood at the edge of the bed. Caleb looked so fragile with his delicate bone structure and his full lips slightly parted in sleep. Jesse thought about what it must have been like for him to lie there, hurt and scared, seeing his house so close, regretting ever leaving the safety of his home. It explained a lot.

Jesse carefully brushed the hair off Caleb's forehead. He heard a door shut down the hallway and turned to grab his pants—he wanted to speak to Kezabeth before she left.

Something had upset Caleb before he arrived and Jesse didn't want Caleb to have to tell him, not if Kezabeth could do it instead. Not after watching and listening as Caleb went through hell telling him about the assault. He wasn't sure his heart could take another round of watching his lover fall apart, not yet, at least.

Jesse fastened his pants and crossed over to the door. As quietly as he could, Jesse opened it, then he paused, twisting around and giving Caleb one last, lingering look. He was sleeping peacefully, and Jesse was grateful for that. He turned around and nearly ran into Kezabeth.

"Shit!" Jesse hissed before he thought and glanced back to make sure Caleb hadn't woken up. His heart raced. He was damned lucky he hadn't screeched like a sissy. Jesse cut his eyes at Kezabeth. "That wasn't nice."

Kezabeth slapped a hand over her mouth as she giggled. She gestured into the living room and waited for Jesse to precede her. "I know it wasn't nice, but it *was* funny," she whispered. "Besides, someone needed to pay for putting Loopy in my room. He kept hogging my pillow, which is fine, except he was pointing the wrong end at me."

Jesse felt his lips twitch. "So where is the little bouncing ball of fluff?"

Kezabeth gestured toward the back of the house. "He needed to go outside and annoy the neighbors like a good boy."

That brought a grin to both their faces. Jesse sat on the couch and was only moderately surprised when Kezabeth plopped down beside him instead of taking the chair. Then again, he couldn't look at that chair without thinking about Caleb.

"Hey!" Kezabeth snapped her fingers in front of his face. "Get your mind out of the gutter! I know that look." Kezabeth paused. "Y'all didn't, uh, you know. In that chair?"

"Why are you even asking? God!"

"Because you were looking at the chair with *that look*! I know *that look*, and I don't want to sit over there if it's been…compromised…" Kezabeth trailed off and Jesse wished she'd shut up earlier. He thought seriously about telling her no, but *something* had happened in that chair. Only the fact that Kezabeth would tease Caleb unmercifully kept him from spilling that secret.

"I'd like for something to happen in that chair." It was as close as he would come to admitting anything. Kezabeth was entirely too nosy at times. *Maybe someone should point that out to her.* "Do you tell people where you and your husband have sex? 'Cause I doubt you've always kept it in the bedroom."

Kezabeth was nearly fluorescent with embarrassment. "Okay, I get it! I was a bitch and I'm sorry."

"Not a bitch, just way too nosy." Jesse flashed her a smile to let her know he wasn't offended…anymore. "Some things should only be shared between lovers. Maybe you have a hard time seeing the line a sister shouldn't cross."

"Yeah, probably, but you're the first guy he's ever kept around." Kezabeth slapped her hand over her mouth as her eyes shot wide open. "Shit!" The word was muffled. She dropped her hand and shook her head. "I didn't say that. I didn't mean to. That's between you two."

Damn it, Jesse had jumped her about being nosy minutes before then she had to let loose with *that* interesting tidbit, and Jesse couldn't even pry! "You did that on purpose, didn't you?"

Kezabeth shook her head again. "No, I didn't. Maybe subconsciously. One of those Freudian slips? And I feel badly about it, believe it or not, so I will tell you this. You're the first guy who's known about Alexander Wyatt — about that side of Caleb. So that must mean something."

Jesse tried his best to keep his face blank and not let Kezabeth see how much her words warmed him. Kezabeth was a fountain of information, and there was no way Jesse wanted her spewing any of his information to anyone and everyone, even if it was done accidentally. He crossed his arms, wishing he'd taken the time to pull on his shirt. Jesse assumed his cop face probably wouldn't be as effective bare-chested.

It wasn't effective at all, as Kezabeth's laugh proved. "That doesn't work on me. I'm married to a detective." Her laughter died and she looked away, blinking rapidly. "Caleb tell you about that?"

Jesse uncrossed his arms and tugged on Kezabeth's wrist until she unfisted her hand. It felt awkward, but Jesse laced his fingers with hers and squeezed. He'd comforted men and women at crime scenes before, but he'd never gotten comfortable with it.

"Yeah, he did. I'm sorry, Kezabeth. It probably doesn't help, but he's got cops across the nation on his side."

Shrugging, she swiped at her eyes. "I don't know what helps right now, but thank you." Kezabeth straightened her shoulders and faced him fully. "So this Officer Asshole stopped by about two-thirty a.m. His name's Monroe."

Jesse felt his stomach drop and his temper spike hot, his already frayed nerves shredding even more. As he listened, he feared it would be impossible to get his anger down to even a simmer before he ran into Monroe again. He'd be hard-pressed not to beat the jackass into the ground.

The need to pound someone made his spine itch and his free hand clench. Monroe, the group of bastards who'd so savagely attacked his lover. His belief in the justice system was wavering, which, considering his profession, could be more than a little problematic.

"Did he say anything to imply he knew about…?" Jesse wasn't ashamed—he only wanted to be prepared. More importantly, he wanted to keep Caleb safe, but how to do that? Should he confront Monroe or ignore the son of a bitch? Or maybe have a talk with the chief?

The only thing he *was* sure of was that he wouldn't give up Caleb, not for Monroe, not for anyone—and not for his job, which answered a question he'd asked himself before.

"No, although Caleb seemed to feel Monroe was definitely implying that, you know." Kezabeth shrugged. "He also called Caleb *pretty boy*. I don't think that was meant as a compliment, more like an accusation. I guess I could have claimed you as my guy, except I mentioned being married to a detective."

Jesse was shaking his head before Kezabeth was finished. "No. I'm glad you didn't. I might not have ever let on at work that I'm gay, but I've never pretended to be straight. I'm cautious, but not willing to lie. I wouldn't do that to Caleb or myself, and I don't believe Caleb would want that either."

Kezabeth's brilliant smile was so much like her brother's that it threatened to steal Jesse's breath. "You're a good person, Jesse. A good man for my brother." She winked and patted his knee. "You might even be the *perfect* guy for him, in which case, I expect you to be around for a long time."

"That works out well, since I expect to be around for a long time too." And it didn't even cause a flutter of panic to admit it.

Caleb stood in the hallway, his heart in his throat. Any doubts about how serious the thing between him and Jesse was had been obliterated when he'd overheard Jesse's refusal to deny their relationship. A new fear stirred in him, one centered on Jesse and the repercussions he'd face when word of their relationship got out. And it would get out.

Monroe's accusatory gaze, his thinly veiled threats — as well as his overt ones — had made it clear the man suspected something was going on between Caleb and Jesse. For whatever reason, Caleb knew Monroe would use those suspicions to out Jesse.

The voices in the living room grew quiet as the conversation wound down. Caleb took a deep breath, then shuffled down the hall, letting his footsteps announce his impending arrival. Kezabeth and Jesse turned to look at him, his sister smiling brightly. Caleb barely noticed her, caught as he was by his lover's tender expression. He was faintly aware of Kezabeth rising. She moved out of his line of vision, probably heading into the kitchen, but he couldn't look away from Jesse.

Jesse's lips quirked up on one side, and he reached out to Caleb. "How much did you overhear?"

Caleb huffed a laugh and hurried to his lover, trembling when Jesse's much bigger hand enfolded his. "How much do you want me to admit to overhearing?" he countered as Jesse pulled him down onto the couch. Caleb settled with his head resting on Jesse's shoulder, one arm around his lover's waist and the other resting across his ridged stomach.

"I'd like to know what I need to repeat for you or if there's anything you think Kezabeth left out." Jesse wrapped his arms around Caleb.

"It sounded like she covered the sheer assholeness and malevolence that is Officer Monroe. She told you — I'm pretty sure — he suspects something."

Jesse's arms tightened around him in a quick, reassuring hug. "I've been walking with you to your mailbox and back for weeks now. It's not surprising someone noticed. The only thing surprising is that it took so long for it to become the subject for gossip. Or I suppose someone could have seen me coming and going from your home at all hours of the day and night. It doesn't really matter how or why Monroe's suspicions were raised. There are no secrets in a small town. I accepted that a long time ago."

Caleb looked at his lover. "Then why did you take a position here? Why not work somewhere more tolerant? It isn't like you have family here." Was that why Jesse had decided to live in El Jardin? "Does your family know you're gay?"

Jesse shifted, his body tensing, until he took a deep breath and forced himself to relax. "They know. We were never really close. Telling them didn't affect things one way or another."

Caleb frowned. "What do you mean?"

"My parents have always been wrapped up in each other, I guess you'd say. I don't think they ever wanted kids, though they never said as much. Just seemed obvious because I was always an afterthought." Jesse shifted again, jostling Caleb slightly, then pulling him in close. "They traveled from job to job, never settling anywhere for more than a year. Sometimes I was homeschooled, other times I went to whatever public school was nearby. They came through El Jardin when I was seventeen because there was a job for my dad at the campground. They parked their RV there, and I got to be the new kid in town. My senior year was, er, different, but at least I earned my diploma. The people here were nice, for the most part. Shortly after that my parents packed up and headed off. I didn't go with them. I'd had enough moving, and while I had to leave to get my college degree, this place was as close to a hometown as I'd ever had, so I came back."

Jesse's voice had been calm and steady, but Caleb felt his lover's muscles tighten and ripple, heard the slight hitch in his breathing. Hearing even that little bit about Jesse's childhood made Caleb ache inside — he couldn't imagine how deeply it affected Jesse. Here he'd been so wrapped up in his own problems, and he'd never known Jesse had spent most of his life feeling unwanted. It broke Caleb's heart, but this wasn't about him.

"Does this still feel like home to you?" Caleb didn't want to be the cause of Jesse losing that security he'd built for himself.

Jesse slipped two fingers under Caleb's chin and lifted. Jesse's soft, peaceful expression was entrancing. The even softer press of lips turned the skip of his heartbeat into a slow *thump-thump-thump* that spread warmth throughout every cell in his body.

"*You* feel like home to me, Caleb," Jesse whispered, his eyes luminous as he snared Caleb's gaze. "Nothing else has ever felt this right before."

This time the kiss was not quite as soft. Jesse's lips were red and swollen, and Caleb knew his must look thoroughly kissed as well. He watched his lover's mouth as more words began to pour from his lips, words that melted Caleb and re-formed him again into a new man, one whose heart was now in another's hands.

"Do you have any idea how much I care about you, Caleb Tomas?"

Caleb couldn't answer, couldn't seem to do anything other than stare like a love-struck idiot as Jesse continued.

"Do you know how perfect you feel in my arms?" Jesse darted a glance toward the kitchen before dropping his voice to a whisper. "How perfect your ass feels squeezing my dick, milking me dry? Or how feeling you inside me makes me feel safe and cared for? The way you touch me, look at me, kiss me... Caleb, do you know I'm falling in love with you?" He chuckled and shook his head. "No, not falling. I think I dove willingly sometime back. Did you know that, Caleb?"

No, he hadn't known any of that, although he did know the sex was mind-meltingly hot and better than he'd ever believed possible. Hearing Jesse's confessions about that alone would have thrilled Caleb, but knowing Jesse loved him — *him*, as he was, flaws and all — was more than Caleb would have dared hope for.

"Caleb?"

Caleb blinked and found himself staring into Jesse's eyes. He'd been stunned into silence, and the note of insecurity in his lover's voice wouldn't do. Caleb reached up and cupped Jesse's stubbly cheek in his hand. He saw the wide smile that had to be echoing his own.

"Oh God, Jesse," Caleb finally got out through his tight throat. "Me too, all of it." For someone who made his living with words, Caleb thought that was pathetic. He swallowed the lump in his throat, ignored the stinging of his eyes. There were four perfect words that said everything, and even he couldn't screw them up. "I love you too."

Chapter Seventeen

Jesse would have sworn the fine hairs at his nape were standing at attention. He turned and wasn't entirely surprised to find Monroe staring at him across the minuscule squad room. The man's smug expression made Jesse grind his teeth together. Now was neither the time nor the place for a confrontation.

Jesse arched an eyebrow and turned away, refusing to be baited. He would definitely be speaking to Monroe soon about his visit to Caleb's house. Depending on how that little chat went, Jesse would decide whether or not he needed to speak to Chief Chapel. Since Monroe was a complete asshole, talking to the chief was almost a sure thing.

The door opened, and Officer Rodriguez came in. Jesse nodded and started to ask how his shift had gone, but the look of disgust Rodriguez gave him had Jesse biting back the words. He glared back at Rodriguez until the man turned away, calling a greeting to Monroe.

Jesse's hands and feet went numb as Rodriguez muttered, "Fuckin' *joto*." Apparently the man would rather be friends with a backstabbing bastard than be associated with the fuckin' fag, even when that *fag* had defended him against Monroe's racial slurs in the past.

Now, unless Jesse was mistaken, Monroe was spreading rumors about his suspicions on Jesse's private life. A quick look at Monroe and Rodriguez huddled together like BFFs convinced Jesse that he wasn't wrong at all.

Fine. Fuck 'em — or not. He had a job to do.

* * * *

Jesse was long past ready for his break. It'd been a busy night for El Jardin's criminal class. He wasn't sure whether it was paranoia on his part, but there seemed to be an unnecessary delay getting him backup when he requested it. He'd never had a problem with Officer Jane Alaniz before, but since he and Rodriguez had always gotten along up until then, Jesse didn't think he could go by his coworkers' past behavior as an indicator of whether they were truly his friends.

Monroe wasn't in the squad room and neither was Rodriguez. No surprise there, as he worked days, and Jesse usually only saw him for a few minutes at the beginning of shifts.

As Jesse opened his locker, he considered taking the rest of the night, or morning, off. The stress of dealing with the looks and whispers and indirect name-calling — that he could handle for a while before feeling the overwhelming need to rip someone's head off. In less than twenty-four hours, Jesse's life had become fodder for the ravenous small-town gossip mill. The one thing he'd worked hard not to participate in was being used against him, and there wasn't much he could do to stop it. The best he could hope for was something more interesting to occur as a distraction from speculation on his private life.

What he didn't want to deal with was his coworkers refusing to do their jobs by backing him up. That went beyond spiteful to attempted murder. However, he knew that taking off would make those assholes think they'd won, so the best he could hope for on the job was that the rest of his shift would be uneventful.

He could hope for a hell of a lot more than that on his break. Maybe Kezabeth had gone home, or if she had stayed over out of concern for Caleb, maybe she'd at least be asleep. If not, Jesse would have to toss Caleb over his shoulder and drag him off to the bedroom. Jesse needed him, and it didn't have to be fucking or sucking, though either of those would be good, but what he really wanted was just to lie with Caleb in his arms, to hold him close and feel the steady beat of his heart, the rise and fall of his chest as his sweet breath tickled over Jesse's skin. That was what he wanted — the warmth and reassurance that the man he loved was healthy, happy and safe.

Jesse spotted another vehicle parked behind Kezabeth's, this one a white late-model pickup truck. Somehow he doubted that truck boded well for his desire to snuggle with his lover. Well, Jesse would make do with what he could get of the man during his break. Just seeing him would help to lift the oppressive weight of his coworkers' attitudes off his shoulders.

Jesse parked and walked to Caleb's house. He'd barely gotten halfway there when the front door swung open. Caleb stepped onto the porch without hesitation, gesturing for Jesse to walk faster. He did, but apparently not fast enough. When Jesse was on the sidewalk, Caleb bolted toward him. The only hesitation came when Caleb was a foot away. Even in the dim light from the porch, Jesse saw Caleb shiver slightly. Then he was smiling, a nervous twitch of lips that warmed Jesse's heart and lifted his mood.

"I'm so glad you're here!" Caleb's words were rushed, and Jesse wondered if his lover even realized what he'd said. It didn't matter, because the cold, bitter feelings that had been building inside him had already been supplanted with the strength of the love he felt for this amazing man.

"You came to me," Jesse murmured, nipping at the soft skin behind Caleb's ear.

"I just did what I had to do to reach you," Caleb pointed out. "Actually, I did what you've made it possible for me to do. You helped me see this isn't a walk to be terrified of, especially not when you're waiting at the end of it."

Jesse was saved from saying something sappy, like *I'll always be waiting for you* by someone else opening Caleb's front door from inside. Jesse kept his eyes on the shape taking up pretty much all the space in the doorway. "Who's the big guy?"

Jesse watched the man approach. He reached for Caleb's hand, tangling their fingers together. It was dark, but if someone wanted to look, they'd probably be able to make out the two of them hand in hand. Right now, Jesse couldn't find the strength to give a damn.

Caleb hummed and glanced down at their joined hands. "You sure you want to do that out here? Even if no one else sees, Remy'll probably give me shit."

Remy? Shit, Kezabeth's husband is huge! "Why would he do that?" Jesse tightened his grip on his lover. He glanced up to find the behemoth standing only a few feet away. Damn, the man moved quietly for his size — or any size.

"He's a bit worried about what would happen to you."

"Probably because I wouldn't want to see your boyfriend here catch a bullet with his head," Remy said.

Caleb jumped and squeaked, and Jesse felt bad for not warning his lover of Remy's approach. But the way Caleb clung to him and the angry look in his eyes directed at his brother-in-law were doing all sorts of interesting things to Jesse's dick.

"That's a bit harsh, Remy, considering—" Caleb snapped his mouth shut and tried to bury his face in Jesse's shirt.

Remy's lips thinned as he looked at Caleb. "Considering I killed a kid?"

No way was Jesse letting this conversation degenerate further. "That was a chest shot, not a head shot. Can you quit blocking the sidewalk and half the freaking yard so we can go inside, man? I'd like to relax for what time I've got left on my break."

Remy blinked, looking dumbfounded that Jesse had casually addressed the shot that had ruined Remy's career. Then he actually snorted.

"You're not scared of much, are you, Jesse?" Remy watched as he kept Caleb tucked tight to his side.

Jesse squeezed Caleb's hip and glanced up at Remy. "I'm scared of plenty of things." He didn't want to add that he didn't believe in running, because he was sure the giant would take it wrong. Jesse didn't know what was going on between Kezabeth and Remy, and he didn't want to interfere inadvertently and piss anyone off.

"Kez made sandwiches." Caleb took Jesse's wrist and led him inside.

Loopy immediately began yipping and dancing around his ankles. He was so happy that Jesse couldn't resist pausing to scoop up the dog. "Think she'll get mad if I slip some to Loopy?"

Caleb laughed as he set a plate in front of Jesse. "If you feed him much people food at all, he tends to have, ah, well, digestive problems. Let's just say it won't be Kez cleaning up the messes, so it won't be her you'll piss off."

"Well, that sucks for you, Loopy, it won't do to have the love of my life kicking me to the curb." Jesse winked at Caleb, ignoring the little gasp from Kezabeth. He still slipped Loopy a piece of lunchmeat when Caleb plopped a thick sandwich on his plate. "Thanks for lunch, well, lunch for me. I don't know what you call eating at three a.m."

"It isn't that unusual for us." Remy stepped forward, arm extended. "We haven't been properly introduced. Remy Cortez."

"Jesse Martin. Good to meet you." Jesse resigned himself to sharing his lunch with two unexpected guests. Then he saw how happy Caleb was every time he glanced at his sister and Remy, and that joy in his lover's expression, his pretty eyes sparkling with emotion, well, it was more than worth Jesse giving up his plans for how he wanted to spend his break.

* * * *

Caleb sprawled out on the couch, waiting for Jesse to get off work. He'd asked him to come straight over — Jesse had the next two days off, and Caleb wanted to dote on him as much as possible. And maybe, as Dr. Gregg suggested, Caleb could get past the assault and have a normal life. He'd have to think about that some more first.

An engine revved up outside. Caleb hurried to look out the blinds. Jesse had parked at the trailer, but it didn't look like he was planning on showering at his place as he usually did before coming over. Was that because he was so eager to see him, or had something happened? Jesse had seemed okay at lunch, maybe a little tense, but Caleb thought that was because he'd wanted more for lunch than food. What if it wasn't? Had Officer Asshole said or done something? A chill slithered down Caleb's spine. Monroe hadn't come off as the kind of guy who'd be able to repress his psychotic tendencies for long.

Caleb opened the door. He stepped onto the porch, then took a few steps forward. The early-morning air seemed laced with tension. Caleb wished there was more light than what the sliver of a moon provided. He had a feeling that if he could see clearly, his lover's body would be stiff, his movements jerky. He imagined those broad shoulders rolling the slightest bit, as if shaking off the bad shit of the day. Caleb didn't want that, wanted the bad as well as the good.

Before Jesse, he might have been too frightened of everything to try to deal with…well, anything at all, really, but that was changing. Now he felt safe enough with Jesse that he might be able to go anywhere, as long as they were together. And if he had a strong sedative, maybe.

"Rough night?" Caleb reached for Jesse.

A frown marred his brow. Fine lines etched the outer corners of his eyes. His lips were pressed firmly together, hiding the plump flesh and showing only a thin line. Jesse clasped Caleb's hand in his and nodded. "We need to talk."

Ominous words—fixing-to-ditch-someone words. Caleb's stomach fluttered as he kept pace with Jesse until they reached the doorway. There Jesse paused, releasing his hand and waiting for Caleb to enter first. Caleb flicked a glance but couldn't read anything in Jesse's expression. What the hell had happened in the few hours since they'd last seen each other?

"I take it Remy and Kezabeth made up?" Jesse tipped his head toward the driveway where Kezabeth's and Remy's vehicles were still parked.

"Yeah, you could say that." Seeing those two making googly eyes at each other all night had been almost nauseating. Only almost, because Caleb had been so relieved his sister and brother-in-law were working through their problems that he'd gladly watched them.

"Am I being too nosy if I ask what the problem was?" Jesse glanced at him as he locked the deadbolts.

Caleb felt his cheeks heat as he shook his head. "No, it's fine." Remy being stupid, much like Caleb had almost been. "Remy thought he was protecting Kez and the girls, with the way the media was dogging him. He had it in his head that if he left, the reporters would leave his family alone."

Jesse's dark eyebrows scrunched together. "Why would he think that? It'd just be another thing to exploit."

"I think sometimes our judgment is clouded by the need to protect our loved ones." That was the only explanation Caleb had as he led Jesse to the bedroom. The door was shut. A big hand landed on Caleb's shoulder, urging him to turn around. Caleb found himself captured by the look in Jesse's eyes, the need and love so plainly shining there.

"Would you do that, Caleb? Did you think about it after Monroe showed up here?" Jesse stepped closer, his hand still on Caleb's shoulder. His other hand rested on Caleb's hip. "Was that why you seemed so jittery that night? Were you going to sacrifice us because you were afraid of what that idiot might do?"

Caleb's throat felt tight, his mouth dry, his eyes were stinging and his nose burning. "I didn't do it," he said, voice cracking. "I'm too selfish. I want you too much, which makes me—"

"Mine." Jesse pulled him close, and Caleb shivered as his lips were nipped, his mouth thoroughly plundered. Rough hands shoved at his shirt, stroking the bare skin beneath the cotton. "It makes you mine."

Then it was Jesse who was clutching at Caleb as he buried his face against Caleb's neck.

"Please, don't. Don't." Jesse lifted his head and rubbed his stubbled cheek over Caleb's. "Please don't run like Remy did and think it will be better for me. I don't think I could take it."

"I won't," Caleb promised, his heart feeling assaulted and exhilarated at the same time. "I couldn't." He was no more capable of leaving Jesse than he was of ignoring the need and longing that caused his eyes to darken with desire, his muscles to twitch, and goosebumps to skitter over his skin.

Right now Jesse needed him as much as Caleb needed to give himself to Jesse. The time for conversation was past. The things left unsaid and unasked would wait while they gave and took comfort and loved each other's fears away.

Chapter Eighteen

Jesse couldn't pinpoint any one thing that made him certain someone had been in his trailer. It was just an uneasy feeling, like an itch between his shoulder blades that he couldn't reach to scratch. The door had been locked when he'd walked over to grab some clean clothes, but as he stood inside the threshold, something felt off.

Carefully scanning the living room, he found nothing out of place. The tattered couch's cushions were all in place, the newspaper from a week ago still folded and stacked neatly where he'd left it. The end table was bare except for his coffee mug, the fine layers of dust coating the surfaces of that and the other furniture were undisturbed. It still didn't feel right.

A faint metallic odor teased his nose when he drew a deep breath. Another stronger sniff brought a deeper odor that easily overpowered the usual musty smell of the small, confined space.

The familiarity of the odor registered seconds before the knowledge of what it was then Jesse was moving, nearly running to his bedroom. He knew instinctively that was where the damage would be. He smacked open the gaping door with his elbow rather than his hand, anger not yet obliterating all rational thought. Jesse's breath rushed from his lungs as though the destruction was to his body rather than his bedroom.

There was nothing left intact other than the walls, floor and ceiling. Even that was debatable, as any available surface had been used as a spray-painted canvas for hatred. Jesse could make out parts of letters on the carpet as well, what part of the carpet that wasn't covered with his broken furniture, shredded and painted clothes, shoes, knickknacks.

Everything. Everything had been destroyed. He spotted pieces of shimmering glass, probably from the framed photos he'd had on the dresser of him and his parents, his graduations from high school, college and the police academy. There hadn't been many things hanging on the walls, but the few paintings he'd had, gifts handed down from his grandmother, those were gone too, buried somewhere in the wreck of a room.

"It's just stuff," Jesse muttered more than once, but his attempts to be grateful that only material things had been lost were only half-successful.

Jesse stood staring at the proof of evil in humanity, trying to decide what to do—not in the immediate future. He'd have to call this in, but the larger issue was, did he want to stay here, in this trailer, in this job, in this town? Could he keep Caleb safe here? He didn't know how long he tried to find the answers to his questions but knew it'd been too long when the front door opened and Remy's deep voice boomed through the small trailer.

"Don't touch anything," Jesse called out. A moment of silence, then Remy's response.

"Shit!" Remy's footsteps thudded heavily, the hall vibrating with his steps as he rushed to where Jesse stood at the bedroom door. "What happened?" Remy grunted as he looked over the room.

Jesse smiled. The man was making mental notes and assimilating the information he found at the crime scene.

"When are you going to call it in?" Remy was still staring at the words sprayed on the walls. "You *are* calling it in, right?"

Jesse's snort had Remy giving him a narrow-eyed gaze, but it didn't faze Jesse. "Of course I'm calling it in. I should have already, yeah, but I started thinking, wondering, you know."

Remy nodded, his bright green eyes narrowing even more as he peered at Jesse. "You're wondering if it's safe here, for you and for Caleb, but more for him, right?"

At Jesse's sharp nod, Remy sighed, his shoulders slumping as he tucked his hands into his pockets. "I don't think it is, and I thought that before this ever happened. It's near impossible for any cop to come out as a homosexual in a big force, one that rants and raves about tolerance. Maybe the brass means it, but most of the peons don't. I've seen more than a few get drummed out of the force. Then there are a few who've stuck it out. They have to put up with a lot of shit and work harder to prove they're good cops, but they've carved out some respect." Remy sighed, an irritated flutter of breath. "I've caught shit once or twice for having a gay brother-in-law, but those idiots learned quickly that I don't have any *tolerance* for their bigoted bullshit." Remy shrugged and glanced back in the bedroom. "Looks like it's gonna be a damn sight worse in a small town."

Jesse tried not to bristle, but he was feeling raw, rough around the edges. "I don't like running. It grates against everything I believe in. And I can't stop being a cop. It's part of who I am."

"Well, sure," Remy agreed. "I didn't mean you should find a new career. There are other places where it isn't so hard being out, I would think. As to running away from a problem, it rarely does any good, as I can attest. I ended up hurting the hell out of the people I love. But that was different, and finding somewhere safer to live out your lives, that isn't necessarily running away. Maybe it's more like running *to* where you belong. I'm not saying you should or shouldn't stay. I have my opinion, yeah, but you gotta decide what to do."

"Except it's not just me I'm deciding for." Jesse got that, loud and clear.

"Right. If you decided to pack up and leave, I wouldn't advise leaving Caleb behind."

"I wouldn't even try. I love Caleb," Jesse admitted, watching Remy closely for his reaction.

Remy's mouth quirked up in one corner. "Thought so. Seems like it's mutual too."

Jesse's neck felt warm with the admission, the flush crawling up to his cheeks. "I'm not much of a reader."

Remy's eyebrows rocketed up his brow. "Really?" He grunted when Jesse shook his head. "Huh. Well, I guess that's a good thing."

"Why do you say that?" Jesse asked.

Remy chuckled and slung his arm over Jesse's shoulders. "Well, he's a very private man, always has been. His books are popular. He's gotten some blatant offers from some of his readers. It has made him intensely aware that there are people who would hook up with him just because of who he is, so he's never really taken a chance."

Jesse thought about that as they walked down the sidewalk. "I guess he would have to be careful not to be taken advantage of. That has to suck, actually."

Remy's laughter boomed loud in the quiet neighborhood and caused Jesse's eardrums to vibrate unpleasantly. "It did, no doubt, but maybe not so much anymore, right?"

"Not anymore," Jesse agreed as he watched Caleb's front door open and his lover step outside. "Not at all."

* * * *

Caleb didn't think he'd ever been so angry before. Not at his attackers, not at himself for his inability to deal with the attack. None of it compared to the anger that caused a roaring in his head when Jesse told him about the vandalism.

Guilt tried to niggle its way into his conscience, telling him Jesse would have been safe if they'd never gotten involved. Caleb batted that shit right back down. There was nothing to feel guilty about. Loving each other was the one thing that was true and right in the world, and he refused to let some narrow-minded bigoted asshole take that from him — from *them*.

Jesse and Remy were still talking to the chief of police. Jesse had felt that dealing with Chief Chapel rather than another officer would be the best way to handle this. Caleb hoped he was right. Caleb couldn't hear, so all he had to judge by was the way Jesse gestured, his hands flinging up and down.

Then there was Remy, standing with his huge arms crossed over his chest and a severe frown that only grew more severe with each flop of Jesse's hands. The chief was frowning as well, and all in all, it didn't look good out there.

"Think the chief's an ass?"

Kezabeth's voice was like a poke in the ribs in the dark when you thought you were all alone. Caleb squeaked and jumped and smacked the side of his head on the window frame.

"Fuck! Kez." Caleb caught himself before he said anything that would leave him lying on the floor cupping his balls. He rubbed his temple and shot Kez a dirty look as she laughed at him.

"You sound like one of those squeaky toys Loopy likes to chew on," Kez got out between snickers. Loopy bounced over upon hearing his name, yipping and pawing at Caleb's calves until he bent to pick him up.

"One word for you, sis. Karma." Caleb ignored his sister's eye roll and turned to peek back out the blind. "Shit!" He thrust Loopy into her arms, then hurried to the front door, surprised to find the deadbolts unlocked.

Caleb jerked the door open and stepped on the porch as Jesse started to reach for the door handle. The brush of his lover's hand over Caleb's hip sent shivers down his legs. Caleb willed his dick to ignore the touch as he straightened his shoulders and braced himself for whatever bigoted crap the chief threw his way. Jesse shifted beside him then Caleb felt his lover's hand on the small of his back, rubbing circles of warmth and support through the thin material of his shirt.

"Mr. Tomas, I'm Chief Mike Chapel." The chief extended his hand, and Caleb shook it firmly, introducing himself while studying Chapel's expression, trying to get some clue to the man's feelings. It was impossible — there wasn't a single hint for Caleb to pick up on.

"I understand one of my officers stopped by and behaved inappropriately recently?"

Caleb had to bite his cheek to keep from making a suggestive remark about just which officer was being inappropriate. Jesse was always deliciously so, but Caleb doubted that was what the chief wanted to hear about.

"He was a completely obnoxious asshole who tried to intimidate my sister and me." Caleb ignored Remy's growling—the man tended to do that when anyone messed with his family. "It didn't work, and really, I'm not sure you want to hear about one of your men doing his best to get your office slapped with a lawsuit."

A rapid tic started at the top of Chapel's jaw. Caleb resisted the urge to look away from the chief's pale blue gaze. He couldn't quite keep from fidgeting as he waited for some verbal response, shifting from foot to foot and twining his fingers together.

"Just what happened that would make you think there are any grounds for a lawsuit?" Chapel's lips barely moved when he spoke, which Caleb decided must mean he was seriously pissed off. "If you were so concerned about Monroe's visit, why didn't you file a report?"

That was an easy one. "Why would I believe you'd take a complaint against one of your men seriously? I mean, obviously Monroe didn't feel he had any reason to be concerned about any repercussions. He was very clear about his dislike for me. In fact, he only became more threatening when confronted about the ridiculousness of his reason for stopping by. That led me to believe that either you had little to no authority over your men, or Monroe knew you'd protect his ass no matter what he did."

Chief Chapel had another tic sprouting up on his opposite jaw. Caleb shrugged, keeping his voice close to bland. "I don't think it matters. I've got the best lawyers money can buy" — he would soon, anyway — "and I'm sure they can come up with plenty of embarrassing, and costly, terms for what happened."

The silence stretched out for several uncomfortable minutes before Chief Chapel finally nodded. "I don't much care for threats, Mr. Tomas, not getting them and not seeing them left for others."

Caleb felt the rebuke heat his skin. It was a not-so-subtle reminder he'd played the bully, much like Monroe had.

"I don't care for threats myself, but I'll do what I have to in order to protect the people I love." God, Caleb hoped Jesse had been clear about their relationship. If not, Caleb had just spilled it all.

"That's understandable," Chapel said without any hint of sarcasm or disdain. "I can't blame you, but Mr. Tomas, you need to file a report — you and your sister both. There needs to be that paper trail. I can't guarantee there's anything I can do about Monroe's visit." Chapel held up a hand when Caleb would have interrupted. "He didn't exactly break any laws, so I can't do a whole lot about it, but I can sit him down and explain a few things, like how easy it would be for me to cut him loose. And if I find any proof he was involved in that mess over there" — the chief gestured behind him to Caleb's place — "I *will* fire him and do everything I can to see him brought up on any charge I think will stick."

It sounded good, but it wasn't enough. "What about Jesse, Chief Chapel? What's he supposed to do while his home is being broken into and his stuff is being trashed? While his coworkers are being assholes? How are you going to fix that?"

Jesse shook his head. "Caleb—"

"No, Martin," Chief Chapel cut Jesse off. "Mr. Tomas has a right to ask those questions, and so do you. You both deserve some answers."

Caleb couldn't tell whether the chief was sincere. If it was an act, the guy was wasting his talent in this dinky town.

"Would it be possible to go inside and continue this discussion? It's hotter than hell out here." Chapel wiped at his forehead.

Chapel's request shot a tendril of fear whipping through Caleb, but it was nowhere near the overpowering terror he'd have felt only a few weeks ago. Jesse still rubbed those soothing circles.

"That okay with you, Caleb?" Jesse asked, never ceasing the caress.

Caleb could do this, invite the chief of police inside, and he could even do it without wigging out.

"Yeah, that's fine." Caleb turned and led the way into his home. There was no way he would let anything, not his issues nor those of any small-minded, hate-mongering jackasses take the security he felt away from him.

Chapter Nineteen

Sunlight peeked through a curtain, singing across Jesse's eyelids, sending a brilliant explosion of white blotches skittering behind his closed lids. He became aware of a weight on his chest, a firm ass cheek in his hand. Soft hair tickled his cheek and nose and one of his legs was asleep. Caleb was draped over him like the best kind of blanket—a warm, sexy male blanket.

Caleb exhaled noisily, the snuffling sound making Jesse smile even as his dick ached. They had talked late into the night, and all Jesse's intentions of fucking Caleb into a state of mindless ecstasy had fallen by the wayside as sleep had snuck up on them.

Now, however, he was more than ready to play. Jesse nudged Caleb carefully, rolling him onto his back. With the sheets kicked off the foot of the bed, Jesse had an unobstructed view of the man in all his nude glory. Caleb was too thin, but he'd put on some weight, enough that he didn't look to be in danger of starving to death in the immediate future. His hipbones still stood out sharply, and when Jesse trailed a finger over one of them, Caleb murmured and shifted his hips, his semi-erect cock filling.

Sliding down the bed, he paused with his shoulder beside Caleb's hip. Lifting his lover's dick with one finger, raising it enough so it was off his stomach, Jesse bit back a moan. His mouth was watering already, his jaws tingling in anticipation. He couldn't wait any longer and didn't see any reason to bother trying.

Jesse lowered his head, his gaze fastened to the pearly pre-cum welling from Caleb's slit. He slid his fingers lower to encircle the base of his lover's cock, then lapped at the leaking slit. The taste of the tangy cream threatened to smash Jesse's control—Caleb tasted so good, salty yet sweet, and as Jesse sucked the spongy head into his mouth, the scent of his lover hit him fully. Musky, masculine and spicy, it matched perfectly the taste of the man.

Caleb's thighs spread, and his hips jerked, shoving the thick cock to the back of Jesse's throat before he could back off. He fought against gagging, his own body jerking.

"Fucking hell. What're you doing?" Caleb muttered, his voice thick with sleep.

Narrow hands grasped at his head, pulling at him until he let Caleb's cock slip from his mouth. Jesse turned and looked at his lover, his chest tightening at the erotic image. Caleb's russet curls were tousled, the vibrant color contrasting beautifully with the stark white pillowcase. The rich green of his eyes glittered through the narrow slits of his lids. Full lips were parted and shaky breaths passed in and out and a rosy flush spread up his chest.

Jesse swallowed noisily, his throat clicking. "What does it look and feel like I'm doing?"

Caleb thrust his hips, his hard dick bouncing as his fingers tightened against Jesse's scalp. "No condom."

"I know." Jesse hadn't been so out of it that he hadn't been fully aware of the decision he'd made. "I want to taste you. You'd have told me if there was a reason I shouldn't."

Caleb closed his eyes and thumped his head against the pillow. "Yes, of course, but I can't think right now."

"You said you haven't been with anyone else in over a year. When you were in the hospital, they'd have run tests."

"It was all fine, and I've always been careful before." Caleb squirmed, rolling to his side to prop his head up on one hand. His expression was a mix of hope and caution. "Are you comfortable with this? Just this?"

Jesse nodded, already reaching for Caleb's dick. "I am. I trust you, I love you, and for this, yes, I am comfortable." He licked the gleaming moisture from Caleb's plump tip.

Caleb gave in with a strangled moan and flopped on his back. Jesse crawled between his lover's legs, nudging them wider so that he could lie between them.

"Bend 'em," Jesse ordered as he propped himself up on his elbows.

Caleb bent his legs, keeping them spread wide. The movement opened the playing field up nicely. Jesse slid one hand under Caleb's ass, cupping his hip. With the other hand, he cupped Caleb's balls, rolling their heavy weight in his palm.

"Jesse, please," Caleb gasped, then groaned as Jesse loved on his balls. He sucked one gently into his mouth, laving it with his tongue, reveling in the low moans being pulled from his lover. Jesse released it, only to treat the other one with the same loving touch, closing his eyes as the taste and scent of his lover filled him.

Letting the nut slip from his mouth, Jesse inhaled deeply, grinding his hips against the sheets. He could smell the heady scent of musk and man. It twisted and fired him up even more inside and drew pre-cum from his dick.

Jesse opened his eyes and buried his nose in his lover's balls. Slick with his spit, the smattering of hair tickled at first. He savored everything about the experience. Caleb's hands slid on his shoulders, patted at his head. Caleb's hips twisted and his dick bobbed as Jesse thoroughly explored him from the base of his dick to the soft patch of skin below his balls.

Jesse sat up and tapped Caleb's hip. "Hands and knees, love."

Caleb nodded and turned over. Jesse gripped his hips and helped him get into position. Once Caleb had his head resting on his forearm, Jesse parted his ass cheeks. The tiny, wrinkled hole clenched then relaxed as if in invitation, and Jesse accepted. He laved the puckered skin with the flat of his tongue, moaning at the taste of his lover's core. Caleb cried out as Jesse licked and teased at his hole, then whimpered when Jesse scraped his teeth over the delicate skin.

Jesse sucked and licked at Caleb's hole until it loosened, and he could work his tongue inside. Caleb was shaking, his voice cracking with each incoherent sound that slipped from his lips. Jesse reached around him with both arms, then cradled Caleb's cock in one hand, and his balls in the other. Caleb bucked when Jesse's fist closed tighter around his cock.

Caleb's needy eagerness was what flipped Jesse's switch. He began eating Caleb's ass, working his lover's hole with his tongue, fucking it with the slick muscle as deeply as he could. His hand formed a rough tunnel for his lover's cock to fuck, and he rolled and tugged on Caleb's balls. Caleb's breath stuttered out of him, his ability to vocalize reduced to nothing more than a high, keening sound that sent heat flaming from Jesse's ears to his spine and into his balls.

Jesse's dick was so hard he ached with the need to come, but he wasn't willing to let go of Caleb long enough to jerk himself off. He scraped his teeth over Caleb's ring and twisted his tongue as he thrust into Caleb's ass. Caleb's cock pulsed in his hand as his inner muscles clamped down on Jesse's tongue. Jesse released Caleb's balls as they drew up. A few seconds later, cum spurted from Caleb's cock, coating Jesse's hand and Caleb's chest.

When the last spurt was released, Jesse grabbed Caleb's legs, tugging them down and out of the way. He grabbed his throbbing dick and straddled the backs of Caleb's thighs, letting his balls rest on the bottom of Caleb's ass. Jesse groaned as he jerked himself off, too horny for finesse. He rubbed his balls against Caleb's ass, then lowered to grind against the taut flesh.

Caleb reached back and grabbed Jesse's thighs, digging his fingers into the muscles, and Jesse screamed, his back arching as he sprayed cum all over Caleb's back and ass. He'd wanted to watch as his cum coated Caleb, marking him in an embarrassingly territorial display, but the force of his climax had slammed his head back, and he hadn't been able to do more than to scream and come until he thought his balls were surely permanently empty.

When Jesse stopped shaking, and he could finally move, the first thing he did was look at his seed on his lover's body. Caleb was watching him, his head turned to the side, one green eye sparkling.

Jesse saw no reason to pretend the sight of Caleb's milky, smooth skin wasn't the hottest damn thing ever.

He smiled seeing he'd shot some of the sticky spunk into Caleb's hair — that'd be a mess if it dried.

"You're looking Neanderthalically pleased with yourself," Caleb murmured, his voice distorted by the pillow.

Jesse nodded, reaching to rub the ribbons of spunk into his lover's skin, or to spread it over more skin, Jesse wasn't sure which, just that he loved the way Caleb looked coated in his juices.

"Neanderthalically isn't a word," Jesse said once his brain cells kicked back into gear.

Caleb grunted, still watching as Jesse continued on with his quest to cover Caleb's entire back in his seed. "Should be. What're you trying to do? Did you get any of that in my hair?"

"I like this, the way it looks, knowing you're wearing my cum." Jesse ignored the blush heating his cheeks. "So yeah, you can have the word. Do you... Is this freaking you out?"

Snorting, Caleb raised his arms up over his head. "Does it *look* like I'm freaking out? Though I do feel like I've been marked, which probably should bother me, but it doesn't. And you never said — did you get cum in my hair?"

Jesse eyed the drying glob in Caleb's curls. "Nope, not freaking out, and ah, maybe a little."

"Then you better hurry up and finish using my body as your cum canvas, because if that stuff dries in my hair..." Caleb trailed off, letting the unspoken threat linger in the air.

"Gotcha." Jesse swiped his hand over his lover's back one more time, then crawled off him. Caleb sat up and Jesse reached out to poke at the back of Caleb's head. "It's kind of right...here." And it didn't feel very wet either. Jesse snatched his hand back. "You should probably hurry up and shower."

"You think?" Caleb stood and grabbed Jesse's wrist. "You made this mess. You clean it up, lover. Let's go."

Jesse thought it was the first time he'd thoroughly enjoyed cleaning up his own mess.

* * * *

Caleb ignored Kezabeth's smirk. He'd been ignoring those looks from her all day, along with Remy's somewhat mortified gazes. He and Jesse had been loud earlier. So what? This was his home, after all. Kez and Remy were free to return home. He and Jesse didn't need them to babysit.

Of course, Jesse wasn't there, and neither was Remy. Both men had gone to talk to Chief Chapel. Caleb would have liked to have gone along as well, but he wasn't sure he was ready for such a big step. He'd had his online counseling session with Dr. Gregg an hour ago and was making progress. Maybe it wouldn't be too long before he could join Jesse on trips away from the house.

Dr. Gregg did agree that moving might be the only alternative he and Jesse had, but he was concerned about Caleb's ability to handle such a drastic change. Caleb and Jesse were worried about it too, but the reality of it was, they might not have any other choice. If worse came to worst, Dr. Gregg could supply him with some type of medication to help him deal with the move. Hopefully something that would knock him out.

Caleb twitched the blinds out of the way again, peeking to make sure he hadn't missed the sound of Remy's truck returning.

"Pacing and checking isn't going to make them return any quicker," Kezabeth pointed out. "Watched pot and all of that, you know."

Caleb dropped the blinds back in place and glared at his sister. "So I'm supposed to sit back and relax while they're at the station, putting up with God knows what from a bunch of bigoted assholes?"

Kez snorted. "Puh-lease. Like either of our men are the types to *put up* with anything or anyone. I know Jesse may seem calmer than Remy, but I have no doubt that he won't take crap from anyone. And you know Remy won't."

Caleb plopped on the couch, waking Loopy up as he did so. The poodle yawned, then stood up before pouncing onto Caleb's lap. Caleb stroked the soft apricot curls, soothing himself even as Loopy dozed back off.

"It'll be all right." Kez patted Caleb's knee as she sat beside him. "Chief Chapel seems like a decent guy and he can't very well let his officers run around committing crimes. Maybe stuff like that went on years ago, but nowadays, with the media looking for anything to exploit, it'd be career suicide for Chapel to ignore or condone such actions from anyone under his command."

"That sounds all well and good, Kez, but there may not be any way to prove Monroe is the ass who trashed Jesse's place." Caleb and Jesse both expected Monroe to have covered his tracks better than that. "And it might not have been Monroe, although Jesse seems certain it was."

Kezabeth cocked her head to the side, waiting for an explanation.

"There's another guy up there, Rodriguez, who Monroe had talked shit about months ago. Jesse put a stop to it, and everything was fine between him and Rodriguez — until Monroe started stirring up trouble."

"How stupid is Rodriguez?" Kez's voice snapped with anger. "What kind of idiots does Chapel have on his force?"

"Is it any surprise to find that there are homophobes on the police force out here? I mean, bigots of all sorts are everywhere. Like roaches." Caleb actually had more sympathy for roaches, even though he doused the nasty suckers with spray anytime he saw one. "Then there's some other cop who Jesse said was suspiciously slow to arrive when he called for backup, some female officer named Jane, I think. He didn't know if it was intentional, but he was going to ask her about it."

Kez nodded and started to reply when a vehicle pulled into the drive. Caleb picked Loopy up before the poodle could scramble off his lap and run for the door. He held the dog in the crook of his arm as he and Kezabeth hurried to unlock the deadbolts. Kezabeth batted his hands aside and had the door open before Jesse and Remy had shut the truck's doors.

Caleb stepped onto the porch, noting the tense set of Jesse's shoulders, the frown tugging his lips down, and the clenched fists at his side. It didn't appear that the talk with Chief Chapel had gone well. A glance at Remy showed the same erect posture, although his hands were jammed into the front pockets of his jeans.

Jesse covered the distance to Caleb in a few short strides. Caleb passed Loopy back to Kezabeth.

"What happened?" Caleb asked as he wound his arms around his lover's neck.

Jesse tipped his head down and brushed a kiss over Caleb's lips. "Let's go inside and sit. We need to make some decisions."

That sounded ominous. Caleb nodded. He slid his hands down Jesse's biceps, then kept on going on until he reached Jesse's wrists. He gave those a squeeze he hoped was reassuring.

Caleb waited until they were all back in the house, then he locked the door. Remy patted his shoulder before walking over and sitting in the recliner. Kezabeth sat on the arm of the chair, while Caleb and Jesse took the couch. Loopy jumped up and snuggled on Jesse's lap.

Caleb looked at Jesse, then Remy, then back at Jesse. "How bad is it?" It had to be bad, since neither man seemed eager to speak.

"Bad enough," Jesse muttered. "There's nothing obvious to tie Monroe to the damage to my place, and chances are all the prints are mine. Rodriguez and Monroe both deny talking shit, and Monroe swears his visit here didn't go down like you or Kezabeth said."

"Of course," Caleb muttered dully while Kezabeth let loose with a searing string of curses. "Next time he shows up, I'll make sure to have my digital recorder in my pocket." Although Caleb really worried that if there was a next time, it'd be violent. And not on Monroe's part.

"That's not a bad idea." Remy tugged Kezabeth onto his lap. "Chapel ordered Monroe to stay away from here, though, so if he does show up, don't answer the door. Call the chief immediately. Jesse has his numbers."

Caleb nodded. "Hopefully that will keep Monroe away. What about that other cop, the woman you said was slow to show for your backup?"

"Officer Jane Alaniz. Chapel brought her in the office while we were there. Jane said she went to respond immediately but stopped to break up a scuffle between two kids on the way. She reported it, filed the paperwork. She didn't seem to have a problem with me." Jesse sounded so relieved that it made Caleb ache for him.

"Alaniz got her ass chewed for not letting Jesse know she'd been delayed," Remy said. "She said Monroe showed up when she was handling the kids, and he said he'd make sure dispatch let Jesse know."

Caleb wanted to peel Monroe's skin from his body. His unprofessional behavior could have gotten Jesse killed. "And nothing is being done about that because—"

"It's back to he said, she said." Remy sneered through the explanation. "Chapel seemed like he believed Alaniz's version, but without proof, there wasn't anything he could do. In the end, it was her responsibility to make sure Jesse knew his backup was delayed. I doubt Alaniz will ever trust Monroe to do anything in her stead again."

"This all just sucks." Caleb leaned against Jesse, blinking against the burning in his eyes. It was hard for him not to feel responsible for this mess. Everything had been fine for Jesse until he came along. "I'm sorry, Jesse."

Jesse cupped Caleb's chin, waiting until Caleb looked up. "You have nothing to be sorry for, Caleb Tomas. Nothing at all."

Caleb was so caught up in the tender stare that he barely noticed Kezabeth and Remy slipping out of the door.

Chapter Twenty

Jesse had a hard time holding on to his thoughts while he stared into Caleb's eyes. The man just melted everything inside him, suffusing Jesse with a warm, fluttery feeling.

"You have no idea how much better you've made my life, Caleb." But Jesse was going to try to make him understand. "I've lived here for years, alone, too worried about the other officers' reactions to who I really am to let them get close. There wasn't any reason to tell them anyway. It wasn't like I had someone important, a one-off here and there when I could get into the city."

Caleb shook his head and looked away. "Yeah, but you were safe. Then I came along."

"No." Jesse hooked his fingers around Caleb's chin, tugging slightly until Caleb faced him again. "I wasn't safe. I am who I am and who I was before you moved in here too. I've always known eventually the truth would come out, but until there was a reason for it, I was content to keep the information tucked away. Now, it's true I wasn't out looking for love, but that makes finding it, and you, that much more special. You're like the best gift, Caleb, and so is your love. I wouldn't trade those two things for anything."

Caleb's eyes had a wet sheen and the tip of his nose was red. His lips trembled. The whole picture was too endearing for Jesse to resist. He cupped the back of Caleb's head, murmuring his approval of the silky, soft curls. Caleb's lips were even softer, and he tasted like the sweetest wine when Jesse's tongue swept into his mouth.

The flavor of his lover went straight to Jesse's head, much like wine, making him almost dizzy with passion and need. He leaned in closer, needing to press his body against his lover's, only to find himself on the receiving end of one small poodle's ire. Jesse jerked his head back as Loopy yipped and let his humans know he didn't appreciate being the filling for their sandwich. With a dignified skittering of paws, the poodle jumped off the couch and ran to the back of the house.

"Maybe I should let him out," Caleb said, "and you could lock the deadbolts and meet me in the bedroom."

"As much as I love your idea, there are a few things we still need to discuss." Jesse stood, pulling Caleb up as well. "Chief Chapel offered to let me take some time off. I have vacation days I can use."

Caleb's eyes narrowed and he flushed, his anger seeming to seep through his pores to tint his skin. "He offered, or he's making you?"

Jesse bit his cheek to keep from smiling at Caleb's sudden fierceness. He didn't want Caleb to think he was being laughed at, when the simple fact was that Caleb in protective mode made Jesse ridiculously happy.

"He offered. That's all," Jesse reassured. "There isn't any way he can guarantee my safety on the job, and while he would like to believe the men and women working for him will always behave professionally, Chapel knows better. He hasn't been in law enforcement for over thirty years without learning a lot about the uglier side of human nature."

Caleb looked like he really wanted to hang on to his anger, but his shoulders sagged the slightest bit and his eyebrows unscrunched, erasing the shallow wrinkle from his forehead. His mouth relaxed, the lips plumping up from the thin line they'd been stretched into. A heavy sigh seemed to release the last of his anger, and he gave Jesse a lopsided smile.

"So are you going to take a vacation, then?"

"I don't think so." Jesse snuggled Caleb to his side. "First off, where would I go? I only want to be with you, and if we went away for two weeks, would we have anywhere to come home to?"

Caleb gently slipped free of Jesse's hold and scooted away. Jesse's stomach clutched painfully as he saw Caleb's wounded expression and replayed his words in his head.

"Caleb, I didn't mean anything. I wasn't criticizing or complaining about you needing to stay near your home." He reached for Caleb who let himself be held, although he didn't relax. "I did mean what I said about going away for a couple of weeks. If someone didn't hesitate to break into my home when I was across the street, why would I believe either of our places would be safe while we took off? I absolutely wouldn't want to go without you, and I don't see a point in taking time off but hanging around this place. If I'm going to be here, I'll do it on my terms. I'm not letting anyone run me off."

Caleb tipped his head up and regarded Jesse solemnly. "Okay, but if I weren't here, none of this would be happening. Or if I wasn't the way I am, maybe."

"Don't even start that," Jesse snapped. "I wouldn't change a thing about you. What we have between us is worth more than any of this other bullshit. That's just the way it is."

Caleb's lips parted as if to say something else Jesse didn't want to hear or argue about, or it could have been to spout words of love and comfort, but Jesse didn't give him a chance. He dipped his head and licked into his lover's mouth, teasing and coaxing, loving away his doubts and fears. His hands slid tenderly up and down Caleb's back, chasing after the waves of trembling muscles.

Only when Caleb calmed, his body becoming pliant, his lips glistening and swollen from kisses, did Jesse feel his fears slipping away. He'd been more than a little concerned Caleb might try to push him away in some misguided attempt to protect him. The truth was, short of them both moving away, there was no way to protect either of them. Even then, who was to say they'd be any safer somewhere else?

"I don't want anything to happen to you," Caleb confessed softly, his head buried against Jesse's chest.

"I don't want anything to happen to *either* of us," Jesse corrected gently. "I don't think running away is the answer. If it becomes necessary to leave for a short period, then it will be necessary to leave permanently. Together."

Caleb's nod was a bare movement against Jesse's chest, but it was enough for now.

* * * *

Caleb had always been an intensely private person. The assault had only increased that attribute, pushing it past reasonable and into the realm of paranoia. Now Caleb found himself wondering if he'd made his life more difficult with his insistence on a pen name and secrecy. Would he have been attacked if his face had been recognizable? Would there have been an outcry from his fans, a demand for justice that might have spurred the police into making an arrest?

More importantly, would exposing himself now be a help or a hindrance? There was no way for him to know the answer to that. Celebrity could backfire, but what were the benefits? He'd never bothered to find out.

He glanced at his website, tapping his fingers nervously on the edge of his laptop. What would happen if he were to post the truth about who he was and what had happened? And about the concerns he had for his lover? He wouldn't have to expose Jesse's name or even his career, but the worries and fears plaguing Caleb's thoughts, couldn't he share those?

It wasn't as if he had a lot of power, but he had a good-sized fan base—his books always hit the bestseller lists. There were even, his agent had recently said, inquiries from people interested in making his books into movies—serious inquiries from some big names that intimidated the hell out of him.

Remy's rumbling laughter breached the heavy walls. Caleb wondered with more than a little guilt if he would have been able to make any difference in his brother-in-law's plight as well. God knew Remy desperately needed someone on his side, and while he had the love of Kezabeth and the girls, that didn't sway the media. In fact, that gave the vultures three additional targets.

How strong was he? Caleb needed to figure that out, along with all the other questions spinning around in his head. Right now, everything rested squarely on Jesse's shoulders. That didn't sit right with Caleb — he needed to help carry the load. But he needed to be certain he was capable of doing so before he tried to lift any of the burden. Otherwise he'd just make it all worse and add to the load.

Decision made, sort of, Caleb opened up his email to write a message. After that, he had a couple of calls to make, and maybe then he'd know whether his plan would work.

Chapter Twenty-One

One week. Seven days. Jesse rolled his shoulders as he sat at his desk, conscious of the looks and whispers around him. He'd made it through one week of this juvenile shit, and his hopes were dimming. The plan had been that Monroe and Rodriguez would back off with their campaign to run him off once they saw he wasn't going to cave. Unfortunately, his plan seemed to have backfired. While Officer Alaniz and Chief Chapel hadn't tried to ostracize him in any way, there were others who did. It was nothing overt, nothing he could take to Chapel and claim harassment, just a sneer from a coworker, cutting glances and whispered words that couldn't quite be made out.

Not everyone in El Jardin treated him like the devil incarnate, though. In fact, most didn't treat him any differently. The cashiers at the convenience store hadn't been anything other than their usual cheery selves, and one of the speeders he'd ticketed yesterday had smiled and slapped him on the shoulder and told him, "Hang in there. Something else will come along and stir everyone else up." He'd been sorry he hadn't given the guy a warning instead, but the fact that the speeder had offered words of support even after being ticketed actually made Jesse feel better about his situation.

Until today, when he sat at his desk and found a crude stick-figure drawing of himself — he knew it was supposed to be him because the artist had written Jesse's name under the crappy picture of the kneeling man sucking on some other anonymous stick figure's dick. At least the jackass, who needed a lifetime of art classes if this was the best he could do, hadn't dragged Caleb's name into it. Jesse tried his best not to let his anger show, but he heard the snickers. The temptation to turn around and confront Monroe and Rodriguez, as well as the two other off-duty officers standing across the room, was nearly irresistible. Only the knowledge that doing so would score a win for the assholes kept Jesse seated. He shuffled the paper to the bottom of a pile and waited until they left before pulling it back out.

Telling the chief wasn't an option. That would only make it worse, because Jesse was as sure as he could be that there would be no fingerprints on the paper, and any surveillance tape would probably just show a group of men walking by his desk. He didn't think sitting down and taking this kind of crap was the answer either, but Jesse didn't see any other option. Confronting Monroe or Rodriguez outside of work would almost certainly result in a physical altercation. If one of them said a bad word about Caleb, Jesse would beat the living shit out of them both, and *that* would result in his arrest and firing. Confronting them at work would be foolish and would probably get him fired too.

So as far as he could tell, all he could do was what he'd been doing. Wait it out and hope that what his speeder yesterday said was true. Something else would happen to capture the townspeople's attention. Hopefully that something would involve Monroe being humiliated and run off. Jesse doubted Rodriguez would be such an ass if he didn't have the obnoxious younger officer prodding him along. Bullies did love to run in packs.

"You look like a man with violence on his mind. It's no wonder if someone left that shit on your desk."

Officer Jane Alaniz's words jerked Jesse out of his musings. He looked up from the drawing and found himself captured in her angry glare.

"It's just stupid shit, Jane. If they don't get a rise out of me, eventually they'll give up." He hoped.

Jane snorted and held out her hand. "Let me see it."

Jesse handed the drawing over, his stomach roiling with embarrassment. Jane examined the paper closely, grunting a couple of times before shaking her head.

"Are you taking it to Chapel?"

Jesse shook his head. He glared at the drawing before shoving it in his pocket. "Do you think he's going to find anything if I do?"

"Probably not, but he needs to know you're being harassed."

"Jane." Jesse ran his fingers through his short hair. He sighed and scrubbed at his scalp, then let his hands drop to his lap. "It won't make any difference, other than to make those assholes think they're getting to me. Chapel will call everyone in for a meeting and emphasize the laws on harassment in the workplace and the morals and standards of professionalism. Everyone will agree and nod and 'yes, sir' him, just like last week, and they'll be pissed off and fired up and ready to cause more trouble. Sometimes it's best to ignore bad behavior."

Jane propped a hip up on his desk and crossed her arms over her chest as she glared at him. "*This* isn't bad behavior, Jesse! *This* is *harassment*. It's not allowed in the workplace, and the fact that it's being done by police officers who are supposed to serve and protect *everyone* is unacceptable. If they think this is okay, then what happens when they get a call about a gay person being victimized? Do you think they're going to do their best to help that person? Or maybe they'll be the ones doing the victimizing!"

Jesse felt a sudden throbbing in his temples. The stress from the past week seemed to be settling there, driving an ice pick into his skull with each heartbeat. He braced his cheeks with his palms and massaged those painful spots with his fingertips, closing his eyes to escape from Jane's knowing stare.

"Just show him, okay? Chapel's not stupid. He won't make everyone sit through the same meeting if the first one was a waste of time." Jane leaned over and bumped her shoulder against Jesse's. The gesture startled and confused him as well until he saw the encouraging smile and the concern lighting Jane's big, dark eyes. That was a look a friend would give, Jesse realized, and the affirmation that he had one person here on his side chased away some of the cold that had been building up inside him.

"At the very least," Jane continued, "show it to Caleb and talk over your options. He has the right to be informed and to know why you're stressed. Don't you think?"

"Yeah, you're right. I'll do that when I get off." Jesse considered nudging her shoulder like she had his moments earlier, but Jane stood and looked down at him.

"I think what you're doing is pretty amazing, you know." She nodded once, then continued before Jesse could ask what she was talking about. "People who are strong enough to make a stand against bigots and narrow-minded fools are rare. I bet you've got more people on your side than you think." Jane nodded again then walked to her desk to answer her phone.

Jesse watched her for a moment, embarrassed and a little flattered. He thought about the people of El Jardin and the way he'd been treated ever since he'd moved to the town.

At first there'd been inquisitive looks, somewhat cautious greetings, as though people weren't sure about him, or maybe they weren't sure he'd be around for long. There had also been more than a little interest from the girls at school, as if he was something exotic to El Jardin. He'd been shy and uncomfortable with their forward ways, only partially because he knew he was gay. Mostly it was because he hadn't ever been anywhere long enough to make friends and he simply didn't know how.

Still, most of the people had been friendly and hadn't pushed when he'd passed up offers of dates. It wasn't until he'd signed on with the El Jardin Police Department that he finally thought he'd seen acceptance in most of the residents' eyes. Like the commitment to protect and serve assured them he intended to stay. Or maybe they realized how desperately he wanted to belong somewhere.

It had taken years to feel he was one of them. He wondered now whether it had been apparent years ago that he was gay. He'd never dated a woman, had never pretended to be interested in one in a personal way. Surely that was a huge hint? Yet his need to be accepted had kept him in a sort of personal limbo—he hadn't quite been brave enough to have an actual relationship until Caleb.

Yet no one had ever said anything, at least not until Monroe had started talking shit. Would it make a difference? Had he been accepted because he'd never flaunted his sexual preference? Or was he accepted regardless of it? Was there some 'don't ask, don't tell' rule in El Jardin? He didn't think so, but Jesse was afraid to believe he wouldn't end up a pariah. Maybe the town wouldn't take Monroe's side over his, but someone like Rodriguez, who was a native, or one of the other officers who'd been here for years...

When it came down to it, did it matter? No, he supposed it didn't, because he wanted Caleb more than he wanted to belong. With Caleb, he *did* belong. When he looked at it like that, the *where* didn't matter. As long as he had Caleb, he was home.

* * * *

Caleb was hovering at the door when Jesse's shift ended. The dead bolts snapped open before he even knocked then the door opened and he was pulled inside by his sexy lover. Loopy greeted him as well, making much more noise than should be possible for a dog that size. Jesse greeted Caleb with a hungry kiss then bent and scooped up the little poodle, cradling him with one arm and petting and scratching those pesky itchy places on the fur ball with his other hand.

"How was your shift?" Caleb asked, gripping Jesse's elbow.

Jesse let Caleb lead him as he rubbed Loopy's slightly damp chin. "It was..." Jane's words came back to him, and Jesse stopped himself from casually dismissing the crap he'd had to deal with. "It was show and tell day at the office, and someone forgot to clue me in."

Caleb gave him an inquisitive look and Jesse set Loopy down. He dug the crude drawing out of his pocket and unfolded it before handing it over.

Caleb looked the drawing over, anger tightening his features and narrowing his eyes. He handed it back to Jesse with a grunt, then let Loopy out. When he turned around after locking the door, Jesse couldn't read a thing in his expression. It was a little unsettling, but Caleb smiled and took his hand, and everything seemed, if not right, then at least better than before.

Jesse followed Caleb into his office, wondering if Caleb intended to seduce him to make up for the shitty day he'd had. It wouldn't be hard—Jesse was already partially erect just from thinking about how he'd fucked his lover on the desk. He was more disappointed than confused when instead Caleb sat down at his desk and pulled up an email on his laptop.

"I've been thinking." Caleb cleared his throat and glanced nervously at Jesse before looking back at the screen. "Maybe. Actually, I talked with Dr. Gregg about this, and he agrees that it might help. Or not."

"What?" Jesse stopped, his attention snared by the attachment on Caleb's laptop. His fingers and toes went cold with shock. "Caleb, are you sure you want to do this? I thought you wanted to remain as anonymous as possible."

Caleb took both of Jesse's hands in his own and rubbed, as if he knew the appendages were tingling uncomfortably.

"I wanted to when I started out, in case my books flopped," Caleb explained, his cheeks darkening as he shrugged. "Then it became more of a marketing ploy. You know, the reclusive writer. My agent thought it would be romantic, secretive. She said keeping people guessing about my sexuality was an added benefit. I didn't argue." Caleb looked more than a little disgusted with himself, and Jesse had to bite his cheek to keep from interrupting. "Macy, she's my agent, she was afraid that if it became known I was gay, my first book wouldn't stand much of a chance in mass market. She used that same argument for the second and the third, and I let her."

"Do you think I would judge you for that? It's not like I ever admitted I was gay. I wish I could say I never hid it, but I did, didn't I? By sneaking away here and there for one-offs, never having the balls to just be who and what I am. I was afraid people here wouldn't accept me, and I wanted to belong somewhere." He stood then pulled Caleb up, too. Jesse wrapped an arm around Caleb's waist and cradled the back of his neck with his other hand. "I realized today that it doesn't matter where I am. I belong with you, that's all that matters."

Caleb's eyes were so wide and luminous that Jesse thought he could see his entire world in those jewel-toned depths.

"That's just it," Caleb said softly. "I wanted to belong, wanted to be famous without it affecting anything other than my ego and my wallet, and I wanted to write. It was stupid, the first two reasons, and somewhere they took the strength out of the third— writing became less important than the image Macy and I had built up. Alexander Wyatt became bigger than the story. I never wanted that. And if I can do anything now, if maybe some good can come from doing some interviews and some book signings, then that's what I want to do. I want to tell people what happened to me and let them know it's okay to get help. If people don't want to buy my books anymore, then they won't, but I'll keep writing anyway. I'll put the stories up on my blog or self-publish or just file them away in a box somewhere, but I'm done being anyone other than myself."

"Are you sure this is what you want to do, to put yourself out there like this?" Jesse wasn't sure it was a good idea. "Are you ready to deal with fans approaching you and reporters maybe banging on your door? I mean, is this going to be a big deal, like where there's national news headlines and stuff?"

Caleb huffed out a shaky laugh and clung to Jesse. "No, it won't be that big of a deal, not to anyone other than fans and people in the industry. I'm not a cross-genres author. Science fiction still isn't the most popular of genres. And" — Caleb's voice hitched a little higher — "I plan on kind of doing this in one fell swoop, so to speak. I've already written up an accounting of what happened to me and my relationship to Remy, who I do name. Maybe, just maybe, it can help sway the public in his favor, you know. I wanted to maybe mention you, though not by name, how lucky I am to have you and how even in today's supposedly enlightened world, there are narrow-minded jackasses who think they have the right to spew their hatred whenever and wherever and however they want to. If you don't mind."

Jesse's head was spinning as he tried to take it all in, but he couldn't, not yet, and when it came down to it, his only concern was for Caleb. "Are you sure this is what you want? And what do you mean, you're doing this in one fell swoop?"

"Yes, this is what I want," Caleb answered, and this time there wasn't even a trace of uncertainty in his voice. "I think that maybe, possibly, I can make a difference to someone, somewhere. Or maybe the only difference will be to myself. I don't know. I feel like it's something I have to do. As for the swoop thing, once I got it through Macy's head that I wasn't going to change my mind on this, she arranged a few interviews.

Some have been like this, via email, but there are a couple scheduled for over the phone too. They're all supposed to come out pretty close together. I'm also posting a lot of this to my website, blog, linking my Facebook and Twitter to it—"

Jesse chuckled. He couldn't help it. Caleb was planning an all-out assault. "You do know it might backfire. There will probably be interest from local stations at the very least, what with Remy being mentioned, but that, along with the rest of what you're putting out there, may be picked up nationally. I'd think if a couple of your books have been turned into popular games..."

Caleb pursed his lips, then shook his head. "I don't know. I don't think it will, but then again, it might, which is why I asked about how you felt about possibly being a part of it. There's a good chance they'll figure out who you are eventually. I can still stop these, refuse to do the phone interviews, an—"

"No." Jesse wasn't sure how he felt about potential national, or broader, exposure, but he did understand Caleb's need to take a stand. It wasn't necessarily what Jesse would have chosen, but Caleb was right to do it. Maybe once it got back to the cops working his assault case, they'd strive harder to solve it and arrest the bastards who'd hurt Caleb. It was more likely his assailants would start bragging once they realized they'd attacked someone relatively famous, and that would hopefully result in their arrests.

"I think we should have a talk with Chief Chapel," Jesse said. "He needs to know there might be a shit storm coming at him if word leaks out that the soon-to-be famous Caleb Tomas' boyfriend is being harassed on the job."

"I wasn't going to mention Monroe's behavior at work," Caleb assured him. "Just how the trailer was broken into."

"That's fine." Jesse could see how this might be therapeutic for Caleb, and he'd do anything for the man. "But people sure like to gossip, and it's amazing how much they do it, especially if running their mouth gets them a few sentences in the paper or on the news. They want to be politically correct too, at least when being broadcast nationwide, so chances are decent that someone will talk, possibly even one of the assholes who thought that drawing was a true piece of art. Of course, going on about what a shame it is that some jerk did it and how they just can't believe the nerve of some people."

Caleb blinked, looking so unsure that Jesse wanted to cradle him in his arms and tell him everything would be okay. "Will this make it worse, then? I can say I'm single or something like that."

Jesse didn't like that at all and didn't hesitate to cut Caleb off. "Get that thought right out of your head, Caleb Tomas! I don't want to have to beat the hell out of guys who think you're free, and once your face is out there, every eligible gay man — and probably more than a few ineligible ones — who spots you will be chasing after you!"

Jealousy was a new experience for him, and Jesse wasn't sure he cared for it in the least. In fact, he decided it sucked. "As for making anything worse at work, right now that doesn't seem possible. I've been rethinking my decision to stay on here. If it gets much worse, we'll move if and when you want to."

Caleb studied him intently, searching for what, Jesse wasn't sure. He assumed his lover found it when he smiled so sweetly it caused a lurching in Jesse's chest, like his heart had expanded and was trying to create more space for itself. Surely his body wasn't big enough to contain everything he felt for Caleb, so his heart had to learn to adjust to the tight confines.

Chapter Twenty-Two

"If and when you want to." Caleb reflected on Jesse's offer to move. It was just the way Jesse worded it, leaving it entirely up to Caleb and using the words *you want* rather than *you're able*. There hadn't been any hesitation either, as if Jesse'd had to think about what he was saying. Instead, there was that complete faith Caleb would be able to do it if he wanted to. When he wanted to.

But he didn't want to take Jesse away from the only place that had ever really been home. Yes, he'd said anywhere Caleb was would be home, but that didn't mean it wouldn't hurt Jesse to have to give up what he'd found here in El Jardin. Caleb could only assume that, with a few exceptions, people here made Jesse feel accepted.

All he could do was assume, since he couldn't yet bring himself to light up the town with his presence. Eventually, and if Dr. Gregg's assessment was correct, and Caleb did have adjustment disorder, well, that was manageable and usually didn't last for more than six months. There could be other lingering issues, as Caleb was well aware. Flashbacks and even PTSD were not uncommon for victims of violent crimes—those were what Caleb thought of as The Big Two, the ones he worried about the most. Anxiety, depression, stress—those were a little less scary, though he thought they probably shouldn't be.

He hadn't had any breakdowns for several days, which Dr. Gregg thought was from a combination of several things, not the least of which was the support system Caleb had in place. With Kezabeth and Remy practically living here while their daughters were with their grandparents, and Jesse, who might as well move his things in since he stayed here more often than not, there was always someone here.

And of course he had Dr. Gregg. He always got back with Caleb quickly if Caleb needed to discuss something. Dr. Gregg was a damn good psychiatrist. He didn't seem to shuffle his patients off to a psychologist and only step in to provide medications. There weren't even any other doctors listed on his website. That was different from most of the other sites Caleb had checked out, which were made up of several different therapists, counselors, and people with so many initials after their names that he'd given up ever figuring out what they stood for. He guessed those people were trying to get the complete alphabet added to their names.

Caleb realized he was stalling. He was, wasn't he? But this was what he wanted to do. Needed to, although it might very well be a pipe dream that making his true name and story known would make any difference to anyone. Still, if there was a chance.

He pulled up Macy Ferris' direct number on his cell and tapped the 'Call' icon. Macy answered after the fifth ring. God forbid she answer any call quickly.

People might think she wasn't a successful, ruthless agent. He'd been in her office often enough and watched her ignore the ringing of her phone for no other reason than because she *could.*

"What'd you decide?" She did, however, have caller ID.

"We're doing it," Caleb answered without preamble. No sense wasting time beating around the bush. Macy was likely to hang up on him if he dared attempt polite conversation before they got down to business.

"We're doing it?" Macy snapped out.

Maybe he should have made this call before Jesse went in to talk to Chief Chapel. "Jesse's talking with his boss right now, giving him a heads-up out of courtesy."

"What's going to stop that guy from running his mouth? Part of the reason I agreed to let you do this was the element of surprise, and now —"

"Now nothing." Caleb cut her off as she'd done to him numerous times. Macy wasn't known for her charm. "Chief Chapel won't say anything until the interviews have been released." Caleb raised his voice to be heard over Macy's arguing. "I understand your concern lies with me." *Or more to the point, the money I can earn you.* "My concern is for Jesse. If he wants to keep his job here, it's in his best interest not to let his boss get broadsided by this. Then again, it may not make any difference at all."

Macy made a noise that sounded like a mix between a growl and a hum, then sighed. "Fine, but if anything gets out before the interviews are released, Jesse might as well apply for his boss's job, because I will run that man into the ground."

Caleb held back a snort of laughter. Macy obviously didn't know how small towns worked, not that he was an expert, but he doubted the people of El Jardin would put up with her going after Chapel. He was, after all, a native, and Macy was abrasive at best.

"It'll be okay," Caleb assured her. "Sales will be fine, the interviews will be fine, and Chief Chapel won't be selling this story to a sleazy tabloid, okay?"

Macy sighed again, then surprised Caleb enough he almost dropped the phone. "Caleb, I know you don't believe it, but I'm not all about the money." She paused and Caleb used the brief moment to wonder if his agent had been abducted by aliens and replaced with a new, kinder pod person.

"Sometimes it is. Most of the time," Macy clarified and Caleb thought maybe she'd suffered a head injury instead. "But you and I have been a team for years. You kind of grew on me, and damn it, now I worry about you! I should up my fee for that!"

Okay, no head injury, just pissed she's developing a human side. But probably not human enough for him to tease her. "It will be fine. I'll be fine, Macy. If there's any chance this will help Jesse or Remy or anyone else who has had to deal with something like what happened to me…" Caleb forced the next words out. Some things were still hard to admit. "If it can encourage one person to get treatment for mental illness, then that's enough for me. I can deal with the repercussions. Besides, isn't it acceptable that writers and other creative types have some issues now and then?"

Macy snorted loud enough that Caleb was surprised the sound didn't whip through the phone and whiffle his hair. "Most agents would say *all* you creative types have issues *all* the time."

"Ha-ha. We only have issues because our agents drive us nuts." If she could poke, so could he.

She chuckled. "So it's the whole chicken-or-the-egg argument all over again." Before Caleb could answer, she reverted back to the brusque agent he knew so well. "All right, then. Send me the interviews, and three-way me for the phone interviews. I'll be quiet, but I want to be able to intervene if the reporters cross any lines."

"Yes, ma'am." Caleb opened his email on the laptop. "I'll send them right now, along with the time and date for the phone interviews."

He finished the phone call and sent the email off to Macy, then went to his blog. After scheduling a post date and time for his new revelations, Caleb felt jittery and ready for everything to come out and be done with. The knock on the office door startled him so much that he nearly slid out of his chair.

"Come in," Caleb called out, repositioning himself as the door opened.

Kezabeth smiled as she entered, but it didn't quite reach her eyes. "I wanted to make sure everything was okay. I know how Macy can be."

Caleb patted the edge of the desk and waited for his sister to plop down on the wooden surface. "It went better than I expected, so that's good. Everything's set."

"I think you're doing the right thing." Kezabeth took his hand. "I'm a little nervous, since you're bringing up Remy, but I think it'll all work out for the best. You've had too much kept hidden away and no one to share it with."

"I can contact the reporters and ask them to omit the part about Remy." Caleb was already reaching for the laptop, feeling panicky. He had discussed this with Remy and Kez, but if they weren't sure—

"Hey, no." Kez batted at his hand. "I'm nervous about how it will affect you, not us. Remy's pretty much decided he's done with being a cop. He's not sure he'll ever be comfortable having to draw on someone, and that could cost lives."

Caleb heard the ache in her voice, the pain she felt for her husband. He tugged her down into his lap and held her, rocking slightly. "I'm sorry, Kez. I know how much it meant to Remy, being a police officer."

"Not as much as my family," Remy said from the doorway, and Caleb nearly tipped both him and Kez out of the chair. "Not as much as making sure I don't endanger anyone else." Remy lifted Kezabeth from Caleb's arms and gave him a nod.

"Don't worry about me." Remy stood holding Kezabeth like she weighed nothing. "I should warn you, though. Kez and I have been talking about finding a place here. The girls miss you more than you know."

Caleb blinked away the moisture threatening to spill from his eyes. "That would be great. I'd love to have them, and you and Kez, a lot closer."

Kezabeth giggled and winked at him. "You might change your mind now that you have Jesse. We're going to be over all the time, and the girls are going to want to be here more often than not."

"Well, I'd been thinking the deadbolts would eventually need to be reduced down to one, but with you telling me that…" It was amazing, he thought, with the love of a few great people how everything could go from being so hopelessly screwed up to better than good.

Epilogue

It was a tie between Caleb and Loopy over who was happier his shift was over. Jesse grinned as he scooped the poodle up with one hand. Caleb locked the door, then lifted Loopy and set him back on the floor.

"I refuse to compete with you." Caleb patted the dog on the back. "Go chase a dust ball or something already!"

"Caleb. Mm, yeah." Jesse found himself with a double armful of horny Caleb and quickly had better things to do with his mouth. He didn't think he'd ever get tired of this—the taste and feel of his lover's lips, the eager sweep of his tongue.

"How'd it go?" Caleb murmured against his lips.

"What?" Jesse figured he could be forgiven for being slow, seeing as how Caleb had melted his brain.

"Oh." He was an idiot. It was his first shift on the new schedule, which meant working with mostly different officers. "It went well. I think if anyone has a problem with me, they're too scared of pissing off the resident celebrity to say anything about it. Plus Chapel moved Alaniz to days so I'd have a friend already in place."

Caleb's look was one of disbelief. "Is that what he said?"

"No, we're police officers, not elementary school kids, no matter what some of the other officers might act like." And Caleb felt so good pressed up against him, his dick rubbing against Jesse's. Conversation really wasn't that important, was it?

"Monroe?" Caleb pinched the tip of Jesse's nose just hard enough to snap his mind back from a lusty haze.

"Gone, but Rodriguez is still there." Jesse couldn't stop himself from snickering. "I hope he likes nights."

"You're nicer than me," Caleb admitted. "I hope he hates them and decides to follow Monroe off to Albuquerque or wherever the bastard went."

"Won't happen," Jesse countered. "He's too entrenched here, with the kids and the wife and the rest of his family, but I doubt he'll give us any crap. He's not a total idiot."

"Well, then, if we're all done here." Caleb reached between them and managed to pat Jesse's dick. Jesse felt that warm touch from his knees to his neck.

"Yeah, we're done."

"Oh good." Caleb squeezed Jesse's package and nipped his bottom lip.

"Fuck," Jesse muttered, groaning as his need ratcheted higher.

"Trying to," Caleb replied, then slanted his mouth over Jesse's with an eager hunger that told him the time for teasing was past.

Jesse tightened his grip on Caleb but tipped his head back enough to ask, "Bed?"

"Chair," Caleb answered. "Stuff's in my pocket."

"But." Jesse released his hold on his lover enough to put an inch or two between them. "Kez and Remy are bringing Jadyn and Jalyn over."

"Don't mention the twin terrors," Caleb mock-growled. "Not when I'm fixing to jump you right in the living room."

"But." Jesse couldn't seem to get past that one lame word.

Caleb grabbed his hand and dragged him over to the big recliner. "But nothing. They won't be here for a couple of hours, so strip." He shoved Jesse, tumbling him into the recliner. "Or at the very least get everything open so I can get to the good stuff. Although it's all good stuff."

Jesse unbuttoned his shirt while Caleb removed his shoes and socks.

"Faster," Caleb ordered, and Jesse couldn't stifle a laugh.

"Aren't you supposed to be saying that in a few minutes?"

Caleb gave him an arch look and began shucking his own clothes. "No, because I'm going to be the one in charge." His last words were muffled as he pulled his shirt over his head then he hit Jesse with the full heat of his vibrant green eyes. "I'm going to ride you until your eyes cross and your balls beg for mercy, until you come so hard you feel like you're being turned inside out."

"Jesus Christ, hurry up!" Jesse kicked his legs trying to get his uniform pants and boxers off at the same time he sat up and whipped his shirt off. His pants hit the floor as a condom package smacked him in the stomach.

"Suit up, lover, 'cause I'm already prepared." Caleb turned away from him and spread his cheeks, showing Jesse the plug stretching his opening. It was slick and lewd, and Jesse thought he was going to lose it in every way possible if he didn't get to bury his dick in Caleb's tight ass now.

Of course his hands were shaking. He fumbled the package, which made Caleb laugh, but it also got him to straddle Jesse and take the condom package. Caleb ripped it open and winked, then rolled it down Jesse's aching length. Jesse reached for the plug and gave it a twist.

"Fuck!" Caleb's back arched. He looked so sexy that Jesse couldn't even use Caleb's earlier retort of *trying to*. He pulled the plug out almost completely as Caleb finished rolling the rubber on. He wanted to bury his dick in Caleb, but he also wanted to drive the man out of his mind, so he reached for one of Caleb's taut nipples. He gave it a pinch as he thrust the toy back in Caleb's ass.

"Fuck!" Caleb's eyes rolled back and Jesse wonder fleetingly if he'd managed to reduce Caleb's vocabulary to one word.

"Now!" Caleb ordered. Jesse figured if he could keep Caleb in enough of a frenzy, two words were all they needed.

Jesse pulled the plug out and tossed it toward Caleb's pile of clothes. Caleb was on him instantly, one hand bracing Jesse's cock while the other hand came down on his chest. Caleb's vibrant gaze never left his as Caleb lowered himself onto Jesse's dick. The warm clenching of Caleb's ass along with the emotions swirling in his eyes was almost too much. Jesse grabbed Caleb's hips, trying to slow the progression of Caleb's ass swallowing his rod, but Caleb made a rumbling, growling sound that shot straight to Jesse's balls.

"Oh God, damn," Jesse panted, trying to keep from blowing his load. "Please, Caleb."

Caleb grunted, then dropped his hips, burying Jesse's dick deep in his ass. Jesse couldn't stop the yell that ripped from him nor could he stop his fingers from clenching, digging into the bit of flesh that covered Caleb's narrow hips. There was no way he could last, not when his cock was being caressed in the velvety soft heat.

Then Caleb shifted, and Jesse's balls were in a different type of vise, Caleb's hand tugging hard enough to send tendrils of pain shooting down Jesse's thighs and up into his gut. But it worked, and... Jesse kind of liked that bite of pain. Caleb's sly smile said he knew it too.

"Fuck me," Jesse ordered, his voice sounding rough and raw, then Caleb began doing just that, hard and fast. Jesse tried to yell and found he had no voice at all. Caleb wasn't working up to a faster speed, a harder thrust—he was taking, demanding, without finesse, nothing but scorching need that threatened to burn Jesse up from the inside out.

He tried to thrust, but Caleb's snarl and the narrowing of his eyes had Jesse ceding control. He gripped Caleb's hips tighter then he managed to move one hand over enough to fist Caleb's cock, watching the flush spread from his lover's chest, up his neck, and onto his cheeks. Caleb's lips were parted, his breath coming out in loud grunts each time he slammed his ass down. His eyes were narrow slits of green and white—his russet hair was sparked with colors that made Jesse ache to bury his fingers in the warm, silky curls.

"Caleb." Jesse wanted to say more, wanted to tell this man how much he loved him, how beautiful and sexy and special he was, but all he managed to do was gasp when Caleb squeezed his muscles. The clenching heat around his dick short-circuited his brain and shut down his vocal cords. Jesse's eyes shut as his orgasm slammed into him, ripping him open inside and setting his nerve endings on fire.

Bright white bolts of lightning fired off behind his eyelids as the first burst of cum raced up his dick. Jesse's body clenched and spasmed as he came, and a keening noise penetrated the air. He felt the warm, wet splatter of Caleb's spunk hitting his chin, then his chest and stomach. Caleb swiveled his hips, grinding his ass against Jesse's hips then he collapsed onto Jesse—and not very gracefully.

The top of his head clipped Jesse's chin, and the weight of his lover knocked the air out of Jesse's lungs. Not that he'd had much in them to begin with. None of it stopped him from wrapping Caleb in his arms and holding the man as tightly as possible.

It also didn't stop them from hearing the rumbling sound of what had to be Remy's diesel engine pull into the drive.

"Shit!" Caleb pushed himself up, clipping Jesse's chin again. Jesse narrowly missed biting his tongue as his teeth clacked together. "They weren't supposed to be here yet! I told Kezabeth I had plans!"

"That was probably your first mistake," Jesse muttered as Caleb scrambled for his clothes. Jesse rose from the recliner and picked up his clothes, then he kicked his shoes under the edge of the couch.

"First mistake?" Caleb tugged his shirt on over his head, then glared at Jesse. "So you're saying there was more than one?"

Jesse nodded as truck doors slammed shut outside. "Shoulda took it to the bedroom." He ducked the plug Caleb threw at him and made a mad dash for the bedroom.

"See if I plan any more seductions," Caleb yelled after him, just in time so that whoever was banging on the front door had to have heard him. "Grab that thing!"

Jesse pivoted around and scooped up the plug, then decided dignity was overrated. He ran bare-assed naked to the bedroom, ignoring Caleb's laughter. He'd get him back later and they'd both enjoy it.

* * * *

Caleb ignored Kezabeth's knowing smirk, although he did whisper in her ear that she was a perv when he hugged her. Remy seemed unfazed and Caleb was grateful his brother-in-law had always so easily accepted him. His nieces were busy running after Loopy. The poor little dog couldn't seem to decide if he wanted to play or hide.

"Where's Jesse?" Jadyn asked.

"He'll be out in a minute," Caleb informed her. Jalyn was too busy trying to talk Loopy into coming out from behind the entertainment center to notice anyone else. "The poor man just got home from work. He has to get out of his uniform and all that."

Kez snickered and Caleb made sure his nieces weren't looking first before he flipped her off. "Actually, Remy said we should surprise you two and take y'all out to dinner to celebrate your latest soon-to-be published book."

Going out to dinner was possible now, thanks to Dr. Gregg and the support of Jesse, as well as Caleb's family. Even the nightmares had finally stopped and Caleb's concerns about depression and PTSD had come to naught.

Caleb arched his eyebrows at Remy. "Oh really? Even after I told Kez it'd be a couple of hours before anyone should stop by?"

Remy blushed and gave his wife a glare that would have scared the piss out of most people.

Kezabeth laughed. "I might have forgotten to mention that part, but not on purpose, I swear!"

"Where's Jesse?" Jalyn asked then, or whined, having given up on coaxing Loopy from his hiding spot.

Kezabeth pointed at her daughters. "That right there, Nag One and Nag Two, is why I forgot. I firmly believe that every time they whine, I lose a dozen brain cells. Not the unused, mysterious ones either, but the important ones I really need. Jalyn, Jesse will be out here soon. Or I'll drag him out here."

Caleb laughed but he agreed with his sister. He thought his brain would bleed out of his ears if he had to hear his nieces whine twenty-four-seven.

The sound of the bedroom door opening then closing was like the waving of a checkered flag for the twins. His nieces squealed and raced toward the bedroom, elbowing and arguing as they fought to get to Jesse first. Caleb sympathized with them—he felt the desire to do the same thing to Loopy every time Jesse walked in the door.

There was a grunt, then more squeals. The girls' laughter was loud and such wonderful proof of love and joy that Caleb's chest ached with happiness. As Jesse stepped into the kitchen with a niece on each hip and a sweet smile on his lips, everything in Caleb seemed to warm and settle in place.

Jesse had needed to belong somewhere, and he'd certainly found that place, not only in El Jardin, but with Caleb and his family too.

Now he was someone who was needed, not just by Caleb, but by the children and Kez and Remy. Jesse had brought them all together.

Caleb was the luckiest man in the world. He'd found his soul mate, his other half. He wasn't going to waste one single minute of their life together.

About the Author

A native Texan, Bailey spends her days spinning stories around in her head, which has contributed to more than one incident of tripping over her own feet. Evenings are reserved for pounding away at the keyboard, as are early morning hours. Sleep? Doesn't happen much. Writing is too much fun, and there are too many characters bouncing about, tapping on Bailey's brain demanding to be let out.

Caffeine and chocolate are permanent fixtures in Bailey's office and are never far from hand at any given time. Removing either of those necessities from Bailey's presence can result in what is known as A Very, Very Scary Bailey and is not advised under any circumstances.

Bailey loves to hear from readers. You can find her contact information, website details and author profile page at http://www.pride-publishing.com.